REBELLIOUS GRACE

Jeri Westerson

**SEVERN
HOUSE**

First world edition published in Great Britain and the USA in 2025
by Severn House, an imprint of Canongate Books Ltd,
14 High Street, Edinburgh EH1 1TE.

severnhouse.com

British Library Cataloguing-in-Publication Data
A CIP catalogue record for this title is available from the British Library.

ISBN-13: 978-1-4483-1475-1 (cased)
ISBN-13: 978-1-4483-1586-4 (e-book)

All Severn House titles are printed on acid-free paper.

MIX
Paper | Supporting
responsible forestry
FSC
www.fsc.org   FSC® C013056

Typeset by Palimpsest Book Production Ltd.,
Falkirk, Stirlingshire, Scotland.
Printed and bound in Great Britain
by TJ Books, Padstow, Cornwall.

Praise for the King's Fool mysteries

"Unexpected twists and a surprising conclusion make this an entertaining read"
Booklist on *The Twilight Queen*

"Historical details mixed with a puzzling mystery make for a fine read"
Kirkus Reviews on *The Twilight Queen*

"The Tudor court . . . comes to vivid life in this sparkling mystery"
C.W. Gortner, bestselling author of *The Tudor Secret*

"Impressive . . . Somers proves an able sleuth, and Westerson does a fine job evoking the period's political intrigue"
Publishers Weekly on *Courting Dragons*

"Jeri Westerson is at the top of her game"
Louis Bayard, bestselling author of
The Pale Blue Eye, on *Courting Dragons*

"Familiar historical figures seen from a different viewpoint add spice to the mystery"
Kirkus Reviews on *Courting Dragons*

"For readers who enjoy accurate, in-depth historical details in a mystery"
Library Journal on *Courting Dragons*

About the author

Jeri Westerson was born and raised in Los Angeles. She is the author of the Sherlockian Irregular Detective mysteries, the Crispin Guest Medieval Noir mysteries, several paranormal series and historical novels. Her books have been nominated for the Shamus, the Macavity and the Agatha awards.

www.jeriwesterson.com

For Craig, keeping that rebellious spirit alive!

'Unthread the rude eye of rebellion, and welcome home again discarded faith.'
—*William Shakespeare, The Life and Death of King John*

GLOSSARY

Archery Butts – Or just butts. The firing range for archery practice. The butts are the targets.

Arquebus – A fifteenth-century long gun or 'hook gun' with a hook or projection under the front of the barrel used to steady it against battlements.

Buckram – A stiff cotton treated with starches to make it even stiffer for women's clothing, and headdresses where a stiff look was desired. See *Gable Hood*.

Buttery – The place where butts of wine and ale are kept, as well as drinking vessels.

Caparison – A decorative cloth spread over a horse's body, saddle and harness.

Carrytale – Gossipmonger.

Chandler – A stand for multiple candles either on a table or a taller one that stands on the floor. A candelabra. Also the office of the one who makes and sells candles.

Cittern – A stringed instrument like a lute, but smaller and plucked with a quill, sounding something like a banjo.

Cock Lorel – A rogue or reprobate.

Cod – As concerns the codpiece, the triangular covering on a man's hose that serves as the flies, as well as the organ beneath it.

Doublet – A man's short jacket worn over the shirt and usually under other garments in this time period.

Ewerers – Servants responsible for linens and for the washing of the hands of the nobility; one holds the basin over which the courtier holds his hands, while a second ewerer pours the water over them from a ewer and provides a towel for them to dry their hands.

Fleet – A prison in London.

Fryture – Medieval fritter, usually battered vegetables, such as parsnips, and deep fried.

Gable Hood – Tudor women's headdresses shaped like an

architectural gable, sometimes called a kennel hood, also for its shape. The parts of a gable hood consist of pastes, lappets, veil and jewellery. A box paste stiffened with buckram was pinned to the back of the hood, with two separate pieces of the veil hanging down at ninety-degree angles. For different styles, one part of the veil might be lifted up and pinned to the headdress.

Hobbledehoy – A clumsy, awkward youth.

Lappets – A decorative piece of material that hangs on both sides of a woman's headdress. At one time, they were allowed to hang down, but during this period, the style was to pin it up on the headdress to overlap itself. See *Gable Hood.*

Leman – Someone you lie with, have sex with, either man or woman.

Messes – Eating meals with alternating groups of people, in this case servants, so some would always be available to serve. The messes were usually between four people, who, when finished, would relieve another four to have their meal.

Motley – What a jester wears; party-coloured clothes, bells attached, with a jester's hood, marking him as a Fool.

Pantry – The place where bread is kept, the 'bread room' from Anglo-French *panetrie*, originally from medieval Latin *panataria*.

Pastes – Stiffened fabric using buckram to make women's hats and bodices, particularly a gable hood, with its rigid shape that resembled a house's gable. See *Gable Hood.*

Pillicock – Vulgar term for a boy, or insult, calling him a penis.

Plectrum – Something like guitar picks, made of quill tips.

Points – Laces tying the waist of a man's hose (now with a trouser, not two separate stockings anymore) to the hem of his doublet, like braces/suspenders, the only way to keep them securely in place.

Prating – Insult to one's intellectual character, long 'A'.

Receptor – A receiver of stolen goods, a fence.

Sirrah – A form of address to inferiors or even gentleman to gentleman meant as an insult.

Suum cuique – Latin phrase, 'To each their own', 'To come into one's own'.

Trimmer – Someone who sways with opinions to please everyone.

Whelk – A large sea snail, eaten at court.

ONE

The man was dead. There was no question it was murder, for he had been found with his throat cut in the king's own corridor of the king's own palace a fortnight ago. And for once, no one asked me, the jester, to investigate it, for what was a Fool like me doing investigating the secret death of an anonymous servant? Still, it *was* my vocation to lighten the king's mood after such a sordid deed.

Though Henry was used to sordid deeds by now. Up to his bearded chin in them. There was the sordid deed of the treatment of Catherine of Aragon, his first queen, and forcing a divorce on her. Which led to the sordidness of biting his thumb to the pope – that is, the 'Bishop of Rome', as he was to be called now – shutting the monasteries and turning out the monks and nuns to shift for themselves. And thence to his marriage to Anne Boleyn . . . which ended in the most sordid of events on the block. And then Henry married his third wife barely before his second wife was cold – and headless – in her unmarked grave.

What can be said of Queen Jane Seymour? Well, she was not beauteous as Anne had been. She was right pale, like marble, and quiet, and somewhat . . . well, not as educated as Queen Catherine or Nan. She was, as best as I could tell, much like a nun or those queens of old, eager to heal, to give charitable relief to the poor, to be a peacemaker. But perhaps this is what Henry craved. His life with Catherine had been lively and at the same time genial like any country knight; pleasant, loving, the three royals – Henry, Catherine and Mary – and how I doted on their company! But when Henry got that wild notion that he needed a *male* heir at all costs, those costs were paid, and his loving, congenial wife became argumentative, steadfast and unyielding . . . when it came to denouncing her and calling her 'Princess Dowager' to the many years' dead

Prince Arthur, calling her daughter a bastard even after a pope had given Catherine and Henry dispensation to marry. And then there was his second wife, Anne Boleyn, who had been loud in her proclamations and recriminations and ended in quite a different divorce . . . her head from her body.

Now we had the peacemaker, pacifying the heart of the king.

Ah, but Henry. As was his taste, as soon as he caught the doe, his eyes roved to the others in the herd, and even *I* heard him remark that had he known there were such beauteous women brought to court, he never would have betrothed himself to Jane. I wanted to tell those ladies, to warn all the new mistresses who would be queen and fell under Henry's gaze; I'd say, 'Flee! Do you dare to think that for you it will be different? That his eyes will not rove from you?'

As always, I listened to the whispering of nobles, for as the court jester, I could arrange to be unseen when I wanted to be. Those whispers came from the likes of Sir Nicholas Carew and Edward Seymour and Gertrude, Marchioness of Exeter. They'd carefully placed Jane Seymour under Henry's nose because they wanted Cromwell to stop the march on the monasteries. They wanted their old religion back. They wanted Henry's daughter, young Mary, back into the line of succession, and though they had connived to push Jane Seymour before the willing eyes of the king, they had not counted on Cromwell. And instead of praise and rewards, they got warnings. 'See what happened to Anne Boleyn,' Cromwell would say, and they drew back into the shadows and said naught more on it.

Queen Jane seemed to have a big heart . . . for lost causes. Though she did not plea for our old religion, being well instructed by King Henry himself not to meddle in his affairs as Queen Anne had done, but for other poor souls who likely did not deserve it.

Well, one thing that Queen Jane did was to ban French fashions, for Queen Nan did love her French ways. No more French hoods, no more French styles of dress. It was good English pastes and lappets instead. My own wife Marion had to put away her favourite French hood and make a good English gable hood that would frame her face in an appealing manner, with the lappets pinned to the frontlet and one of her veils pinned up on one side. Methinks she made it slightly smaller than was quite the fashion so as to be less . . . weighty.

In fact, today, she looked quite adorable in her little gable hood, and I told her so over the breakfast table with the other servants, and kissed her loudly and publicly, to the hoots and whistles of my fellow citizens of court.

Marion – who one would think would be used to my cavorting and jesting by now – blushed a deep crimson and turned her face away from me. 'Must you make a mockery of your wife's affections?'

'My dear Marion! It is not a mockery I make, but a proud display of all my love for you and *you* alone!' And it was at that moment that my dog, Nosewise, scrambled forth, jumped into my arms and licked my face. 'Well,' said I, wiping my lips and cheek with my doublet's sleeve, 'I reckon it's not *quite* you alone.'

And, of course, all laughed. And Marion along with them, for she could not seem to stay cross with me, which was just as well.

I carried my dog away from the table – Nosewise was some sort of white and brown terrier of many breeds – and, with my basket of foolery hanging from the crook of my arm, I set off to find Henry, for, after all, I was *his* Fool and I served him first.

When I finally came upon him in his withdrawing room, I was surprised to find him quite alone. This was his private space, between bedchamber and privy chamber. It was wainscoted with golden oak polished to a sheen and filled with tapestries of royal hunts and summer frolics in gardens. Chandlers burned brightly with beeswax candles, and the friendly aroma of big oaken logs in the hearth bloomed. It was Henry's happy room for games with his male friends . . . and *other* kinds of games with womenfolk. Not that I spied on the king, never did I. But I was most times simply . . . *there*. For a jester needed go hither to first find the king or the queen and get himself in there for to entertain. And I was most often greeted with a smile, which is a merry way to live one's life.

But here was Henry by himself. I looked about, even behind tapestries and tables. Henry was never alone. There were always courtiers around him, above him, below him, laughing whenever he said something humorous, smiling and nodding when he quoted his own poetry or sang his own composition. They fawned, they 'yessed' him, they defended, but mostly they surrounded him like a forest of protective trees. And yet today – naught.

'What ho, Harry!'

He looked up from the documents he was reading. I scrambled to him.

'Harry, are you actually *reading* your papers of state? Is there not a man to do that for you? Where is Cromwell?' I rushed to the screen around the close stool and frantically looked under the lid.

'You silly whoreson,' he muttered. 'I am on my own today by choice.'

'But Harry! You never do this.'

'Well, today I do! Have you nothing better to do yourself?'

'No, sire. I have naught better to do but to serve you as your loving Fool.' And here I got to my knees and laid my head in his lap.

He pushed me off him. 'Go elsewhere, Somers.'

'But, Harry . . .'

And then Nosewise trotted in, and the king groaned. 'That cur. Must you bring him into my chambers? He's a filthy dog.'

'Not so, Uncle.' I scooped the dog up into my arms. 'I bathed him myself just yesterday.'

'Bathed or no, jester or no, leave me.'

'Well . . .' I kicked at the floor, catching the edge of a carpet. 'If you do not wish to play . . .'

'Play elsewhere.'

'You have but to command it and I will obey.'

'And yet you are still here.'

'I go, Harry. I go! I leave you to your static boredom, wondering where your smile has got to. Alone in your chamber with naught but the farting of the Yeoman Guards for company.' And the one standing in the doorway with his halberd twitched an eye towards me. 'No quips, no jocularity, no songs to soothe or to hoot in bawdy laughter to. I go!'

'Your leave-taking is longer than your entering ever was.'

'I just want to make certain you *desire* to lose my presence from you.'

'By Christ, Somers! Is this clear enough? Get out!' He thrust his beringed index finger towards the door.

I bowed again as dramatically as possible, sighed, put my hand to my brow and dragged me feet, leaving him at last.

As I stepped over the threshold, I had the satisfaction of hearing a soft chuckle from His Majesty's breast, and that suited.

But, of course, now I was at a loose end. What's a jester to do when left on his own? Well . . . seek out trouble! And that trouble was mostly in the person of my current lover, Nicholas Pachett, Lord Hammond.

Leaving Henry's many outer chambers, I came upon the watching chamber, where hopefuls wishing to see the king waited, some in unfulfilled expectation, for Henry had to be in the mood to see those suing for his favour. And they had to be well dressed, for Henry could not abide the look of a poor or slovenly man.

And then it occurred to me to seek out our lady queen. And so, on I went to see what Queen Jane, though not yet crowned so, was about. Oh, she had her own jester, simple-minded little Jane Beden, known to one and all as Jane Foole, who had been Queen Catherine's and *then* Queen Anne's *and* Princess Mary's Fool – though we were not to call Henry's daughter 'princess' as she was banished from the line of succession. She was '*Lady* Mary', Christ mend me.

Jane Foole cared little for such things. In fact, she didn't understand any of it, and she reaped, perhaps, the most benefit of all creatures in the kingdom for her ignorance. It was all too heart-breaking. Too melancholy a thought. For I, being Henry's court jester, used to call both late lady wives of Henry my family and counted the children of these marriages mine as well, not having any of me own. I sorely missed Madam Elizabeth – as *she* must now be called – torn from her mother untimely. My little Bess.

As I approached Queen Jane's court in her apartments, I could hear laughter and merry-making. When the Yeoman Guards allowed me in, I saw Queen Jane and her ladies, and my Marion sitting amongst them, showing them intricate stitches – for being a bastard herself, she was not amongst the ladies as a peer, but as the premier embroideress of the court, though the queen was also very fine with a needle.

The room was much like Henry's withdrawing room with its tapestries, chandlers and warm wainscoting, with the difference of embroidered curtains at the tall windows with a lovely view of the great garden.

Lady Mary herself sat beside the queen. Brought to court at last in July through much negotiation by our queen, being the peacemaker that she was, Queen Jane managed to foil even the toughest connivences of Cromwell, who tried to argue that she no longer belonged at court. A kind-hearted soul was Jane.

Lady Mary had been a cheerful child, yet now her chin was always burled, and her brow always furrowed, and who could blame her? She looked up from her own embroidery when I entered. I gave her my dearest and sincerest smile, and I saw it brighten her face. For in those mutual smiles, we both remembered better days together. She knew, in the only way I could convey, that I still loved her.

Lastly, of course, Jane Foole was there, cavorting as only those in my guild can. She was a small creature, with shorn hair as was the fashion for witless fools (and I followed the fashion with shorn hair of my own simply to make it easier to wear the wigs and masks I often donned to make fun of various courtiers). Her dress was of simple cloth and not quite in the fashion of the day, with the Dutch headdress she favoured.

When she spotted me, she gave a hoot and ran for me headlong. I had no choice but to drop my dog and basket, and spread out my arms to capture her, or I would surely have been toppled over.

'Will!' she cried.

'Janie! My lovely.'

'Come with me for to entertain the queen and her ladies.' She grabbed my hand and dragged me before them. They sat in a semi-circle facing the royal Jane – with a bombardment of coloured gowns all about me, which served as nicely as any ancient amphitheatre.

I bowed to the queen. 'Since I am devoted to these two Janes, I cannot refuse.'

'Indeed not,' said the queen, acknowledging my bow. 'My Jane Foole is an amusing lass, but not as clever as you, Master Somers.'

'We each have our own specialities. With Janie here, it is her ability to tumble and prattle in her innocence. With me, it is my songs and my wit. Each good in and of itself, just a different flavour.'

Jane was the kind of fool that was known as a 'natural fool', one without her full wits about her. The most guileless of folk, for in her simple-mindedness, she could not scheme evil as the rest of us could do. No, her mind was filled with butterflies and pastry and the soft fur of animals. There was nothing inside that shell that could do any harm. Some say this was the best kind of fool . . . though, to my mind and in all humility, the witty sort – the sort like me – was more supple.

'You brought no instrument, Master Somers,' said the queen.

'Oh, but I can sing anyway. Janie can sing with me. What shall we sing, Mistress of Fools? The King's Ballad.'

She clapped her hands. 'Oh yes! And I shall sing the high part.'

'And so I would agree. My manhood would never allow me to hit those notes again since I was a lad.' The ladies tittered in laughter. 'And our Janie here has a tolerable and pleasant voice. And so we shall begin.'

> *'Pastime with good company*
> *I love and shall until I die;*
> *Grudge who lust, but none deny,*
> *So God be pleased thus live will I.*
> *For my pastance*
> *Hunt, sing and dance.*
> *My heart is set:*
> *All goodly sport*
> *For my comfort,*
> *Who shall me let?'*

We finished all the verses with an exaggerated flourish and, at the conclusion of the song, held hands as we bowed together. It was King Henry's own composition . . . that he wrote for his first queen. Aye me. How the time flits away like a mayfly; here one moment, gone the next.

But Queen Jane either never knew its history or was generous in forgetting, for she smiled and clapped like the rest of the ladies. Henry's tune was popular throughout the continent . . . or so it was said.

But they didn't wait to see what other merriment Janie and I had to give, for the ladies turned to one another and – as ladies and groups of young men are wont to do – they gossiped.

'Have you heard of the killing of one of the king's servants?' asked Lady Anne Bassett to her seat mates. 'It was simply awful! A fortnight ago, right down *this* corridor.' Some had heard, it seemed, whilst others were just hearing the old news. All had ghastly looks on their faces at these tidings. I wondered that they were just now hearing about it.

And when I turned to Jane Foole, she had the ghastliest look of all. She was covering her ears with her hands and shaking her head. I would have gone to her, but the queen urged me forth. 'Is the king safe?' she asked, rising.

'Fear not, sweet lady,' I said to her. 'The king's men are on it like a dog on the hunt. They will find the culprit. But in all truth, it was a fortnight ago. I shouldn't worry.'

But alas, they all grew silent and looked at me with pointed enquiry in their eyes. I well knew their minds and I shook my finger at them. 'No, no. This jester will remain the Fool he has made himself out to be. There is no need of Will Somers as an inquisitor. Better men than me are at it.'

'But, Will,' said the queen, 'you have proved yourself able at this. Will you not assist to find the vile offender?'

'Madam, what could a poor Fool as me add to the doings of Sir Nicholas Carew?' (For I had heard that Henry assigned the task to him, his bosom friend.) 'No, no. This jester will remain the man of quips and song, as I have ever been. As proof, I must present this.' I postured, one foot elegantly forward, my opposite hand open, palm up to tell my jest. 'A man gave his wife a valuable dress. But now he complained that he could never exercise his marital rights in the bedchamber without it costing him more than a gold half-angel each time. "The fault is yours," answered the wife, "why do you not, by frequent repetition, bring down the cost to one silver penny?"'

The queen blushed, as I thought she would, and the ladies tittered behind their hands, watching the queen carefully lest they displease her by their bawdiness. I cast a glance towards my wife, and she merely raised a brow at me. But I had made them forget, for a time, the horrible crime.

Jane Foole seemed to have recovered from her anxiety – if she were ever troubled, it usually didn't last long, for I believe she forgot it easily – and we did tumbling and pratfalls, and I used her as a foil for my quips. But before I tried to take my leave, the queen stopped me. She set her embroidery down in her lap and looked up with bright, cheerful eyes. 'I have saved this news for last,' she said to her court of ladies. 'It is good news.'

We leaned forward in anticipation. For the best news she could convey was that she was with child. But even as our ears were pricked as hard as they could be, she breathed a satisfied sigh. 'Madam Elizabeth is coming home to court.'

It was the last thing any of us expected. The queen's countenance gave little doubt that this was her doing, for she had tried to reunite the king to his daughters, to Lady Mary foremost, for Jane, as I have said, was a kind soul and had wanted that reconciliation between father and daughter, king and . . . well. Certainly not heir, for the queen had begged to have the Lady Mary back into the line of succession . . . to be *after* her own issue, of course. But Henry was immovable.

What had brought about this miracle? Madam Elizabeth! My Bess! Oh, I longed to see her.

Though when I flicked an eye towards Lady Mary, this was far from good news to her.

The other women of her court looked on askance, for Madam Elizabeth was Anne Boleyn's child. The adulterous traitor's child. The now *bastard* child.

'She should arrive in two days,' said the queen, not noticing the silence that had followed her pronouncement. She blithely picked up her embroidery again – one of Henry's shirts, it was – and continued pushing the needle through the fabric, pleased with herself and oblivious to the turmoil that made the room heavy with a sudden, darker mood.

TWO

I watched as the ladies of Jane's court slowly returned to their normal discourse, chatting about this swain or that, and arguing over who was the most handsome courtier. But my eyes searched for Jane Foole. *I must talk to her*, I had decided, but she was already forgetful of the crime, as was her way, and I had not wished to remind her. But I knew I would have to speak of it to her at some moment after this, for it was best to know all the secrets of court. It was folly for the jester to be left out in the cold on gossip. I thought it best to leave the queen's company, and as I bowed to her and quit the chamber, I moved through the palace back to Henry to see if he would be more amenable to my presence, but he was now in the midst of his privy council. This time I had fetched my cittern, and I sat in his window as I usually did, Nosewise at my feet, as I softly plucked a tune.

Henry glanced once at me but made no other acknowledgment of my arrival. At least he hadn't shooed me away. Yet he did not look pleased with what his men were telling him. I knew how he moved his body when he was tired, bored, displeased, needed to empty his bowels, was merry . . . No, nothing was a secret to my keen eye. I spent more hours with him than his own wives did.

I listened to their speech rather than my tune. My tune I could play in my sleep. What the men were discussing was the rebellion in the north, in Yorkshire. The 'Pilgrimage of Grace', they called it. It was not just those traditional nobles at court who wanted their old religion restored, but there were many all over England who would see the mass said as it used to be. And so many common folk had relied on humble monks or nuns for their sustenance. They had lost the labour they had done for generations for the abbey lands. And my dear Henry – the stumbling oaf that he sometimes was – never even realized that all those who depended on the monasteries for their wellbeing lost far more than religion when he dissolved them, tore down their roofs and sold their land to fill his coffers. He did not see that the enclosure of once common land was a disaster to those who used to tenant there. How grain prices had risen. And further, he did not see that the people did not like a base-born man like Thomas Cromwell, who instigated what they saw as destroying their way of life.

Perhaps the king did not hear the people cry out, but *I* did. Those like me – the unlanded, the poor, the weak – who had only the comfort of their faith, didn't even have that left to them.

Oh, Harry, I wondered. *How can your Will ever help you in this? It's a right mess.*

And so, this Pilgrimage of Grace had begun. It started in Lincolnshire last year and spread to Yorkshire and other places in the north. They had flung Henry's men from the monasteries and restored some of the monks and nuns there. They wanted Henry to attend to their cries and do this work, but mostly to bring back their faith. It was only the more tolerant – like m'self – that didn't mind the reform of religion: to free us from the pope, to hear the mass in our own language, to give up all those statues and saints. Anne Boleyn had felt the same way too, by the bye. Verily, I always felt that God would rather be left in peace than be harried at all hours with constant prayers and the smell of incense. And so I happily let the Almighty alone, and, in turn, he let me go on my way.

But none of this pleased the king, for his command was to be obeyed, and no barrister from London would stand in the way of it.

It was Robert Aske, said barrister, who led the rebels. Last year, Aske led some nine thousand followers on their march, so it was said, and in order to be allowed into their company, they had to swear the Oath of the Honourable Men. This oath was simple:

'Ye shall not enter into this our Pilgrimage of Grace for the common wealth but only for the love ye bear to God's faith and church militant and the maintenance thereof, the preservation of the king's person, his issue, and the purifying of the

*nobility and to expulse all villein blood and evil counsellors
against the common wealth of the same. And that ye shall not
enter into our said pilgrimage for no peculiar private profit
to no private person but by counsel of the common wealth nor
slay nor murder for no envy but in your hearts to put away
all fear for the common wealth. And to take before you the
cross of Christ and your heart's faith to the restitution of the
church and to the suppression of heretics' opinions by the holy
content of this book.'*

And such *sounded* reasonable to me. If they meant it. Still,
there were even those at court who secretly maintained priests
and celebrated the mass in Latin with all its Catholic accoutrements of saints and incense. Even some of Henry's own
gentlemen of the privy chamber. I mentioned to Henry that
perhaps he should let those who wished to celebrate like
Catholics and those others like Protestants to do so, but he
became quite cross with me. '*I* am the Head of the Church in
England!' he had bellowed, and would take no apologies. Well,
I am not a scholarly man. I had had no church training, and
little tutoring in other ways. What I know I had to garner from
listening to others, and even reading a little. Henry himself
had been called 'Defender of the Faith' by one pope . . . long
before he disinherited the whole of those that followed the
seat of Peter.

Methinks religion is best left to one's conscience. But Henry
is too loud and drowns out all sound before one's conscience
has a chance to speak a word.

The upshot was that it was Henry's way and no other. And
yet, as I listened, his counsellors were suggesting that they
bring Robert Aske to the palace to negotiate.

Henry's face flushed with angry red. 'I am king,' he said,
voice low and dangerous like an animal's growl. 'I do not negotiate with rebels. Rebels are to be executed and disposed of.'

'But, Your Grace,' said Carew – and such a one as him
would argue with the king, for he was one of those tradition-
alists that wanted Catholic ways again – 'these so-called rebels
swore an oath; they march under the sign and banner of the
cross. They mean well . . .'

'Whilst trying to undermine my authority.'

'I say, let them come,' said that oily voice. I turned, and there he was in the threshold, joining the meeting at last. The Chancellor of the Exchequer himself, the right hand of the king, Thomas Cromwell – piggy-eyed, corpulent and widening like his old master Wolsey, who died before he could be executed these six years ago now – strode into the chamber. He never even slowed when another counsellor rose from his chair and offered it to him, whilst the poor counsellor sought a chair from across the room to sit himself in.

'Thomas,' cried the king. '*Let* him come? *That* man?'

'We will negotiate in good faith. Show the people that you can listen thoughtfully to his demands just as God's anointed would, promise them that much shall be as they wish—'

'Thomas!'

'Promise them . . . but form our words carefully, listen still harder and make certain that their words will be used against *them*. The Crown shall appear mightier in its beneficence and swift in its retribution for their forswearing *their* oaths.'

Henry rubbed at his flaming red beard. 'Can this be done?'

'Of course, Your Grace. Leave it to me.' Like a vulture on a branch, he scoured the faces around him and picked out his minions. At a jerk of his head, they rose, bowed to the king and left with Cromwell. No doubt his secretary, Rafe Sadler, was also waiting in some dim chamber to do the chancellor's bidding.

'Bring Aske here?' I said from my windowsill perch. 'That seems unwise.'

'I find it distasteful,' said one of his privy gentlemen, 'to allow the *jester* to suggest court policy.'

I focused my attention on the popinjay sneering at me. 'Better to *listen* to the advice of a fool, than to *be* one yourself.'

Henry dismissed the man with a wave of his bejewelled hand. 'My chief minister has said it. And I agree with him.' But he didn't much sound convinced.

Of course, why should Henry disagree with Cromwell? He got him Anne when he wanted Anne . . . and equally quit him from Anne when he so wished it. He should add 'Queen Maker and Queen Destroyer' to his titles, for Cromwell could indeed be trusted to do the bidding of the king . . . even before Henry ever thought of it. Or wanted it.

Sir Francis Bryan, the king's Chief Gentleman of the Privy Chamber tilted his head in a carefree way, his one eye merely flicking a glance at me, whilst his other was covered with a patch to hide the missing organ. 'It may be a wise move to listen to Cromwell in this, Your Grace.' He took in all the other gentlemen with a sweeping glance. 'It will be as he says. We can play our part and allow Aske to bury himself. For if Cromwell stumbles, it isn't Your Majesty's fault . . . but the Chancellor of the Exchequer's.'

Henry tipped his gaze towards the man, measuring him. Oh, Sir Francis was a trimmer indeed. It was said that he never had a fresh opinion, for he was always stealing that of the king. He was a man who knew how to keep his head.

I shrugged and deferred to Sir Francis. When Henry had too many opinions shooting his way, it was best to stay away from the archery butts.

Instead, I played my cittern and hopped off the sill. I plucked and strummed as I walked a circuit around him in his chair. 'It matters little, Harry. All will be well. I will make sure of it.'

'*You* will? Are *you* one of my ministers now?'

'Harry, that would be the most intelligent thing you might ever do. For what makes better sense than to employ your jester to help you craft laws for the kingdom? You've already got a pack of fools in place. Why not a professional one?'

Henry turned towards his privy council who looked like crows in their dark motley, and they stared back at him, sallow-faced and mute. Puppets, they were, like the ones I carried with me to entertain the king. But they did not entertain. They mouthed back all the things that Henry said to them. Not a fresh idea to rub together amongst them, for they all feared for their place on the council . . . and for their own necks. Thomas More, ex-chancellor, said 'no' to the king, and look where it got him: head stuck on a pike on London Bridge.

'You may go, Somers,' he said at last. And verily, I was glad in that instance to quit him. Sometimes Henry made me so cross with him. The fact that his jester must instruct him on what is right and what is wrong strikes me as the height of mismanagement. But I take the job seriously, even though I am not technically counted amongst his counsellors. Despite what that sneering gentleman said.

I strode through the corridors, Nosewise on my heels for once, and I, thinking of nothing, when I heard a 'Psst!'

I stopped and turned round. And out from behind a curtain in a window alcove was my courtier paramour, Nicholas Pachett, Lord Hammond.

I bowed to him. 'Did you "psst" at me, sirrah?'

He glanced about too. 'I did. You are the devil to find, Somers.'

I approached him, still wary of our secret meeting, for little is secret in a corridor in the palace. 'You need only skulk near the king. That is where I can usually be found.'

'And you spend a great deal of time there. I could not await outside, like some fawning courtier waiting to see *him* . . . when I wanted to see *you*.'

'Why not? Everyone else does it. Wait to see him, that is.'

He stepped closer, until we were but an arm's length away. 'I am not like everyone else.'

Oh, he was a handsome devil. Dark hair with a curl of it on his forehead, and a dark beard and moustache close-cropped to his face and enhancing that smile of his, like Lucifer himself, with his bright eyes under dark, thick brows. There was much mischief there. The kind that this humble jester enjoyed.

'Oh ho, my lord! Are you not? Looking for the king's favour as every other lord looks to do?'

'You know I promised you, Somers, that I would not use your influence with the king for my own betterment.'

'And so you have not. But what, then, could you want with the king's poor servant?'

He edged ever closer. 'You know what I want,' he said under his breath.

'It seems I currently have the time.' He led, I followed, and then I elbowed him. 'And stop calling me "Somers" as if I was your servant.'

'You *are* my servant. You are the servant of any courtier here.'

'Oh, well, if you are going to make courtly matters into country matters . . .'

We three – Nosewise, me and Nicholas – went to his apartments. I shooed the dog away when Nicholas opened the door, but the damned dog whinged and threatened to sit outside Nick's door howling, and that we could not have. The one time I wanted that dog to disappear, and he stubbornly would not!

'Come in, then, you cur,' I said. 'And don't make a sound or get on the bed. We will be, er, busy there.'

And so we were. We did close off Nosewise in the outer chamber, whilst we moved to the bedchamber. Nick didn't wait. He wrestled me roughly against his bedpost and yanked at my clothing.

'My lord,' I gasped, 'mind the clothing. I am not made of doublets.'

He eased it off me then and, with his teeth, clamped on to my neck in that way he knew I liked, and when I was sufficiently undressed for him, he pushed me on to the bed.

The man had a way of consuming me, leaving me breathless and leaden, but I was still able to roll over and pleasure him, spent as I was.

We lay side by side atop his quilts, gazing at one another. He liked to fawn upon me afterwards, caress my cheek, my brows. I closed my eyes to fully feel the sensations.

'I never imagined I could fall in love with a jester,' he said softly.

My eyes drew open and gazed at him. 'Now, now, my lord . . .'

'Do stop calling me that. It is rude upon *your* lips. I prefer you use my Christian name.'

'Nicholas. You mustn't think that way. I love my wife.'

He rushed me across the sheets, scooping me up by my shoulders that were not as broad as his and held me close. 'But can you not do both? She cannot give you what I can. Oh, besides the obvious, there are also riches. Well . . . modest riches.'

I leaned my forehead against his bearded chin. 'And you cannot give me what she can. This is a futile argument, Nick. For I do love my wife and I . . . I am very fond of you.'

But the truth of it was far deeper. For over the months since I had known him, my feelings for him had grown, shifted, made little sense to me. Verily, I wasn't certain if I *didn't* love him . . . a little. But I couldn't succumb to that. I had promised Marion. Promised her, as loyal a husband as I could be, that I would not love my male paramours, that I *would* only love her. But in this little country that was Will Somers, the borders kept changing. And that meant that I would have to give up our dalliances, Nick and me. And I didn't know that I could do that either.

I meant to push him away, but I drew him tighter to me. For he was dear, and in truth, I was not brave enough to send him from me just yet.

'What nonsense you say,' I whispered, my voice too shaky to speak louder.

He said nothing more. We lay in each other's arms in the afternoon, and dinner was soon to be served in the banqueting hall. We would *have* to leave one another.

'It is warm with you,' I couldn't help but say. For, indeed, winter had crept through the palace walls, and sometimes fires and furs would not do.

'And with you, my silly jester.'

Reluctantly, I pulled away and began to gather my clothing. 'Your groom will soon return to dress you for dinner.'

'I know.' But instead of rising to dress, he lay amid the bedsheets and watched me.

'Get up, you layabout,' I said as cheerfully as I could, though my heart wasn't in it. I pulled my chemise down over my head and shook it into place before I grabbed my doublet and donned it, and drew my green serge coat on over that.

'What if we were to run away to my estate?' he said dreamily. This was a common refrain for him. For his family was urging him to marry, as every young man with land should.

And I always replied to him, 'You know the answer to that, Nick.'

He sighed. 'I know.'

Dressed, laced and buttoned, I stood before his bed. 'You must get dressed, Nicholas.'

He said no more and rolled off the bed on the other side and, like an angry child, he frowned and grunted as he pulled on his things. He *was* a child, sometimes, thinking that because he was a lord, albeit a fairly poor one, he could do what he liked. But Henry had instigated the Buggery Act three years ago – though it mostly concerned congress with farm animals. Even I was not as twisted as that. Still, the law would put such men as were we to death for these bedchamber antics, regardless of our passions. And surely, Nick did not want to die for love of me, with all the disgrace to his family to follow.

'I must go,' I said. I had to be there at the same time as the king. It wouldn't do to be late.

'I will drink all my toasts to you, Will.'

'And . . . I will do the same for you.'

He smiled finally, and it was a passing marvellous smile.

Nosewise was glad to see me as I opened the chamber door, and he trotted in a circle and followed me out of the chamber through the rooms of Nick's apartments and finally into the corridor, where poor, weeping Jane Foole came trotting forward.

I caught her in my arms and held her tight. 'Janie, Janie. What's amiss? Calm yourself now. Dry your tears and tell your Will what the matter is.'

She sniffled and wiped at her face. Her Dutch headdress sat askew, and I helped her put it to rights. 'It's that man, Will.'

The mill wheel in me head slowly cranked, trying to find sense in the nonsensical. 'Man? What man?'

'The one that was murdered.'

'Well . . . what about it, then?'

'It's terrible, Will. I saw him! I was there!'

'You saw what, dear heart? Shhh. Shhh. Calm yourself.'

She tried again, her lips trembling. 'I saw it. Just now. Someone . . . someone has dug him up from the churchyard and disembowelled him. Why did they do that, Will? Why do that to a poor, poor man?'

THREE

I managed to quiet her sufficiently, but now *I* was far from becalmed. First, someone kills a servant to the king's courtiers, and not satisfied with that, they dig him up and tear him open? What devilry was this?

For her, I kept m'self straight-faced. 'You must not weep about this. You must put on a good aspect, Jane. We are going to the king's banqueting hall, and you must serve the queen whilst I serve the king. Do you understand?'

She nodded. Though she was a natural fool, she was not an idiot. She understood much. And with a flash of heat to my chest, I realized she also understood *where I would be*, for she seemed to have been waiting for me outside of Nicholas's chamber, pacing before it. Cuds-me. I would have to ask her later what she knew, and I feared mightily the answer. Perhaps it *would* be the better part for Nick and me to cool our ardour.

I first went to my spare rooms to gather my basket of foolery – with Nosewise trotting after. Then I brushed down my coat with its pleats, and I secured a festive collar for my dog and a jester's hood for him as well, though I did not wear one, and the two of us headed for the banqueting hall.

Marion was not high enough in rank to be seated in the hall, though her father, Yeoman of the Records Lord Heyward, was seating himself on one of the far tables. She, being a bastard and all, and the wife of the jester to boot, did not belong in such august company. She ate this day, no doubt, in the servants' hall as she usually did.

Preparations from the kitchen servants were already started, with every man working like bees in a hive, moving hither and yon across the hall, but mostly tending to the high table and the tables immediately below it that would seat the privy council and other lords and their wives that Henry favoured.

Gleaming white tablecloths were laid on the trestle tables that had just been set up, whilst other servants brought forth

the chairs for the high table and the benches for the lower tables
that were usually placed against the walls. Still more servants
lit the candles in chandlers, others set the tables with salt cellars,
plates and goblets of silver for the high table, of pewter for the
lesser tables, and wooden plates and goblets for the lowest
tables. It is ever thus. There will always be the richest men with
the best of all, and there will always be those middling men
who have only a touch of finery, and always men of the lowest
estate who must dine on wood and sup without salt.

And where was I in this mix? Oh, I was my own agency,
for though I had my own goblet of silver that Henry had made
just for me with a jester on its face, I ate not from my own
plate but from Henry's whilst sitting *not* beside him, but *before*
his table on a stool, like the meanest of servants . . . and yet
not like one at all, for a slave or peasant might kneel at his
master's feet and be fed from what a king *tossed* from his
plate. But I had the singular privilege to *take* from his plate
without his complaint. And I tried my damnedest to take the
juiciest morsels, just to rile him up.

The sideboards were beginning to fill with dishes that could
sit covered for a time, whilst the hot dishes of meats and
pottages would await the call to come to dinner, as I was just
beginning to hear.

The lords and lesser courtiers who had a place in the
banqueting hall – for not *all* of court could gather there – began
to arrive, and a buzz of conversation of the day's happenings
rumbled throughout. I thought it a most pleasant sound, the
sounds of humanity with its shuffling feet, tittered laughter,
rustle of fabric and reverberations of voices converging, for
though we resided in London, we were also our own city here
behind our palace walls, and we knew well all its citizens.

And then, from the kitchens, the heavenly perfumes of
roasted meat, aromatic sauces, the fragrance of herbs in baked
dishes and the smell of sugar and fruit made into colourful
tarts. Oh, the king's table was the most pleasant of affairs.

Some of court acknowledged me with a nod, for they knew
if they were not cordial to me, they would be made a fool of
at some point and in the most public of ways. I was not a
man to be trifled with, even Fool that I was.

In the gallery above, I noted my musician friends were all in place, and I waved my jester stick with its small jester hood atop it to my fellows. And when that trumpeter, John Blanke, a foreign man as black as soot, stood and, with the flair of a dancer, raised the shiny brass instrument to his lips and began his processional, everyone stood, for they knew that Henry and Queen Jane would arrive at the archway, and so thence they came, he holding her hand upwards as if they were in a dance. They had both changed their clothing to dine. Henry was resplendent in a gold doublet with artful slashes on the chest and sleeves, with his silken chemise pulled through each one and held in place with bejewelled pins. Oh, how he sparkled. The jewels in his hat, the feathers, the furs that covered his shoulders and lining of his coat. My Henry. In truth, he always took my breath away, and once again, I could scarce believe I was allowed in his company as I was, insulting him, chiding him, singing to him, making merry for him – and the joy I felt when I made him laugh. Was there ever a man as blessed as me?

And the queen, bedecked in a white gown with pearls. Her gable hood was white to match it, with one side of her golden veil pinned up. She was as pale as her gown, but she seemed to glow, like porcelain. She was not one to dress resplendently on her own, being like a simple maid in her heart, but she dressed as a queen because the king wanted it so. Henry was proud of this wife, though . . . well, he did not seem *enamoured* of her as he was once with Catherine, and once with Nan. But thinking of Nan Bullen saddened me, which made me think of disembowelled corpses, and I knew I mustn't let my mind tread there, for I must needs devise things to entertain Henry.

Henry took his seat under the canopy of state, and Jane took the place beside him at the head table. Sir Nicholas Carew, the Master of the Horse and Henry's bosom friend, sat on his right side. A long-faced man was he, as long as a horse's face. Thank *Jesu* for the beard.

A few chairs down from him was Cromwell. Growing fat like a toad, he puddled in his chair, looking not at the court but at his place setting, perhaps marking it down that it was not polished enough or grand enough.

Queen Jane had her court of trusted ladies on her side, but sitting closest to her was the Lady Mary. Jane smiled at her, patted her hand, made brief comments to her, but Lady Mary kept her eyes downcast with a rosy blush high on her cheeks.

John Blanke the trumpeter – a most congenial fellow who came to court as a young man under Henry VII – finished his entrance salute, thrust the cup of the horn into his side and sat, all with the precision of a military legion. A pompous bishop intoned the grace, and then Henry gestured to his musicians, and they began to softly play.

'What shall we dine on tonight, Harry?' I asked, pulling my stool up to the table before him, the stool being low enough not to block the view of the king from the others in the hall. 'Game or . . . *foul*,' and I glanced at the row of his privy men lined up beside him.

'Will,' he said, like a disciplining father to a son, as he washed his fingers over the basin the ewerer was holding, 'we will not make ourselves bilious from troubling talk. You, sirrah, should entertain. Stand and give us all a jest or a rhyme.'

I pushed the stool back and rose. Nosewise sat beside me and gazed up with adoration. With my hand to my heart, and facing the gathered at their tables, I began.

'A riddle, Your Majesty, and for all of court. A riddle to test the wit of your men . . . and ladies,' I added with a bow to Jane's court beside her. 'Listen carefully and reason it out: I carry a greater load dead than alive. Whilst I lie, I serve many; if I stand, I serve but a few. If my entrails are torn out to lie open out of doors' – and here I paused, thinking of that servant – 'I . . . I bring life to all, and I give sustenance to many. A lifeless creature which bites naught; when loaded down, I run on my way yet never show my feet.' I turned to Henry. 'Well, Uncle? What am I?'

I could see that he was stumped, as were his privy men, reluctant to answer at any rate lest they show up His Majesty.

The queen shook her head and looked to her ladies.

So I turned to the court and opened wide my arms. 'My lords! Who has an answer for the Fool?'

Someone from the back yelled out, 'A ship!'

I could not see the gentleman but pointed to him. 'You are correct, sirrah. And win . . . nothing.' I put the back of my hand to my cheek as if speaking confidentially, but bellowed in a harsh whisper instead, 'Especially for besting the king.'

But Henry laughed and slapped the table with his hand. 'Bring that clever fellow forward. He should sit with me.'

And never was I so surprised to see that it was my own Nicholas Pachett! I quickly wiped the shocked look from my features and greeted him as if he were a stranger, grabbing his arm and patting him on the back.

Henry extended his hand to shake across his table and he gestured for Nicholas to come round to sit on the other side of Lady Mary, moving the ladies down till one had no seat and, with flushing cheeks, was forced to replace Nicholas at his chair at the far end of the hall.

'And who are you, good sir?' asked Henry.

He bowed low. 'Your Majesty, I am Nicholas Pachett, Lord Hammond, and your servant.'

'I seem to have met you before, my lord, but cannot recall where.'

'We have talked before, sire, on little matters.'

'Well, we shall talk more. Perhaps on bigger matters. I cannot allow a man as clever as this to go unnoticed any longer. And look you, Will. I'll wager you thought none could answer your riddle, and this right smart lord did.'

'Aye, Harry. I admit, he's at least as smart as a Fool.' I waited for the court's laughter to subside. 'Perhaps you should make *him* your Privy Seal.' And I gave a little pout towards Cromwell.

More laughter followed, and Nicholas shot me a quick look with a sparkle in his eye before we all sat again and the servants began to approach the king's table.

I ate sparingly from Henry's plate as the dinner continued. My stomach was thinking of dead men and of Nick having the gall to make his move without my help at all. Yes, he was ambitious and wanted to make a name for himself . . . and get himself a knighthood too. I couldn't blame him. I just didn't like the idea that anyone might have thought I had tutored him.

Tut, what a pillicock I was! Of course they wouldn't know! How *could* they? We had kept our association secret. Even if someone had noted the two of us talking together, they wouldn't suspect him any more than any other courtier who hired me to entertain their fellows, as so many did when they played at cards or had gatherings in their lodgings.

Except for Jane Foole.

And *that* thought made my belly roil. I glanced at her, and she did a simpleton's dance for the queen's ladies at the other end of the table, but I could tell that her heart wasn't in it. I had to talk to her. Not only about this servant, but of what she might know – or *think* she knew – about Nicholas and me.

Yet, as the afternoon rolled on, and when I was in the middle of juggling a pullet leg, a boiled egg and an onion, a servant approached Carew and whispered in his ear, a worried look starching the servant's face to white.

Carew, for his part, jolted back, eyes turned towards the king.

Henry noticed. He always noticed.

'What is it, Nicholas?'

'Nothing to upset yourself over, sire. But I fear I must leave the table to tend to certain matters.' He rose, but Henry stayed him.

'What matters are these?'

'Your Grace, do not interrupt your feast. The music is merry, the food is delicious, and your Fool is entertaining.'

'And yet,' said Henry, never letting go like a dog with a bone . . . just as Nosewise was doing on the floor barely under the tablecloth below Henry's feet, 'I should like to know.'

Carew glanced back at his fellows, catching the one eye of his brother-in-law, Sir Francis Bryan, Chief Gentleman of the Privy Chamber and Henry's long-time and *debauched* friend, who wore an eyepatch after losing that eye in a joust some years ago. Some say the Devil demanded payment for being wickeder than he and took the eye from Sir Francis to keep in Hell, awaiting the man's arrival. Indeed, Cromwell (of all people) called *him* the Vicar of Hell.

Carew finally sighed and spoke low. 'Sire, it is in regard to . . . to the servant, Geoffrey Payne.'

Geoffrey Payne! No one had mentioned his name before,

and I sent up an extra prayer. I knew him. Of course, I knew everyone, but never imagined it would be someone so close to the king. He was a part of the queen's own household. Beshrew me for a whelk-headed dolt!

Henry frowned and dropped his eating knife with a clatter to his plate. Queen Jane leaned in and put a hand to his arm in comfort, for all at the high table could easily hear this exchange.

I nearly dropped the items I was juggling and caught them, one, two, three, tossing the pullet leg to Nosewise. I listened as intently as I could whilst not *looking* as if I were listening. I fussed with the onion and set it down and proceeded to peel the shell off the egg.

'What? Have you found the knave that killed him?'

'Not yet, my liege. But . . . sire, perhaps we can go to some private place and—'

Henry slammed his hand to the table and did exactly what Carew *didn't* want him to do. He bellowed, and all of the court silenced, listening to him.

'My patience is ragged, Nicholas. Tell me now, or by St George I will . . . I will . . .'

Carew bowed. 'Very well, Your Grace. Payne was found earlier today, dug up from his grave and deliberately disembowelled.'

Queen Jane and her ladies shrieked. They turned their faces away and paled.

Henry shot to his feet, upturning his plate and goblet upon the tablecloth. It ran red with the wine, like blood. And the carnage left behind from his plate was reminiscent in my mind of the innards of that poor man. I promptly lost my appetite.

'By God and all his angels! I will strangle that cur m'self! My wife's own servant! How was this allowed to happen? Answer me that, Chief Gentleman.' And here he turned viciously on Sir Francis.

Sir Francis stood to face his king and bowed. 'Your Grace, there are no clues to discover. No reason why someone should have done this deed. And still no further clues on this latest abuse.'

'This cannot be,' said Henry, angrier than I have ever seen him, though deadly quiet. 'I want more guards night and day on the queen's chamber. I tell you, Nicholas, I shall not stand for this.'

'We have been trying, Your Grace, but . . .'

And then, in the quiet that followed, both Sir Nicholas and Sir Francis slowly turned their heads . . . to me.

I took a step back, my breath captured.

Henry turned to look, too, without comprehension. To help Henry, I turned to look behind me.

'Your jester is good with an investigation,' said Carew with a sly tone.

I couldn't help but stab a glance towards Cromwell. Oh, how well *he* knew the jester was good at it.

'*My* jester? Will Somers?' asked Henry, astounded.

Please gentle Jesu, please don't let him ask me. There were certain things that Henry did not need to know about my extra activities. No, indeed.

Thank Christ Henry only stared at me, as if divining the answers from the very look on my silly face.

'He has done admirably a few times, Your Grace,' said the voice of my paramour. I could not believe he spoke. *What the hell are you doing, Nick?*

Henry turned to look at him, already forgetting who he was and why he spoke. But I could see as it passed over his face his remembrance of him, and a gentleness enlightened his eyes. He stepped forward and laid his hand on Pachett's shoulder. 'Is it true?'

'I have seen it for myself. Your jester is a very clever fellow, and loves and serves only you, Your Grace.'

And that, in Nick's way, was saying to the king that I had no fortune to make, no title to earn, as opposed to the king's bosom friends. That I only served Henry. And that was true enough.

But Christ save me, Nick!

Henry, having measured his Chief Gentleman of the Privy Chamber, his Master of the Horse and this new unknown lord with the gentle smile, finally turned back to me.

'Somers, is this true? Do you solve more than riddles?'

I bowed and couldn't raise my head. 'Uncle, it is true. I–I have. I have sorted murderers from common men, but it is not my *vocation*. That is to entertain *you*, Uncle.'

Henry's ginger brows furrowed. 'That Spaniard,' he muttered, remembering from years ago, and then shook it away, for he did not wish to think of Spain. It would only remind him of Catherine and their child Mary whom he had declared a bastard, the child he once called his Pearl. Now the young woman who sat beside Queen Jane at the high table.

'Then, Somers, you are excused to help Carew with this murder question. I want that knave found and executed. Go with him now. And Edward. You go as well.' He was talking to the ambitious Edward Seymour, Viscount Beauchamp, the elder brother of the queen. He rose and bowed with a stiffness to his face. No doubt he found himself too good for this task.

And me? I froze for but a moment, and the king's face softened, for he could see that I was frightened. 'Go, and God bless you, Will. There's a pouch of gold in it for you, and the love of your king.'

I softened then. 'Aw, Harry. You know I would do anything for you, gold or no.'

'I do know. Go with these men, then, for Sir Francis will go with you as well. Go, and save the household of the king. I trust you, Will.'

I could do naught else. I left my basket and my dog behind and followed those three varlets out of the banqueting hall.

FOUR

What, by Christ, was a jester to do? Cuds-me. I had to obey and follow those lords throughout the palace and out to the churchyard, and me with just my coat and no cloak. And it was cold this December afternoon, with a sun slanted low in a white sky painted with slashes of winter colour, with patches of snow upon the ground and puddles with ice glimmering upon them. *They* had boots and fur-lined coats. I had naught but shivering to warm me. And a belly roiling with the thought that I could offer them naught. If *they* had no clues, what could *I* find?

The Thames had frozen solid, and I recalled well how the court had progressed through London to Greenwich – the king, the queen *and* Lady Mary – with the friars standing along the way with lit candles and incense, making our path fragrant. Marion and I were both given horses for the occasion rather than riding in a wagon with servants, and though the air had been cold, it was filled with the sweet aroma of incense, reminding us of the old days of our religion. At least it did me. Marion and I seldom spoke of it. One never knew who might be listening.

And always, Eustace Chapuys, the Ambassador to the Holy Roman Emperor, was there with us, like a conscience. Watching, judging, reporting back. I wondered why Henry allowed him nigh since he was on such poor terms with His Imperial Majesty, but one must keep discourse open . . . especially when one might want a favour in the future.

I was well bundled for travelling back then, with a cloak and hood lined in fleece, with gloves and travelling boots.

But today these worthies had given me no time to collect my snow apparel, and I went as I was from the table to the grave, as it were, with just my simple shoes and my coat for warmth. They were silent as we crossed through the still yard, filled with new stones and older tilted ones, as if trying to release the souls of those buried there for Judgement Day. There were men along our path, bowing as we passed them. Alas, they were not bowing for me, but for my grand companions, who were all scowling. I don't think Carew or Sir Francis cared much for Beauchamp, Esquire of the Body to the King, but from what I heard, one did not want to be on the wrong side of the queen's brother. Though it seemed to me that Carew would welcome him, them both wanting Jane as queen and urging her to plead to the king for the return of the old religion. It concerned me that they had urged the king to bring Robert Aske to court for Christmas, for his pilgrimage had such specific demands: that the monasteries be restored – and the friars of London weren't burning candles and blowing incense for naught! That Lady Mary be restored to the line of succession. That Cromwell, Richard Rich – Speaker of the House of Commons – and others who had worked to destroy the monasteries, be executed, and that heretic bishops like Cranmer be burned at the stake. Aye, I had heard it all from the whisperings amongst the courtiers and some few reliable servants on such matters.

But knowing Henry as I did, he wouldn't be agreeing to any of that. Henry was not one that went back on his orders. And woe to the man who naysaid him. Except for me. I was likened to a light-fingered cutpurse; I got away with little things.

We rounded the corner of the church and walked through the slushy, muddy snow to a place where more men were milling, with a cold wind slicing through the thinness of my coat. As we approached, the men bowed and stepped back from the piled mud and the twisted corpse that lay amongst it. And the smell!

One leg was in the air but drooping. Rigor had long ago come and gone. I was familiar with it from my childhood on my father's farm. But it wasn't that. It was the bloated corpse, the bones of his ribs and the offal spread out from them.

I put my hand to my nose for the stench of it. It seemed sharper in the cold air . . . or was it only my imagination?

Carew stepped forward and stared, looking it all over. He must have seen something similar many a time from the battlefield. He motioned for Sir Francis to approach, and with

an exhaust of air in a cloud, he did so. Edward Seymour
stood slightly before me but would not approach, and I
thought, for that hairsbreadth of a moment, that *I* wouldn't
be called forth . . . until Carew cast his eyes back at me.
'Somers,' he said gruffly. 'Come.'

Oh blessed *Jesu*. Oh Almighty God and His angels. Why?
Why had I been so cursed?

I dragged me feet forward, my already hunched shoulders
hunching even more to make m'self as small as possible. I
got in as close as I dared so my belly wouldn't give up me
dinner. But that whoreson Carew made a harsh motion with
his hand to impatiently urge me closer.

'You're this great investigator,' he said to me with a scowl.
He pointed sharply to the corpse. 'Investigate.'

Sir Francis stared at me as well, and I was forced to look.

As I expected. A man on his back, neck extended from the
slashing it took to kill him. And now belly opened for whatever devilry was at hand.

But hold! No one ever said the nature of his death blow
before. When a man's throat is cut, one expects it to be from
east to west or west to east . . . not north to south, as his was.

I glanced around the man's hasty grave. No chance of foot-
prints since all the men had trod that ground like a muddy
field. There was no weapon at hand left carelessly behind. Too
bad. The crudeness of the operation indicated no one in
particular. What was I to gain from this?

I raised my head to my worthies. 'My lords,' I said as
seriously as I could make a silly face like mine, 'I see no
evidence either.'

Carew snorted. He well knew he was wasting his time with
me, but the king had ordered it. Sir Francis was equally
incensed . . . before I opened my mouth again.

'The only thing, then, is to identify *why* it had happened at
all. Why *this* man? And why now . . . this disembowelling?'

'What's that, you say, Somers?' said Sir Francis.

'The *why* of it, my lord. The purpose. For the killing and
the way it was done. For no man's throat is cut in such a way.
And then for the . . . the disembowelling. Something about
this servant is important. He was one of the queen's, after all.'

'You think he was attacked because he was the queen's servant? He is not an important man. He is a servant like hundreds of others here at court. There is no great conspiracy here,' said Sir Francis.

'You're wrong,' Seymour piped up, still from a distance, but his words were meant for me, for he was staring directly at me. 'How could there be a reason for this? The jester is an idiot. It was a madman's folly. Look for a madman.'

The others swiftly agreed, wishing to be dismissed from this duty that was surely up to the Captain of the Yeoman Guards, and when they walked past me and said naught more, I almost tended to agree with them. Almost.

For *I* had seen no madman. And surely we would have noticed one running amok through the court, through the servants' hall at least.

Once the nobles had left, I took in the men around the dead man – gravediggers, possibly. Other servants called to assist. 'Good sirs,' I said, bowing to them. 'Have you ever seen the like?'

'What?' said a man with ginger hair. 'Someone killing the queen's servant? Never!'

'What of the manner he was killed?' said a man of my height and brown-haired. 'I was the one that came upon him when he was first discovered, and I marked how strange the cut to his neck was. Bruises on it, too.'

'It would have to be a right sharp one, the knife that done it,' Ginger added. 'Clean through, one stroke, like slaughtering a pig, though that was no stroke as this is to his belly.'

'Strange.' I bit my lower lip in thought. 'Would it have been a sword or dagger?'

'I have no sword, mind,' said the brown-haired man. 'But I don't think a sword done it. I would think a dagger. Close up.'

'Bruising, you say?' I said to Brown Hair. 'On his neck? But then *you* say' – and I turned to Ginger – 'that it was one stroke, clean through. Perhaps he was throttled, and not succeeding in that, the killer cut him.'

'Or held him down to cut him,' said Ginger. 'That seems a right foul deed there.'

'Verily,' I agreed. Desperate. Angry. To squeeze a man's

neck one-handed until the life was leaving him, finishing the
deed with a dagger stroke . . . Aye, marry. Horrible.

'But then,' I mused aloud, 'what of this disembowelling?
After you kill a man, it is done. Why do this?'

The last man, little better than a boy, likely some servant's
lad, said, 'The man wasn't moving by then. It would be an
easy butchering. Just beginning to bloat.'

My belly was almost at its wits' end. 'But why? So much
hate in such vicious doings.' They all nodded in agreement.
I girded m'self. 'I hate to ask . . . but is there anything, er,
missing?'

'Of his insides?' said Ginger.

'Aye.'

He shook his head. 'Naught. Just cut open, and a few bits
cut through too.'

'Which "bits"?'

Ginger measured his fellows, then squinted at me as if I were
an idiot. And what sort of idiot would even ask such a question?
'Liver, stomach, intestines. All sliced. But none removed.'

'That *is* puzzling,' I agreed.

'Aye. Are *you* exploring this? The *jester*?'

I shrugged. 'His Majesty believes I have some facility
with it.' I shrugged again. The others exchanged glances
and shrugged as well.

'Did any of you know Geoffrey Payne, the dead man? Did
anyone know if he had any enemies? Gambling debts and
such? This seems like the work of criminal men.'

They exchanged more blank looks, and it was then I bade
them farewell since there was little more to be said. None of
those lords that had left me behind believed I could achieve
anything. Which was why I was suddenly determined to do so.

I deemed a trip to the laundresses was in order.

FIVE

I hurried back out of the cold through the palace and out the other side into the cold once more to the place set aside for the laundresses – a few outbuildings and a grassy court-yard for laying out the linens, which was beginning to sparkle from frost. I went into one of the outbuildings, blessedly warm and steamy from the hot vats.

The women had split their work into messes, with four eating their pottage for the afternoon meal, whilst the others were still stirring the linens in the vats with wooden paddles, some batting them to get out the wet. I knew from frequent visits in the past that they would take turns: some eating, some still working, and then they'd switch.

'Why, if it isn't Will Somers,' said a plump lass, stirring the vat. Her chemise sleeves were rolled up past her chapped elbows, and she gave me a bawdy, gap-toothed grin. 'We haven't seen you in many a day.'

I glanced at the other women, many of whom had been my leman back before I had married Marion. Yes, both women and men were to my taste. I was just that way. And though Marion and I had not been chaste with each other throughout our court-ship – I did stray from time to time – but had vowed – once we'd married – that I would lay with no woman but her.

Men, on the other hand, were a different territory.

I held up my hands to placate. 'My turtle doves all. I did not come here to dance in love's garden with any of you.' They made sounds of disappointment. 'Now, now. I did tell you that once I married, I would not gambol with you further.'

'A shame, that,' said the woman at the vat. 'I miss that skinny arse of yours.'

'Skinny?' I spun round, trying to catch a glimpse of said arse. 'I'll have you know it is a fine arse, a noble arse, the best arse in Shropshire. But none of that. I am here to ask a serious question of you all.'

The woman at the vat stopped stirring. The women at the table stopped eating.

'A serious question?' asked a woman named Kate. Oh, I remembered that she had a clever mouth when it came to bedroom matters.

'Indeed. Do you all remember the day that Geoffrey Payne, the queen's servant, was killed in the corridor?'

They stared at one another, trying to divine why I would ask *them* such a question.

'Ayes' were answered all round.

'Well, then,' I said, unconsciously rubbing my hands together in anticipation. 'Do any of you recall washing an unnatural amount of blood from anyone's chemise on that day or the day after?'

They searched each other's faces. Then a wench called Isabel raised her hand at the other end of the vat. 'I do.'

Eagerly, I turned to her. Could it be this easy? 'Who then? Whose chemise was it?'

'I don't know, Will. I found it.'

'Found it. Where?'

'It was discarded near the rubbish pile. I found it and took it to the laundry for cleaning. Oh, it was a right mess. Like someone butchering in his good shirt. Sleeves dark with blood. Front too. Thought if I could clean it good and all, I could sell it.' But then she seemed to understand the implications of it and frowned.

'Was it a servant's shirt or a courtier?'

'Courtier. Embroidered at the cuffs and neck. A right good shirt it was.'

'Where is it now?'

'Sold it. To a servant in the hall. Couldn't quite get all the stains out, so it was good for little else but the rag man. I got a penny for it.'

'Who'd you sell it to?'

'That ruttish fellow Edward. Always grabbing every arse he can. That man.'

Edward? My sarding former *lover* Edward? Christ mend me.

* * *

Edward. He had not given up hope that he and I would tumble together again, but I refused him. There was my wife to consider, and there was Nicholas now. And my wife and Nicholas had made some sort of truce between them that it would be only her and him, and that I would love only her.

Oh, didn't I mention that they were acquaintances? That they were even now friends of a sort since they had both saved my life? And that Marion knew full well what went on between Nick and me? Aye. I lived a . . . complicated life.

But cuds-me, I knew I had to talk to Edward. With great reluctance, I betook m'self back through the palace to the kitchens where most of the servants gathered at one time or another. And, of course, it was all a-bustle from the meal that had finished and was being cleared away. I wandered amongst them, through them, trying not to get in the way. No one wanted a jester in the midst of actual work. In fact, I knew my presence was a hindrance and I tried to be as unobtrusive as I could be.

I searched on my own but could not find him. I know he served many other courtiers, but I didn't feel that I could interrupt any of the servants to ask after him. Well . . . that was not quite true. The truth is . . . I didn't *want* to find Edward.

Aye me. But I knew that I must. Perhaps Marion would know. She always seemed to know.

I left the kitchens through the servants' hall and poked my head into the banqueting room. And there was faithful Nosewise, sitting on my basket, waiting for his absent master. I whistled to him. His ears pricked up, his face opened into a smile that only dogs could achieve, and he leapt off the basket, took the handle in his mouth and trotted towards me, neck curved and head held erect like a stallion.

'Good boy, Nosewise.' I took the basket from his teeth. After all, he wasn't a large dog or a young pup anymore and I didn't want to strain him. 'Come along. Let's go see Marion.' He brightened at that prospect, and through the many corridors we went to our lodgings.

When I opened the door, our servant Michael was there, dusting this and polishing that. 'Good evening, Master Somers.'

'Good ev'n, Michael. Is Mistress Somers nigh?'

'At her embroidery.' He nodded once to me and carried on. This was always the gist of our exchange. He wasn't a garrulous man, was Michael. It was as if he did not wish to know me as a private man. Or perhaps he knew me to be a gossip. Well . . . it wasn't so much me doing the gossiping as it was me doing the listening.

I set my basket aside – and Michael knew enough not to touch it, not even to move it, lest I failed to find it when Henry called for his Fool.

'*MAR*-i-on!' I bellowed. Nosewise followed me to our bedchamber, and there she sat under the failing light of winter through the panes, candles around her at her embroidery frame. I wish I could have hauled Master Holbein into the chamber to capture her in paint thus, for it was a homely sight of comfort and piety, this simple tableau.

'There's no need for such noise, Will.'

I sat with a gusting sigh. 'All the saints both Catholic and Protestant preserve me!'

'Hush, Will, lest Michael hear you.'

'Marion . . .'

'I know where you went. I heard it from the servants that the king charged you with finding the killer of that servant. Well? What did you find?'

'*That* servant was Geoffrey Payne, know you that?'

She gasped. 'The queen's Geoffrey?'

'The very same.' Marion was one to acquaint herself with the high and the low. Her heart was big. 'There are so few clues. I'm trying to find Edward.'

I noted that her shoulders stiffened at mention of his name. Nothing had been kept from Marion. She knew we had dallied at one time. 'Oh?' she said nonchalantly.

I couldn't help but smile at her artifice. 'Only to ask him about the chemise he bought from one of the laundresses. I went there first. I reckoned a man who plunged a dagger into the neck of another man would be covered in blood.'

'That's very clever of you.'

'Not clever enough.' I toyed with the cuff of my shirt. 'I couldn't find him and feared asking anyone when they were so harried.'

'Will Somers,' she said with the sighing shake of her head. 'I cannot imagine you fearful of anyone at court but the king.' The little snipping sounds of her scissors through her stitches was a small comfort under such great *dis*comfort.

'Oh, I fear, my love. I fear many at this court. But servants most of all. They toil long hours—'

'As do you,' she interrupted.

'Aye, but my toil is joyful. I sing, I dance, I rhyme and make Harry laugh. That isn't the same as hauling tables about, fetching water, scrubbing plates and bowls and goblets. I think at times they are envious of me. And that provokes anger.'

'I think you work very hard. Making jests about his privy counsellors and avoiding a clout must be very vexing.'

'Ah, Marion. It is the difference between a fool on the street and a professional one who spends all his time at court. If I didn't live here, I wouldn't know how far to go with Harry. As it is . . . well, I mistime it occasionally. Still, I count it as much better work than rubbing my hands raw in the scullery.'

She nodded her bonneted head. 'That is true.'

'Might *you* know where Edward is? I moved through the kitchens, the buttery, the pantry and the like, but see him I did not.'

'He serves all over the palace.'

'Aye me. I suppose that will have to wait.'

'What of the killing weapon?'

I rose and strode to her, laying my hands on her shoulders, running my finger delicately up the side of her neck and making her shiver. I liked how she shivered. After all, from where I was standing, I could look directly down into her bosom as it shivered, and what a pleasant sight it was. 'Weapon?'

'Surely you have looked for the weapon.'

'There was no weapon to be found. Not at his grave. If I had been there at the beginning when his body was found, then . . . But here, Marion.' I pushed her round to face me. 'Have you ever heard of cutting a throat this way . . .' And I slashed gently with my finger down her white neck from chin to base of the throat. 'Rather than this way?' And I slashed gently again with my finger from right to left.

Her eyes were wide. 'Up and down?' She covered her neck with her hand. 'How strange. And . . . awkward. Why should someone do so?'

'That's what I'm asking *you*. It seems nonsensical.'

We both paused to consider it in our private thoughts.

'I'll think on it, Will.'

'It's getting late, Marion,' I finally said.

She slowly returned to her stitchery. 'Shouldn't you see to the king before you retire?'

I threw my head back upon my crooked shoulders with a sigh. 'Aye, I should. But I so wanted to see you before I did if I was late.' I leaned in and kissed her cheek. Her skin smelled pleasantly of rose water. By my oath, the woman must bathe every day!

'I go! And when I am done with the king, I might see about Edward. Or I might not. In any case, I will come speeding back to you like a swift.'

'Swifts are summer birds.'

'Very well, then. A sparrow. Constant and everywhere.'

'A sparrow,' she muttered with a smile, shaking her head likely at the absurdity of her foolish husband as a sparrow.

I kissed the top of her head behind the headdress and over her veil. 'And *you* are my turtle dove. I love you and bid you farewell till later.'

I left Nosewise with her but grabbed the stick with the pig bladder atop it. It was a great tool for slapping recalcitrant men in the face with. And then I took my cittern and pulled the strap over my arm. She glanced over her shoulder at me. I did love Marion. What a foolish notion that I could ever love another. Woman . . . or man.

I skipped along through the corridor, something only a Fool might do, and arrived at Henry's watching chamber, sidling by the two Yeomen of the Guard of the King's Body, eyeing me without turning their heads. I only had difficulty passing them when they were new to their jobs and did not know me, for I wore neither Fool's hood nor motley and bells. I learned these important men's names right quick, for it was only neighbourly to acquaint myself to them since they were in constant attendance.

I passed through the presence chamber, the dining chamber, the privy chamber – and each doorway set with guards – and finally found him in his withdrawing room with his groomsmen and, much to my surprise, *my* Nicholas! The man had managed to work his way into the king's heart by his wit, for Henry did like clever men about him. Perhaps Nick would go far. As long as his liaison with the jester remained unknown, that is.

With a sudden jolt to my heart, it occurred to me that Nicholas may wish to leave *me*.

It would be better for him if he did, I mused. *No incumbrances for a knighthood or some other title bestowed upon him. He'd see that my involvement in his life, no matter how brief, would get in the way of his ambitions.* It made all the sense in the world. But it saddened me. Oh, how dreadfully it saddened me.

I swallowed hard and girded m'self. It was my solemn duty to entertain the king, and entertain him I would!

'Greetings, Harry!' I said, saluting him with my bladder on a stick, my eyes adroitly keeping away from Nicholas.

'You have been scarce, Somers.'

Already he had forgot he sent me to investigate the killing of the queen's servant. Aye me. It made little matter. 'But I am here now, Uncle. Listen, I knew an old bishop who had lost some of his teeth, and complained of others in his gob being so loose that he was afraid they would soon fall out. "Never fear," said one of his friends, "they won't fall." "And why not?" enquired the bishop. His friend replied, "Because my testicles have been hanging loose for the last forty years, and if they were going to fall off, they would have by now."'

Henry guffawed and slapped the arm of his chair. The others laughed too, most of it genuine. I tried not to look yon at Nick, but I could not help it, and he was laughing with the rest of them. *Was* he like the rest of them? Fawning on the king to curry favours? Laughing when *Henry* laughed, stifling it when Henry did not?

I was reluctant to think it, but of *course* he was. How long could he truly dally with the jester, catering to his own whims? One day he would have to marry, and that left little time for extravagances like his favourite bedmate. I knew all this. It's just that . . . I was never on the other side of it before.

'Play a song, Will,' said the king, 'whilst I talk with these men.'

I took up my cittern, grasped the plectrums from the pouch hanging from my belt and plucked a tune for him.

They talked of this upcoming visitation from Robert Aske and his compatriots from the Pilgrimage of Grace. There were furrowed brows and frowns all round at the prospect, and all the while as the privy men talked, Henry's scowl deepened. I wondered if I should do something about it. It was my job, after all, but I wasn't certain. Henry could blow up at me, and I wasn't in the mood this night to take that abuse.

Henry's sudden explosion took us all by surprise.

'Enough!' he bellowed. Everyone froze, even me with my fingers suspended over the strings of my instrument. 'Have done,' Henry said, swiping the air with his hand as if erasing it all from a slate. 'Make your preparations, but I don't want to hear of it. Leave me.'

The men gathered their papers and satchels, bowed to the king and hastily left his privy chamber. With head down, I gathered my cittern and stick and made to depart as well, but with a world-weary sigh, the king said, 'Not you, Will.'

'Oh? What may I do to soothe your heart, sire?'

'Just your presence does that. Sometimes I think you are my only friend.'

'I am a loyal friend and servant to you, Harry. And well you know that. But you have other friends at court.'

'Is that so? Name them.'

Cuds-me. An opportunity of a lifetime. But as soon as I found joy at the idea of naming no one, it occurred to me that I couldn't leave Henry with not one peer as a friend. Besides, I knew it to be so that Charles Brandon and Nicholas Carew were his bosom friends, even though the latter sought to reverse the king's edict on the Catholic Church.

'Ah, Harry. You well know that Charles Brandon is a long-time friend of yours. As is the Master of the Horse.'

'Yes, yes,' he said softly.

'They are true friends. But . . .' I strutted a bit. 'You know I have naught to gain. So *I* am truly your bosom friend.'

'So it would seem to me.'

He smiled a little sadly, I thought. I sat on the arm of his chair and dared to touch the royal shoulder. 'I am yours, Harry. You must know that. How can I ease your burden, for you look full tired today?'

'I am. I am against this meeting with a traitor! I am to give him gifts and spout hollow platitudes to the scoundrel.'

'But, Harry, this is mere politics. In diplomacy, you aren't supposed to tell the truth.'

He had the grace to chuckle slightly at that. 'How I wish I could send my loyal jester when it serves.'

'But you *can*, Harry. I shall be hard by if you want it.'

His eyes were suddenly alight. 'And *you* can say the vilest things, because you are the Fool.'

'And *you* can look magnanimous because you can admonish me publicly for them.'

He laughed and clapped his bejewelled hands. 'Now *that* is the most sensible advice I have been given in a fortnight.'

I hopped off my perch and bowed to him. 'Your servant, sire.'

When I left him, Henry was happier than I had seen him in a long while. He had cares, did Henry. Oh, not the cares of the common man as to where the next meal would come from, or if they had enough pence when the rent was due. But larger things, like traitors trying to shift you off the throne. Vile creatures seeking to put *your* head on a pike. The thought made me shiver. For Henry had put enough of his own friends' heads on pikes, but I never wanted the same for him. Not my Henry, my patron, my king. My friend. He was mine, you see. And I was his. He was like an uncle to me, and so I was free to call him so. Ours was a companionship like no other. I wasn't a rider to go on the hunt with him, though he insisted on bringing me time and again. I was no diplomat, but he wanted me nigh when negotiations were afoot. I reckoned that Henry – even surrounded as he was by hundreds of people – was truly singular and alone. And so was I. For when it came down to it, there truly could be only one king at a time and one jester at a time in any court.

And then there was the other care of having a wife, for methought he had already tired of his new wife. He might have told himself he wanted a meek and mild companion, but the reality was not as pleasant as the dream. He was a lusty man, and he needed a lusty playmate, and she was not it. Still, the moment he got her with child, the clock would tick. If a girl, he would be done with her. But if a boy, she would be celebrated as no other wife had been. Though I would imagine that he would not be often in her company again. For she was . . . well, dull, for a word.

And Henry was never dull.

I yawned as I made my way through the corridors. No, not dull, but a heavy burden for so slender a jester. I was only one man, and sometimes it was the job of many to assuage the heart of this king. Ah, but I took to the task. For I knew Henry. Knew his heart and soul. He was not an evil man. He was strict and harsh at times, yet he valued some of his closest courtiers. He valued the two friends I mentioned. He valued me. He even valued Cromwell in his way, but more for what the man's efficiency could do for him than to have him on the hunt with him. No, he valued the working man's work that Cromwell did, the work Henry did not wish to do himself.

I passed a window and saw the pale moon wash the clouds with the colour of milk. I hadn't been that late with Henry. Mayhap I could visit Nick . . . but just as the thought occurred, I dismissed it as hastily. Nick had got his foot in the door with the king, and I could not be in the way of it. Though . . . bless me, I craved his presence. His attention. His . . . kisses. I craved them in a way that made my heart sick. I could not love him. It wasn't right. Swive him, but never love him. I loved my wife! So I told myself. Aye, marry. Why was I complicating my life more than it already was?

Gentle Lord, I prayed, *can you not take this cup from my lips? Can you not make me faithful unto my wife alone?*

I listened hard. But as usual, there was no reply.

As I walked, I saw before me a figure, just closing a door silently and stealthily making their way away from me. It seemed curious, because I knew the apartments from which this figure came, and then I recognized the tall lankiness of this person . . . and he definitely did not belong in this lady's chamber.

I followed him for a while, devising what I could make of this in my jests at court . . . until I turned a corner and he was waiting for me . . . with dagger in hand.

'Hold, Master Blanke,' I hissed with hands raised to guard me.

'Why are you following me, Jester?' he said in that strange and musical accent he had, from the wilds of Africa.

'I'm not . . . I mean, I . . . oh, cuds-me, I suppose I was.'

'Why?' His eyes shone in the gloom, for his face was nearly as shadowed as our surroundings.

I stared at his dagger, and then he looked down at it and, seeming to think better of it, sheathed it again.

'Well, the truth of it is, I saw you coming out of Lady Agnes's apartments. And, well, a man does wonder . . .'

He made a scoffing sound. 'Don't be a fool, man.'

'Too late.'

He rolled his eyes, crossed his arms and leaned against the wall. 'It isn't as you think. I . . . cannot speak of it.'

'Well, far be it from me to shake a finger at your amorous doings . . .'

'It's not amorous.' He swore in a language I did not understand. Raising his head and staring distantly, he heaved a sigh. 'Trust me, Will. And I beg you to keep your own counsel on it. Please.'

'We are friends. Of course I will. But you must be careful. You might encounter anyone in the corridors. At least this time it was a friend.'

'How well I know it. This is the second king I have served. And King Henry's father was no less suspicious.'

Indeed. John Blanke was not just any musician. He was a trumpeter. He announced all grand things at grand celebrations. Not just any man could rise to this special post, and he had done this task for *two* of England's greatest kings. But I wondered if he felt strange being the only black man amongst so many white faces. I suppose this made him exotic, and to women this can be an attractive thing. But being exotic did not always make life better. *I* was exotic in a way. Oh, I wasn't the only jester at court, but I was the one who was almost exclusive to the king, and all knew it. Which was why I had many admirers, both women and men. I suppose they thought I could bestow special favours upon them because of it. Alas, the only favour I had to bestow . . . was my person. And that was no great prize.

He offered no more explanation. Indeed, he owed me naught. We exchanged our good nights, and I promised once more not to make public sport of him and so watched that lean figure disappear into the gloom.

I turned, and then decided this was my night to see mysterious figures lurking in the corridors, for there was yet another. For a heart-pounding moment, I thought it might be Nicholas . . . but when he stepped into the candlelight, I saw that it was the servant Edward. My heart sank.

'I hear you are looking for me.' He said it sullenly, but his eyes were bright in anticipation, hoping that it meant what he wanted it to mean.

'Be at ease, Edward. I want you for naught more than information.'

'Then the Devil take you!' He spun on his heel.

'Wait,' I hissed in the quiet corridor. 'Edward, I need to talk to you.'

'I thought you didn't need me anymore,' he hissed back as I caught up to him.

'Your friendship would suffice. My other paramours are still friends with me. Why not you, Edward?'

'Because I love you,' he rasped, emotion choking him.

'I am so sorry. You know I am.'

He said nothing as he continued his march down the corridor. I kept pace.

'Edward . . .'

He halted so abruptly that I had gone two more steps ahead of him before I stopped to face him.

'What, then? What?' he asked petulantly.

I got in closer and glanced behind and before, but there were no shadows, no spies. 'You recently bought a shirt from the laundress.'

His eyes showed his utter surprise at the direction this had taken. 'Aye. And so?'

'May I see it?'

'Why?'

'It's important.'

'I say again, why?'

'I just need to see it, Edward.'

'You can have it. For three pence.'

Why the . . . '*You* bought it for *one*.'

'And now the price is three.'

'Why are you selling it?'

'Because you want it so badly. And . . . it is too stained to wear.'

I screwed up my mouth. 'Very well,' said I, tightly.

We returned again to the servants' area near the kitchens. We went in step throughout the corridors, down some stairs and to the kitchens, through some rooms and thence to the many cots with many bodies snoring and farting in them.

He went to his own bed, pulled a small coffer out from under it and took a key from his belt. He quietly unlocked the coffer and pulled a wadded-up cloth from it before closing and locking it and sliding it again under his bed. I let out a whoosh of air when he shoved it hard into my chest. Waiting, he looked at me coldly, and I reluctantly reached for my pouch at my belt and handed over three coins into his hand. 'There,' I whispered. 'And good luck to you.'

I left him. But I couldn't resist looking back. Still, he stood by his bed, watching me. And a forlorn figure he was, standing in the dark like a shadow amongst the sleeping men.

SIX

I hurried back to my lodgings when I suddenly *did* encounter Nicholas Pachett. I seemed to be a light gleaming in the darkness, attracting all the moths!

He grabbed me before I darted away . . . and captured me with his smile. 'Hold, Fool. Why do you career so recklessly throughout the passages of the king's palace?' And then he said more quietly for my ears alone, 'And into my waiting arms.'

'My lord, my apologies.' I glanced about and saw no one. 'And into your arms I would gladly fall, but . . .' I clutched the wadded shirt to my chest and bit my lip. He watched my lips and began to lean in. I jerked away from him and his grasp. 'We can't. Not here.'

'Then why not hence to my chambers?'

I sighed from the depths of me. 'Nick.' I shook my head and stepped around him. 'How can we continue to meet? You have only just stepped through the king's portal. This is your chance now.'

'Yes! And I wish to celebrate with you. For it was you who opened that door, whether you intended to or not.'

'Because you are a clever man and can discern my riddles? Tut, Nick. You know what I am speaking about.'

'I am afraid I do not.'

'Nick, the king *sees* you now. And his eyes are keen. Don't muck it up with a sodomite bedmate.'

Now he searched into the shadows for the ears of others. 'You do put things plainly.'

'Aye. I must. You must understand the situation.'

'I do. I do know how serious it is. But Will . . . my . . . my love. I would not give you up for the vanity of a title.'

'It's not mere vanity, and you know it. It is your future. And you must think on it.'

He finally frowned. But, Jesus' mercy, not for his future but for his present. 'I won't give you up.'

'You . . .' I turned away, for I did not want to look at him as I said it. 'You must.'

I felt him approach. Was there that much heat radiating from him? He took my shoulder with one hand and turned me, even as he took the other to lift my beard-stubbled chin. 'I won't,' he whispered and laid the softest, gentlest kiss yet to my lips. 'I love you,' he said, pulling back a little. His finger was still holding up my chin. Verily, it was holding up me whole body, for I surely would have swooned like a maiden. And *that* pulled me up short. I was no maiden to be falling this way and that for a swain. Thus awakened, I was able then to step back on my own.

'Nicholas. My lord . . .'

'Don't call me that.'

'*My lord*,' I said more firmly. 'We must not. For your sake. And for mine.' I turned to leave, and it would have been a dramatic exit, something to be memorialized on a stone at a crossroads . . . had I not dropped the sarding shirt.

He said nothing but instead gracefully scooped it up and shook it out. He looked at it this way and that. 'What are you doing with my shirt?'

My heart stopped. It surely did. I staggered back and could not speak.

Then, as quickly as I had suddenly died, I was resurrected when he shook his head. 'No, I am mistaken. But it is very like my shirts. Though stained. I should never wear such a thing again. What are you doing with it?'

'Christ mend me, Nicholas. Don't scare me like that again.'

'Scare you? Over a shirt?'

'It is the murderer's shirt.'

Then *he* was brought up short. 'Murderer. Oh Christ, Will. Your investigation?'

'Yes!'

He held it at arm's length, looking it over. 'But it isn't my shirt. I swear to the Virgin it isn't.'

'And thank God for that.'

'But look here. There are the remnants of initials at the cuffs.'

I snatched a sleeve to look at it closely. And there – if the jester had cared to look in the first place – were initials.

Well . . . partial initials. The first. For the other had been rent from the cuff. 'E.'

'That's not very helpful, is it?' he said. 'The first name, which must surely be Edward.'

'It could be Eustace.' And we both amused ourselves silently that it could be Eustace Chapuys, Ambassador from the Holy Roman Emperor. But unlikely on two counts. He would never murder one of the king's servants, and the shirt seemed much too broad for the Imperial Ambassador's frame.

'Edmund,' Nick recited. 'Elias, Edwin, Ellis . . . I can think of no more.'

'This is foolish. I can't investigate every "E" name of the court.'

'Then you shall have to do it with your usual aplomb and cleverness.'

'That I will.' I stood thinking for a moment, unconsciously tapping my chin with the bloody shirt . . . until I noticed Nick drawing closer to me. 'Nick!' I hissed and jumped back as if an adder were after me.

'This is most foolish, Will. Let us to my chambers and we can . . . talk.'

I shook my head and backed away. 'Talk usually turns to other things. As well you know.'

'Why are you being so stubborn?'

'Because *you* are not being sensible. I want you to become the man you should be. With titles and power and . . . and a wife and heirs. And you can't do that whilst dallying with me.'

'But . . . I can have both.'

Oh, how young he truly was. I forgot that. 'No, my sweet friend. You cannot. Secrets need to be kept. But at court there are too many eyes and ears. Someday, a cleverer jester will come to court and push me aside, and he will know and jest about us . . . and then all will be lost.'

He gazed at me, questions dancing over his face. 'I never knew that there was such a melancholy streak about you . . . funny fellow that you are.'

'Didn't you know?' Oh, how I wanted to kiss him then! When he was pensive, he was most handsome. No, when merry. No . . . what was I saying? He was always handsome.

'Every man full of mirth has the other side of the coin on his soul. For a man cannot see the amusing side of life when he has not encountered the wretched. It is why the witty Fool is so comical.'

'I never thought of that.'

'Of course not, my lord. No lord ever thinks about the lowly man.'

'That is a wretched thing to say to me.'

I bowed. 'I apologize.' But when I raised my head, I could tell he was thinking about that too.

He sighed. 'Then . . . I don't suppose you will allow me to investigate with you.'

'Well . . . I shall keep your offer in reserve. But for now, I must return . . . to my wife.'

He nodded. His arms drew in, and he raised his chin and pushed his shoulders back, composing himself. 'Very well. Then I shall await your call.'

'Nick . . .'

'There's no need, Will.' His head nodded in a sharp gesture. 'Good night.' And into the shadows of the corridor he retreated.

I looked at the place he had disappeared from. This battle was won, but was I strong enough to win the war?

With no other stealthy figures vexing me in the corridors, I returned to Marion, who was sitting in the corner of our bedchamber with a candle beside her, darning one of my stockings. I sighed in relief. At least here was contentment. Here were no questions of this or that. It was faithful Marion, loving Marion, the jester's poor Marion.

I dropped myself into a seat opposing her and watched her for a time.

She never looked up from her careful and precise stitches when she said, 'I wasn't expecting you back tonight. I understand Lord Hammond has made himself known to the king.'

Cuds-me. Even Marion?

'What's that you've got there?' she said.

I had forgotten the shirt. I shook it out for her. 'It's the murderer's.'

She dropped the stocking to her lap. 'Blessed Lord.'

'And there is an initial embroidered on the sleeve, but the rest is gone. This isn't one of yours, is it?'

Her trembling hand reached across between us and took the cuff with two fingers. She shook her head. 'No. Not one of mine. It is finely done, though.'

'Would you *know* the hand?'

'I . . . I am not certain.'

That evasion in her eyes concerned me. I knelt before her. 'Marion? You *do* know.'

'And your eye is too keen, sir.'

'You know I have been charged by the king to investigate, God save me.' I waited. 'Marion?'

'I can't be sure—'

'Can you not?'

'Oh, very well!' She rose and made a tight circuit around her chair. 'I *am* certain of the hand.' She came round to the front of her chair again and squared with me. 'But I do not know what you could do with that information. It isn't—'

'For God's sake, Marion!'

'Very well. The hand belongs to Queen Jane. Of *that*, I *am* certain.'

All night I tossed and slept little, and in the morning I looked like something Nosewise had dragged in from the rubbish pile. But I washed my face, shaved it and presented m'self to Marion for inspection and approval before we joined the others in the servants' hall for our morning meal.

We had talked little after her pronouncement of last night. We harboured our own thoughts on the matter, not wishing to dig deeper. But this morning I was all questions. Why would the queen embroider a shirt for a murderer? Ah, but this was a man who killed a servant to the queen. Mayhap he found the man to be acting improperly, even insultingly to her. So the killing was justified. But what if it weren't? What if it were for something entirely different and *un*justified?

And so was my task. One had to be sure of it to pronounce it done. Else a murderer would be free to do his deeds again. And the next might be to a higher person, a person of note to the court. One of the queen's ladies, perhaps . . . or the queen herself! No, until I was satisfied, I would continue on. Marion must have noted it in my eyes, for across the table I recognized that expression of hers, the one that said, 'Will has a feather under his nose.'

I began to wonder if I couldn't simply present it to Queen Jane and ask her to tell me for whom she embroidered it. But that was folly and I quickly dismissed it. She might reckon why I wanted to know, and if it were a person close to her, she might not wish to say. She was a peacemaker, after all. She did not wish to rend, but to bring together. She was very like a saint in her comportment, and I often felt she would have been happier as a nun and not the brood mare of Henry of England.

I hadn't realized most everyone had eaten their allotted and was rising and going on to their work, and so too must I. I kissed Marion goodbye and hurried to my first lodgings where I stored most of my jester trappings. I bundled some things into my basket and, with my cittern strapped behind my back, I set off for Henry.

I heard him bellow even as I passed through the first hurdle of the watching chamber. I glanced at the Yeoman Guard, who gave me a side glance as well that had much warning in it, and hurried on through the presence chamber, the dining chamber, the privy chamber and finally the withdrawing room where his bellowing was the loudest.

'For the last time, Thomas, I do not want that traitor here! I do not wish to bestow gifts upon him as if he were a bosom companion. For all I know, he wants to oppose me in more and more and wish me dead.'

I stuck my head into the doorway. There was that perpetually frowning Thomas Cromwell. And there was my Henry, drawing himself up like a boar to defend himself against a hunter. He was all bristles, was Henry, and he looked imposing in his fur-trimmed gown, his padded doublet, his legs still like pillars of strength, though I know how they ached him.

'You take too many liberties, Thomas. You force me into situations I am not content with. You have displeased me of late.'

At the word 'displeased', Cromwell flinched. To discontent the king was to get your head on a pike.

Cromwell paused, thinking what to say. And I was wondering if I should blunder in and discontent Cromwell when he hastily said, 'Sire.' He bowed. 'It pains me to think I have hurt you so. Never would I do such. My only desire is to see you rise higher.'

'I think your desire is to grow in stature yourself, get more titles, eh? Lord Privy Seal, *Baron* Cromwell.'

'Your Grace, the fact that you have conferred such beneficence upon me only serves to prove that I am performing your will. And part of my service includes thinking beyond what is evident. To seeing possibilities. To know men's hearts. And Robert Aske is not a guileless man. He may be the leader of this rebellion, but it does not come from a godly place. And if we must cozen him to discover all his deceits, then it is blessed by the Lord Himself in order to secure the peace of the kingdom. And part of that plan . . . is to bring him to the palace.'

Oh, what a schemer was this man! What gutless deceit! For I had little doubt that this Pilgrimage of Grace came out of the *goodness* of men's hearts, not their guile, torn as they were from their religion and from the upheaval Cromwell himself had instigated. They took an oath, after all. Maybe Cromwell supposed all men were liars and blasphemers like himself.

I could take it no more. Just as Henry seemed to be deciding Cromwell was right, I whipped out my Cromwell puppet and loudly proclaimed in my best Lord of the Privy Seal imitation, 'I am all the things you granted me, King Henry, and more: Lord Liar, Baron Deceiver, Sir Crumbled-Well. Oh, I know what is in men's black hearts because I simply look beneath me own doublet.'

I snatched a glance at Cromwell, and there were hot coals burning in his eyes. If he could have drawn his dagger on me, he would have. *This time, Will, you might have gone too far.*

Henry merely frowned.

I lowered the puppet. 'Oh, Harry, I know you told me not to abuse your ministers, but verily, here is Master Cromwell, painted with gilt and ermine. Oh aye, he has your best interests at heart, but might he be mistaken in this? They march under the sign of the cross. They swore oaths.'

'You will not meddle in my doings, Somers.'

'But, sire, do you listen to this man? How he measures his speech, how he cajoles . . .'

'I advise, Master Somers,' said Cromwell, eyes settling down to mere cinders. 'It is my duty to my king. My conscience is clear.'

'Cuds-me! I didn't know you had one of those.'

He turned to the king. 'Must I suffer this, Your Grace?'

'No, you must not. Somers, begone, or I shall have you whipped.'

That was clear enough. I bowed. 'I would not offend you for the world, my king. Him, on the other hand . . .' I thumbed over my shoulder at Cromwell.

Harry picked up an orange sitting on his side table and hurled it at me. It caught me on the side of my head. It did not hurt, but it did wound, and I bowed my way out of the room. He was furious. It wasn't often I dared to make him so, but I knew he would be forced to remember my words and to consider them. I wished I had a way to stop Cromwell completely, but short of murder, I did not have an answer to that puzzle.

I wandered the corridors, cheered somewhat by the greenery festooned about the walls for Advent, with pinecones and acorns tied with red ribbons to the branches. Downhearted, I stopped to admire a swag of it, to inhale the sweet pine scent, and nearly ran into Charles Wriothesley, Windsor Herald of Arms in Ordinary. I bowed and begged his mercy. He was polite, as always. A subtle man, a quiet man. He mostly went about unnoticed, but I recognized a fellow listener. He was a herald, a chronicler. It was his vocation to take notes of the life and heartbeat of the court, to write it down for posterity and to find no recognition for it, for he seemed to glean very little out of all his work.

'Master Herald,' I said, placing my free hand to my heart. 'Perhaps you are just the man I am looking for.'

He shook his head. 'No. I beg of you, Master Somers, I want no part of your foolery. Jests and rhymes do not interest me.'

'Oh no, Master Wriothesley. I do not wish to irk you, but only to ask you a question. No foolery at all. I give you my oath, sir.'

His moustache and beard were a light chestnut colour, almost reddish-blond, and a little vague like his slender person and character. Everything about him was more shadow than solidity. He twitched said moustache and narrowed his eyes, measuring me. I seldom talked to him, never mocked him, for he was barely there.

'Very well. But I warn you, I will not bear your folly.'

We began to walk along the corridor in slow, measured strides. 'My question to you, Master Wriothesley, is this. Do you trust Robert Aske and his ilk? Do you believe this Pilgrimage of Grace is of the heart?'

He glanced at me but for a moment before turning his face ahead. 'And why would the jester ask such a serious question?'

'There are many more layers to me, sir, than most men care to ever think about. I worry. Because this man is being invited to court.'

'Invited, is he? To what end? To execute him?'

'No, for it is Master Cromwell's idea that he and our king can discuss and come to a mutual agreement.'

'The devil, you say,' he muttered.

'You do not believe that?'

'I . . .' But he never finished that thought. 'It is not for me to gainsay Master Cromwell.'

Nor was it prudent. I understood his position.

'You are an observer and not a player. You are very like me in many ways, Master Wriothesley. Does that surprise you? For I make it my job to observe, but I also make judgements based on those observations. And a jest or two, of course.'

'I . . . chronicle what transpires. I do not make judgements, for that is not the chronicler's task.'

'Is it not? Then how is one to interpret that which has come before? Histories are studied so that men may learn from the past.'

'Well, I suppose I do inject *some* commentary to explain what has transpired and why, but I do not believe in being verbose about it.'

No, indeed, for this was the most verbiage I have ever heard pass his lips.

'Then what of this man Aske who leads this so-called pilgrimage?'

'I know he is a barrister. I know that those who speak of him seem sincere. I know that he may be honest in his dealings and genuine in his requests.'

'Do you think he will be dealt with fairly if he comes to court?'

His gaze drifted here and there into alcoves and shadows, and ahead to where courtiers had gathered. He slowed his steps. 'I believe that any man who comes to court who is not a courtier should watch his step.' He stopped and squared with me. 'And I believe, also, that anyone who sides with him may be considered a traitor and should also watch *their* step.'

'I side with no one,' I was quick to add. 'No one but King Harry.'

He slowly nodded. 'That is wise indeed. And now if you will excuse me, Master Somers, I have my own tasks to attend to.' He turned away to go back the way we had come, and I got the impression it was because of the courtiers ahead of us that he did not wish to mingle with. But then he paused and looked at me again. 'It was an interesting discussion, Jester. I would not mind further argument on it.' He nodded, as if reassuring himself of the idea, and finally left me.

Well, that was enlightening. In a way. But I already knew that Cromwell never intended to play fairly with this Robert Aske, and it was only a matter of time till it all came to a head.

Or . . . a beheading.

SEVEN

Since I wasn't welcomed in Henry's company for the nonce, it seemed meet to wander to the queen's court and see about asking the servants some questions. After all, they were the most likely to know the circumstances that got poor Geoffrey into such a foul situation.

And I needed to make a list. A list of 'E' names for whom our queen would have embroidered a shirt.

When I came to her apartments, a musician was making merry with a tune, the ladies were playing games, and Jane Foole was shrieking in delight. Queen Jane had brought forth her casket of jewellery for the little fool to play with, for she did love sparkly things. Didn't most of us? Especially when it came to gold or sparkling gems.

I almost turned to leave, for it seemed there was already much merry-making, and I did not see what I could add to it all, especially as melancholy as I felt, when Jane Foole caught sight of me. 'Will! There you are. Come sit beside me and I shall adorn you.'

I couldn't turn away a request such as that, so I scampered forward and sat on the floor beside her. She pulled out lengths of pearl necklaces, gold chains, gems of enormous size, and draped them around my neck. 'Janie, you silly fool. Did the queen give you leave to play with her baubles?'

'I did,' said Jane Seymour, leaning forward. She held embroidered ribbons in her hands, and she seemed to be choosing amongst them. 'My Jane likes to play with them, and I am loath to refuse her. I am not one to adorn myself so, except as the king wishes of me.' No, she was not. What had I said? She'd rather be a nun, methinks.

'But, lady, she might lose something or break it.'

'She is careful.' She tapped below her eye. 'And I am careful to keep watch.'

'Oh!' cried Janie. 'My favourite is not here.'

'And what is your favourite, my dear?' asked the queen, like the Virgin herself, all care and alert to the sorrows of others, for indeed our Jane Foole seemed to be quite distressed.

'The brooch,' she said, her voice very much like a weeping child. 'The one with the purple stone and the twisted wire about it.'

I stepped back, startled, as the queen flew from her chair and knelt beside the girl. She grasped her hand and laid one of the embroidered ribbons within it. There was also a dangle of small pearls sewn to it, ending in a pearl droplet. 'My foolish Jane,' she said in calming appeasement. 'This I gift to you, for the most happy occasion of the birth of our Lord.'

Janie stopped her caterwauling as abruptly as a shutting door and stared down at the gift from the queen. Her stubby finger touched the dangling pearls. 'These are pearls,' she breathed. 'Oh, it's lovely. For me? Thank you, my queen. I love you!'

Queen Jane had returned to her chair and smoothed out her skirts with the help of her attendants, one being the Lady Mary who, for once, looked grateful to her patron. 'And I love *you*, my little fool.'

But though it was a kind gesture, I stared long upon the queen. For I had seen her expression before Janie began to fret. There was not the idea to soothe a crying child. There had been surprise and then alarm upon her face, and quickly, so quickly that no one else would have noticed, her eyes darted here and there to see if anyone observed, before she launched herself to distract the girl. Queen Jane regained her seat, breathing hard from the exertion.

But the jester saw it. And marked it down.

For what brooch was this?

I tarried and sang a song with the musician, told a joke and bustled from lady to lady to see what thing they embroidered, but also to boldly listen to their gossip and to comment upon it. I waited for my moment to sidle close to Janie when the court was preoccupied elsewhere and drew her even farther away from the others.

'My Janie,' I said, as she continued to admire her ribbon, flicking the dangling pearls to watch them swing. 'My dear, what was it that so vexed you earlier? About some brooch?'

She brought the ribbon close to her eyes to examine the stitchery. 'It was my favourite.'

'Aye. I heard you say so. Where has it gone, do you suppose?'

She put a finger to her chin and raised her face. 'Oh. Geoffrey must have taken it.'

'Geoffrey Payne? The servant?'

'Aye. I saw him once. He tried to before, but someone came.'

'He tried to take it before?'

'I saw him, but he didn't see me. The black man told him not to. They were close friends, you see.'

I sat back on my haunches. How dare there be something at court that I didn't know about! I was bewildered. I reached forward and put my hand on hers, lowering the sarding ribbon. 'Janie, dearling, John Blanke, the trumpeter, was friends with Geoffrey Payne?'

'Oh, aye. I thought everyone knew.'

Clearly not.

'Why was Geoffrey trying to take the brooch?'

She shrugged, now bewitched by her new gift. 'Maybe it was his favourite too.' She looked up suddenly. 'Is that why they killed him?'

I fell back in horror. Cuds-me. Killed for a piece of jewellery that was not his to keep? And now my suspicions fell on John Blanke. He tried to stop him. Mayhap it was an accident. A dagger gone awry . . .

But that's a dagger gone well too far awry to dig him up and follow the accidental execution with a disembowelling. There was something much too strange here.

I turned back to Janie, and as hastily as the lucid moment had shown on her face, it just as quickly dispersed again, like a cloud passing across the sun. 'It was my favourite.' Her gaze looked deep into the mist only she could see.

'It . . . it was that particular brooch he seemed fond of?'

'Not many brooches. But this one was a lovely size. This big.' She extended her hand, palm upwards, and curled in her stubby fingers to show me. A little larger than a gold sovereign.

I whistled. 'What did it look like, dearling?'

'The stone was purple. Pretty. All chiselled till it sparkled. And there was twisted wire all around it. Oval in shape.

There were three pearls like teardrops hanging from it. Like my new ribbon. Do you like my new ribbon, Will? The queen gave it to me.' She held it up and swiped a finger through the dangling pearls. 'It was very pretty. Belonged to Queen Jane. But *this* is mine!' She clutched her ribbon with pride.

'Is that why you seemed so upset at mention of him yesterday?'

She pushed out her lower lip and shook her head.

'No? Because it seemed—'

'Don't want to talk about it. No.' She shook her head vigorously, threatening to come to tears again. When I saw that there was little more to be got from her, I knew I had to leave her to it.

This Advent, Henry had many a meal with his court. It seemed the proper thing, and he did enjoy his entertainments. It seemed to make him merry when the court enjoyed them as well, and so we feasted. Modestly, for it was still Advent. Henry liked the Christmas songs and bid me sing one as his court ate.

My eyes swept the high table. There again, two ladies sat on the other side of Queen Jane, and then there was my Nicholas. And with a flash of hot regret, I realized he was to be *my* Nicholas no more. I turned away to my task, stood and sidled closer to where Cromwell sat a few seats from the king at the high table. I strummed my lute and began, looking at Cromwell's frowning countenance. Did naught make the man smile?

'*The boar's head in hand bear I*,' I sang, jerking my head towards Cromwell with my insinuation.

> '*Bedeck'd with bays and rosemary.*
> *And I pray you, my masters, merry be,*
> *Quot estis in convivio . . .*'

Henry snorted a chuckle but tried to hide it in his wine cup. Cromwell's big boar's head made no change of expression as I sang the old carol.

When 'twas done, the court tossed coins to me, which I ably scooped up. I allowed the musicians up in the gallery to take on the musical work as I sat on my stool before the king and ate as heartily as I could from his plate whilst I juggled the thoughts in me head: a cut throat and a disembowelled man, a bauble from the queen's jewellery casket, the black trumpeter and a man with the initial 'E'.

I managed to stab a piece of fish and ate its flesh from off my knife. I glanced at the king and got my mind set back upon him. 'You know, Harry,' I said, with mouth full, 'a man I know was set to buy a horse, and he haggled with the dealer. "One crown," he said. The dealer shook his head. "Very well, two crowns." The dealer shook his head again. "Well, then, *three* crowns, and that is my final offer." The man paid one, not being a gentleman of great means, and led the horse away, promising to pay the remainder. On the following day, when the dealer encountered the man and asked for the balance, the buyer all of a sudden refused, saying, "We must keep our agreement; it was settled between us that I was to be your debtor; I should be so no longer if I were to *pay* you."'

Henry and his court laughed, and by that I could finish my meal. When I glanced above to the gallery again, it got me to thinking about John Blanke . . . but I did not see him there up above. I thought to seek him out but had to wait for Henry to excuse me.

It didn't take long. Henry was full of his meal and merriment and bid his court farewell and took the hand of his wife, who had eaten less than a doe would have done, and they exited the banqueting hall. Soon, all the others began to leave, but I noticed out of the edge of my eye that Nicholas lingered.

No, blessed Lord. Not this. I was trying to forget him, and I was scrambling to collect my cumbersome lute, my basket and my dog when he came round the table and stood by me. I couldn't very well ignore him now, and so, very reluctantly, I turned. 'My lord.'

'Do stop calling me that,' he said softly.

'But, my lord, I thought this was settled.'

'It is *not* settled.' He reddened in fury for but a moment. It was a rare sight on him. He seldom used anger to get his way. 'Will . . .'

'Nicholas.' I could not look at him. I feared bursting into tears like a woman. I wanted him. I wanted him in ways I hadn't thought my jaded heart could. I wanted him like I wanted Marion. With love, devotion, desire.

'Nicholas . . .'

'Come to my bed tonight. Please, Will. Please come to me.'

I weakened. I was no kind of man, with no substance inside me. I was an empty pasty, crumbling crust, no filling.

'Yes,' I said, still ducking my head as I hurried away.

'What kind of man am I?' I asked Nosewise as we tramped through the corridor to my lodgings, the lodgings I share with my *wife*.

He looked up at me with pure devotion. Ah, such is the life of a dog. They have no cares, no worries, no philosophy to wonder about. His master paid him heed, gave him food and a scratch behind the ears. Did he need any more than that?

How I envied my dog.

I reached my lodgings . . . and hesitated. Marion will know. She will take one look at my face and know that something plagued me. So I would put a mask on it and smile and chuckle and be the courtly Fool I was paid to be.

I thrust through the door and made a merry sound. I released the dog from his lead, and he rushed through, seeking out Marion, for she was as solicitous to him as I was.

'How was the king and his court tonight?' she asked from the other room. I put my lute and basket in a cupboard and came to greet her with a kiss upon her cheek.

She had some of the silver of our board in her lap and was polishing the spoons and goblets.

'It went well. Look. Coins from the court.' I spilled them from my pouch and dropped them into her lap as well.

She smiled at the bounty. 'You must have been *very* good tonight.'

I swept down on one knee and took up her slightly chapped hand. 'I am good every night.' And I kissed it. 'Oh, Marion. I miss you when I cannot dine with you. I long to see your merriment, for it is your pleasure I seek.' I pulled her forward into a proper kiss. I felt her begin to complain, for some of the coins and a spoon or two tumbled from her lap to the floor, but as the kiss went on, she clutched at me and kissed me back fervently. Had I not kissed her of late? Was she so desperate for love from me?

I drew back and touched her face. 'My Marion.'

'You won't be here tonight, will you?'

The Devil take it. She knew. She always knew. And now I felt guilty as I had not felt in a long time. 'W—well Marion, I—'

'Is it Pachett? Or someone new?'

I froze. 'Why, by the Rood, would you say that?'

'I merely wondered. He has the king's attention now. I thought you and he would . . . would have . . .'

'I must not see him. But . . .'

'But you wish to.' She returned the fallen silver to her lap and just as swiftly brought her face up in a hopeful smile. 'Is it the investigation? I should accompany you!'

And quicker than one could snap their fingers, she was up, putting away her work and affixing her headdress to her hair.

'Erm . . . Marion . . .'

'You must solve this riddle, Will. You'll be plagued by it until you do. And I willingly offer my help.' She stopped checking pins and laces and raised her chin. 'You do want my help, do you not?'

'Oh. Well, of course.'

Smiling, she adjusted her sleeves and slashes, and then strode towards the chamber door.

Apparently, we were *both* to go see Nicholas.

EIGHT

There was naught I could do. I shut my mouth and followed her. She was so cheerful in her reckoning what I was about. I *couldn't* tell her no. But I prayed that Nick would be in a proper state of dress to receive us. *Both* of us.

As we approached through the nearly empty corridors, but hearing shrieks of laughter and conversation as we passed the many doors to courtiers' lodgings, we finally arrived at Nicholas's, and it was here that I finally said, 'Erm . . . Marion. I should tell you that he is expecting me . . . alone.'

But I wasn't quick enough for she was already knocking on the door, and an undressed Nicholas answered – in only his chemise and hose. He stared at Marion and she at him, before I pushed past her and shoved my lord into his rooms.

'Marion wanted to see you,' I hissed in explanation, but it turned out not to be any explanation at all when Nick's eyes widened to mazers. 'I didn't mean *that*!' I quickly amended. 'She wants to help solve the crime I am investigating. *Jesu.*'

He stumbled back and took another moment to come to his senses. 'If you will excuse me . . .' He escaped into his private rooms and returned with a dressing gown over his shirt and hose, and he had put some shoes on. 'Er . . . won't you please sit down. Shall I serve you wine?'

'My lord,' said Marion, 'I cannot allow you to serve us. Allow me.' She rushed to the sideboard and proceeded to pour three cups.

Nicholas stared at me with silent pleading, but I could only shake my head and shrug.

Marion returned and set the goblets before us, first serving Nicholas. 'I know you weren't expecting me,' said Marion in her best diplomatic tenor, 'but Will must solve this murder. We cannot have the murder of servants at court, especially servants to the queen.'

'I quite agree,' he said mechanically, and downed his wine. 'Well?' he said after a moment of pondering his empty goblet. 'Then, er . . . what have you learned so far?'

I sighed and rose to get the flagon to fill his cup again. 'Geoffrey Payne was murdered by having his throat cut. But not this way' – and I demonstrated on my own neck from side to side – 'but this way.' I moved my hand up and down. 'And then as if that weren't strange enough, the poor soul was dug up and disembowelled. As you clearly heard at dinner the other day. Someone seemed very angry with him.'

'That's diabolical.' He slumped in his chair and merely toyed with the goblet.

'But that's not all,' said I. 'He was friends with John Blanke, the black trumpeter, and he seemed to fancy a brooch belonging to the queen and tried to snatch it once. And now it's gone from the queen's jewellery casket.'

Nick frowned. 'The trumpeter tried to steal it?'

'No, Geoffrey Payne, the murdered servant.'

He shook his head. 'Didn't the man know he could be executed for stealing from the queen?'

'Perhaps he was.'

We all stopped and looked at each other. 'No,' I said at last. 'This was no execution. It was foul and unnatural what happened to him.'

Nick shook his head again. 'What the devil does all that signify?'

'I don't know. That's why we're here. To tumble it about.' But as soon as I said the word 'tumble', Nick and I shared a look that Marion did not like.

'My lord.' She nodded to Nicholas. 'My husband.' She nodded to me. 'Shall we talk it through?'

It looked to be her job to put out the fire between Nicholas and me, and so she did, pouring common sense all over us to quell it. But further than that, she was right. Faith, she was *always* right. Talking it through is the stepping stone to furthering our cause, that of finding a killer. 'Look you, we should not think of the why for the nonce,' I said, standing and pacing. 'We should make a list. Do you, my lord, have paper and ink?'

Nicholas rose and went to his ambry and brought out a box. In it were leaves of trimmed paper, quills and ink. He set it before him and, like a secretary, dipped the quill and poised it above his paper, waiting for me to recite. I felt suddenly very important.

'Now, let us think of names around the queen that begin with an "E".'

'Why?' said Marion.

'Because the murderer's shirt had an embroidered initial on it, an "E".'

'Well, obviously,' said Nick, 'the first must be Edward Seymour, the queen's own brother. But truly, Will . . .'

'Mark it down,' I said sternly, just as if I knew what I was doing.

'There is Doctor Ellis Dawlish,' said my wife. 'He is the envoy to the queen's charities.'

I pointed at her. 'Aye! Good. And Doctor Edmund Bonner, who is a trimmer to the king and has often been in the queen's company as an adviser, though he is frequently absent from court. Is he here now?'

Nick nodded. 'Yes, I have seen him and shall mark him down.'

'Who else, my gentles?'

Nick tapped his beard with a finger. 'Edmund Bedingfield. A vile man. The late Princess Dowager was in his custody, as you will recall.'

Recall I did. My poor Lady Catherine. *Queen* Catherine, I shall still call her in me own head. 'Princess Dowager' indeed!

'And mark him down.' But then I was at an impasse, for I could think of no more 'E' names. 'Well, a blessedly short list. How shall this be done? Is it meet that we talk to each man or . . .'

'The truth of it is,' said Nick, concern stirring his grey eyes to swirling cauldrons, 'that I am still no one at court. I do not think any of these men will pay me any heed. I have only just come to the attention of the king. And that attention could just as easily fade.'

I looked to my wife who was nodding solicitously. 'Too true,' she said, with perhaps a little too much venom. 'Will, I cannot see that anyone can match you in the way you can poke and prod at these men with no one being the wiser.'

'Except that all of court now knows the king has charged me with this investigation.'

She sighed. 'Still. You have a way about you. Even in their deviousness, you are far cleverer.'

'That may be so,' I conceded with a little puffery. 'Well, my dears, there is naught for it. I must. The stealth of my investigation is all but gone. But if I am shrewd enough . . .'

'If,' said Nick with a sly grin.

And how that grin discomfited me. 'Er . . . erm . . . aye. If I can be clever enough, they will never know . . . until it is too late.'

We looked at one another again in the silence that followed. We seemed not to be the merry company back when we started. When my wife decided that my antics with select males of the court were no longer bawdy stories but her own husband carrying on in another's bed. The shine was off the coin. I owed Marion my oath of love and loyalty. But coward I, for I still wanted Nick too.

'If, er, anything else comes to mind,' I said, mostly for Nick, 'then you know how to contact me. I am . . . everywhere.'

'So you are,' he said softly. *Everywhere but in my bed*, he seemed to be saying with his eyes. I gazed at my wife instead and extended my hand to her.

'Good night, Lord Hammond,' she said with a curtsey.

He bowed as solemnly as a man in his dressing gown could do.

I slipped Marion's hand in the crook of my arm and walked back with her through the corridors, neither of us speaking. But when I heard a shoe scrape against the tiles ahead, I pulled her close against the wall. The oil lamp in a niche across the passage allowed only enough light to see the path and not us in the shadows. I turned to Marion, her eyes wide and bright, the rise and fall of her breast under her kirtle spellbinding. I put my finger to her lips and crept to the corner as the corridor turned, and with the stealth of a snake, I slowly pushed my face to the edge to spy ahead and saw a figure. He was creeping into a door soundlessly, a door not his own for I recognized him.

'Marion,' I whispered oh-so-silently to her ear. 'Go on back to our lodgings on your toes. I must stay and spy a while.'

'Is it our murderer?'

'I do not know. But I want you home and safe.'

'But—'

'Wife, do not argue the point! Go home.'

Surprisingly, she said nothing more, but carefully looked around the corner and scampered into the gloom.

I waited against the warm wood of the wall as the sounds of her careful feet disappeared. I waited until I heard the soft whinge of the door, its closing and then feet moving on. As I peered round the corner, I saw the retreating back of my quarry. He couldn't have been in those quarters for more than five minutes. Methinks any lady would be disappointed with that result. So what was the miscreant up to?

My steps mirrored his own, so if hear me he did, he might take it for but an echo. Indeed, he did stop once to cast a look over his shoulder, but I had hastily got m'self behind some curtains.

On he went, whilst his shadow pursued. And again, he stopped before a door not his own and tried the door latch. Foiled! It was locked. But then he reached for the pouch at his hip and withdrew . . . keys!

By the mass, what is this?

The scoundrel unlocked the door as well, just as quiet as you please, with a mouse whisper, and in he went.

This was not to be borne. It was true that I could not stand a mystery and must know the answer, and this time I cast aside all pretence of stealth. I got m'self against the wall opposite the door, crossed my arms and my foot one over the other, and waited.

Anon, not more than five minutes, out he came, carefully locking the door so quietly I could not discern the sound from any other. He turned, saw me and halted.

'Well, John Blanke,' said I. 'What's the news?'

NINE

'Christ, Will,' he said, his hand to his chest. He was not wearing his usual doublet of fine linen with its tabard of the king's arms when he served as a trumpeter, but a finely embroidered doublet of scarlet. His shirt was embroidered at the cuffs and collar with blackwork and with his initials.

'What say you, John? You're having a busy night.'

I flicked my glance at the movement of his hand to his dagger hilt, but he did not clasp it. Cuds-me, but it gave me a scare.

'My nights are my own.'

'Of course, of course.'

'And what are *you* doing out in the corridors in the middle of the night?'

Ah, how I loved his speech, for it was far more melodious than a Frenchman, with none of the fiery speed of a Spaniard. It flowed like a vine, with pronunciations that spoke of far places, places I will never see. Africa. They say it is an expansive country, and I do not have the means to doubt it. I saw a map of the world once, but it did not look that big to me.

'Oh, you know me. I go everywhere at any time. All the guards know me well.'

'Is that a fact?'

'Indeed. Whereas you . . . well, I have never seen you flit from door to door so easily.'

He took long strides across the tiled floor and stood close to me. His dark face lay in shadow and all I could see were his eyes. 'It would be best that you not speak of it. For I will not be the butt of your jests.'

'Never would I, John.'

'I have heard you promise such before and break that promise.'

'I? Oh, well. If there is a joke in it, then aye. I find it a struggle not to when I know it will be funny. I am a jest hunter, always after a laugh.'

'Not at my expense, Fool.' His hand neared his dagger again. I took a chance and rested my hand on his.

'John . . . what is amiss? All jesting aside. You look disturbed.'

'It is not your affair, Somers.'

'But, John, we are friends. You know you can come to me in a difficulty.'

He stared down at me before turning his head and his gaze away. 'I have nothing to say.'

'I am no cleric like Cranmer, but' – and here I did my imitation of the man – 'omission is still a sin.'

'Is it a sin now not to tell the jester something to satisfy his curiosity?'

'*I* consider it so. Because I am an ever-curious fellow, and to me, a mystery unsolved is, well . . . a crime!' But as I said it, I was of a mind of that terrible crime against Geoffrey Payne, and my light-heartedness faded.

And then I noticed his cuff. I grabbed at it, and he started to yell but cut it off.

There was an 'E' embroidered on it. 'John, is there some strangeness about the alphabet that makes a J-name into an E-name?'

He yanked back his arm and pulled at his cuff. 'You are the only one to have noticed that.'

'Perhaps . . . perhaps you got the shirt second-hand?'

He twiddled with his cuff a moment more before he dropped both hands to his sides. He spoke softly, for our ears alone. 'John is my baptized name. My birth name . . . is Ekene.'

Ee-KEN-ay, I rolled over my tongue, not quite giving it breath. A foreign name from a foreign, faraway place.

He flashed a brief smile of remembrance. 'It is strange. I have been "John" longer than I have been Ekene now, and living in England longer than I lived in Africa. But when I think of myself in my head, it is "Ekene" I hear. My mother's voice calling it over the tall grasses of home.'

'Ah. You and me, Master Blanke, we are of a kind. We are both far from our homes. And 'tis true that I am also almost longer in Henry's court than on my father's farm. It has been long that I have heard my mother's voice, but she has been long gone from this earth. It is odd to think on it. Would you rather I call you Ekene?'

'No, it would not do to eschew my baptized name now, would it? The priests would be most displeased.'

'Yes, there are far too many clerics' eyes about with big ears.' My cheerfulness again diminished. 'Then who made this shirt for you?'

His expression looked abashed. 'Why should you want to know that?' He had gathered himself and began walking down the corridor to his own quarters. I walked beside him.

'As I said, I'm a curious fellow.'

'You are, right enough. Well, it's one of the queen's ladies. She's taken a fancy to me, and when she began the stitchery of the initials, I asked her to.'

'What a darling lady. And who is this paragon of sweetness?'

'You are being more than curious, it seems.'

'I am. Oh, this is foolish, John. You and Geoffrey Payne were friends.'

His tread slowed. 'And what has this to do with shirts?'

'I will be plain with you. He was killed by a man wearing a shirt like yours. With an "E" embroidered on the cuffs.'

He stopped again and appraised me with widened eyes. 'And you think I killed him? My friend? One of the few friends I have at court for all these years?'

'*I'm* your friend.'

Pulling back from me, he glared. 'Friends do not accuse their friends of murder.'

Cuds-me. I did get my foot in it. 'I am not accusing you—'

'Just the shirt, then.'

'This is coming out all wrong.' Who was it that said I was clever? My wife and my lover? This was a good show of that! 'I wasn't accusing you. Truly I wasn't. I–It is the shirt that has confounded me.'

'And knowing the lady would help?'

'Aye, it would. It might . . .'

'Need I say that . . . well, the lady is all but betrothed . . . to another.'

'It need not be said at all. Just the name.'

He sighed deeply. 'Lady Margery Horsman.'

I did not gasp but I could not help my brows lifting into my hairline. 'Horsman, Keeper of the Queen's *Jewels*?'

He drew back again. 'Yes. Why do you say it like that?'

Instead of his hand on his dagger, he pressed it to the pouch at his hip.

I forced a smile. 'Say it like . . . what? I was merely making certain I got the right lady.'

Eyes narrowed, he scrutinized me. 'There's only one Lady Horsman.'

'But . . . forgive me, Master Blanke, but neither of the doors I saw you make your way through this evening are the lodgings of Lady Horsman. And having a set of keys is, well . . . quite . . . opportune. As well as quite . . . unusual.'

He raised his chin and glared down his nose at me. He said not a word.

'And you'll not tell me what you were doing for so brief a time in either door? Nor the door I saw you pass through yestereve?'

A sneer was added to his overall suspicious appearance. 'You think yourself clever, Somers.'

'I used to. But I must confess, this encounter has me rethinking it.'

'Bah!' He waved his hand about. 'I need not talk to you further.'

'Oh, John! Please don't be cross with me. I'm just trying to find a murderer.'

'It is not me, Will. I swear by Jesus.'

What was I to think? Why was he going to these apartments? They couldn't be trysts, for he hadn't stayed long enough. And just what was in the bulging pouch he wore . . . that he laid a protective hand over?

A jewel was stolen. Master Blanke's lover is the Keeper of the Queen's Jewels. Aye, marry. I did not like such an association.

I shrugged and gave him my sincerest expression. But the offence I had given him would not be appeased so easily. He spared me barely a glance as he swung away and hurried down the passage.

*   *   *

In the morning, Marion made me return to that encounter, repeating the conversation, lingering on certain words and actions. As she rolled up the stockings on to her shapely legs and gartered them secure with a ribbon, she paused in thought.

'It is obvious to me that you think this John Blanke was stealing jewellery from these lodgings.'

'I don't. I mean . . . mayhap.'

'So is it any coincidence that he is ensorcelled by Lady Horsman, Keeper of the Queen's Jewels? It's ideal. Might she know a receptor to sell them for her?'

'Receptor? Where is my innocent wife getting these terms?'

'Oh, Will. Everyone knows that.'

'*I* don't know it,' I muttered.

'If he's a thief—'

'Wait, wait, Marion. I've known him all the years I've been at court. True, this is the first that I learned he had another name, but . . . the character of the man surely could not have changed. He was here during the old king's reign. And he must be paid handsomely. Far more handsomely than I am. What would he have need of more money?'

'People gamble, get blackmailed, require funds for houses and finery. Any number of reasons. Just because you don't have a robber's bone in *your* body does not mean others aren't greedy.'

'But, Marion . . .'

She threw her skirts down over her legs and looked up at me with an exasperated expression. 'Will Somers, sometimes you act like a babe in arms. You, who make merry on the human condition; you, who can quote a quip without a thought, you don't know the minds of men?'

'I suppose I do not wish them ill. Or wish to think ill of them. And yet . . . cuds-me, I all but accused him, a *friend*, of murder and thievery. That's inexcusable.'

She wrapped a hand around my neck and pulled me down for a kiss. She was sweet and got me of a mind to stay and toy with her, but alas, I had to go to see the king. 'It was ill done, Marion. I hope to make it up to him. But confound it, I still need to know what he was doing.'

'It could be perfectly innocent.'

'Aye, it could be, but I must be certain that it is.'

I bid my farewell, for I had to make an appearance to Henry almost at cock crow so he would know I was still his. He needed the assurance that his Fool loved him well, and I would spend as much time with him as he desired, no matter what else it was that I was doing. It was my life's work and my most fervent desire to please him. It was a vocation, as much as a monk or a priest . . . only I was more pious.

As it was, Henry and a few of his ministers had gathered in his privy chamber. The king raised his head at my entry but otherwise did not acknowledge me. I led Nosewise to the window alcove into which I perched with my cittern, and began to pluck a wayward tune. In truth, I wasn't paying attention to it. My mind was on John Blanke. I could not imagine the man a murderer . . . but what did I truly know about him? Only that which he deigned to tell me. He was anonymous to most of us. Did anyone ever ask him from whence he came? His life before England? Even his name wasn't true.

And now he was another 'E' name added to the list.

'What rubbish are you playing, Somers!' bellowed Henry.

Christ mend me. I reckon I wasn't paying any attention at all. 'Oh, forgive me, Uncle. I was twittering about in me head and my hand forgot what it was supposed to be doing.'

'Play or do not play, but in the name of God, do not give us that useless plucking further.'

I bowed low, my arm sweeping away from my body as the courtiers do it. 'Forgive me, Your Grace. I was lost in thought about a priest I knew. He was preaching one day to his flock and thundering loud against adultery. "It is such a horrible sin," said he, "that I had rather undo ten virgins than one married woman!" Well, you never heard such an uproar in the church . . . and such a rush of men out the door to get themselves on to it.'

Henry paused but for a moment until all the words reached his ears. He roared with laughter and pounded the table with his hand. He smacked the shoulder of the lord beside him and gestured towards me.

Ah, Henry was pleased. Even when he doesn't want to laugh, I can bring it up like a sorcerer burbling up water from the ground.

He bid me back to my station to play a tune. 'And pay attention this time.'

That I did. And paid attention right well to the conversation at the same time. It was about that Pilgrimage of Grace yet again. It was concerning to the king, for it was a true danger to his reign. Aye, I had done some thinking on it. And though one could plead to the king for this or that – and Henry, like the kings of old, did see the people on occasion to take their petitions – this cut right to the heart of what he had done by taking control of the Church. Why, it had been a true catastrophe! No more popes, no more cardinals, different liturgy. Monasteries being shut or the roof taken down and left to rot as an example to others. But that part was Cromwell. Cruelty was *his* game.

I awoke again to Henry standing and shooing his men away. They left in a rush of gathering papers and quills, and just for added fun, I set Nosewise to bark them out the door. Especially when Henry jerked his head at me and said, 'You stay, Will. Fetch us both some wine.'

'I am very amenable to that suggestion,' I said, and hurriedly walked to the sideboard. I poured Henry a generous amount, myself a goodly dose, and raised my goblet. 'To your very good health, my Harry.'

He nodded his thanks and drank. I followed suit. Henry had the best wine, of course. But sensing his wanting to talk privily to me, I set myself down on a footstool beside him, stretched out my legs and crossed them at the ankles, and sipped as I gazed up at him. Poor Henry. He wasn't as merry as he had been in the past. Methought his past was catching up to him, with all the losses he and his minions had brought down upon him. Anne Boleyn could have – *should* have – been divorced. Not this other. And though I knew he was glad she was gone, there came a darkness to his eyes sometimes, a veil of . . . guilt?

'What troubles you, Harry?'

A sigh rumbled under his moustache, rippling it. 'The Lady Mary.'

'Your daughter,' I said quietly. His eyes didn't track towards me, but distantly, into that irretrievable past. I decided to press on, see how much I could poke the badger. 'Remember so long ago, Harry, when she was but a little thing and so pretty? And you called her your Pearl of the World?'

A smile flickered at just the edge of his mouth, but never took flame. 'She was a pretty girl.'

'And a pretty young woman now. And she so loves you. All she wants is a father's love.'

Before his growing scowl could blow up, I interrupted. 'My wife is the bastard daughter of Lord Heyward, your very own Yeoman of the Records. And he loves her dearly. Has always treated her well.'

'He does not have a throne to see to.'

'No, true. But he is, in the end, only a man, as you are, Harry. And she, your daughter, is your child. You have never denied that, eh?'

'This is a swirling whirlpool you are swimming in, Somers.' But I noted that his voice never rose above our normal speaking volume. Yes, he wanted to talk to someone about this. Cromwell would not do, for he would talk of succession. And I could tell by my heart that what he wanted to speak of . . . was his flesh and blood.

'Oh, I know it, Your Grace, but 'tis about love . . . and family. Your daughter Mary. Do you . . . have you talked to her since she came back to court?'

'She loves me?' This time his tone was as if he did not perceive speaking it aloud – oh, but it was a clanging gong. Henry, Henry. This man did not lack for love if he wished to pursue it. This man who wore a crown, a greater crown than many of the rest of the world, desperately desired love in return. And perhaps, in his strange pursuit of it, would never find it.

Setting my goblet aside, I gave him my best loving attention. 'She does, Harry. She is the sweet girl of our days together at court. The four of us. Remember? We'd sit by the fire, and Mary would play the lute and sing with her strong voice, as strong as yours sometimes. And I would make jokes and we'd all laugh.' His hands closed into fists for a moment . . . before they fell open on the chair's arms. He cast his mind back and he did not yell at me for it. Maybe he was desperate for simpler times as well.

'I suppose . . . I must begin to think of marrying her to some noble or other.'

'Why have you not?' Aye me. I knew. We all knew. She was no longer a princess. She would not inherit a throne. She would not be a good bargain to marry a foreign prince, for Henry had declared her a bastard and no prince or king wished to marry an illegitimate daughter of a king. What alliance could you make? Where was the benefit of it?

'She is sad, Harry. Sad that her . . . her father the king rejects her.'

He struggled in his seat. Full of umbrage, he was. 'I brought her back to court, didn't I?'

'And that was good and gracious of you. And the queen was kind to ask you. But she's still a girl, Harry, not merely a pawn. She's your *Pearl*, remember? You should send for her. Do it now, Harry.'

'What an absurdity.' Yet he thought on it. And then he stared at me suddenly as if seeing me for the first time. 'Call for the guard. Have her sent to me.'

I rose and slapped him on the back. He was so distracted that he didn't react. I skipped to the door and stuck my head through. 'His Majesty requests that someone fetch the Lady Mary to him. Now, man.'

I turned back to the king in his chair. Though he wore no physical crown from day to day, it wove about his head by his magnificence alone. Flat cap he wore, with its feathers and jewels, but it was no crown. That blazon of ginger hair was crown enough as surely as any golden one.

We waited. I stood beside him. He seemed nervous. He had greeted her personally when she arrived back to court, but the attention was on the queen, for she had arranged it, and the woman had glowed with the inner light of doing God's work. And Mary, poor little Mary. She had fought long and hard to return, and little Elizabeth, who had usurped Mary for a time, was also to return.

Aye, marry. A king's life was not a personal one. Even after all these years, he had yet to contend with that. His life was political, every scrap of it. But he didn't see it that way. He wasn't allowed sentimentality, only expedience, and he had cast aside his daughter as easily as he had cast aside his first wife. He'd had to. His ministers insisted. And I feared that Henry had pressed it so far down inside his heart, like a stuffed goose, that it was irretrievable. But now I knew that it was not true. Henry wanted to love and to have that love returned. He remembered it as well as I did.

I hoped it was so. I hoped that he would take this moment to take something intimate and return it to the bosom of his heart and always keep it there.

A Fool can only hope.

We sat in silence until we heard steps at the door. I urged him to stand. He was reluctant but he did rise, seeing the sense in it. Lady Mary entered, saw me with but a fleeting glance and cast herself upon the floor at the king's feet.

'Now, now,' he said, using that voice I well remember from the past. That fatherly voice when he would gently correct his child when she recited Latin (which she was quite good at, and I learned a thing or two by sitting in on her lessons). He reached down and pulled her gently to her feet. They gazed at one another until she fell into his arms and wept. 'Mary, Mary,' he cooed, rocking her a bit before he took her arms and set her on her feet again. 'Let me look at you. My, what a beautiful young woman you are.'

'Your Grace,' she peeped, lowering her face and wiping the tears from her cheeks.

'It has been a long time,' he said, even though she sat night after night at his dinner table, and he never invited her to speak to him.

And that's when I made to leave, but Henry reached out with his hand. 'No, Will. It was you who brought about this meeting. You should stay. I'm certain that you have something to say to Princ—' He caught himself and started again. 'To Lady Mary.'

'Oh, Will!' And then she fell into *my* arms, and there was weeping all around. She was taller now, and we could rest cheek to cheek, the beautiful maid and the ugly jester. Oh, how silly life can be. How remarkable when a man such as myself, with such humble beginnings, could preside over such a reconciliation.

'My precious lady,' I said softly to her bonnet, sniffing, the tears rolling down my own cheeks. 'You are so well grown. I shall have to call you my turnip now.'

She laughed softly and pulled back. 'Turnip, am I? And are you a radish?'

'Spicey, am I? It must be so. And your father. What must he be?'

She daren't say anything, so I did. 'I say he is a . . . cabbage. Strong and hearty.'

'A cabbage?' bellowed Henry good-naturedly. He laughed.

'Have you ever dropped one on your foot, Harry? Trust me, they are strong.'

'A cabbage it is. Come, daughter. Sit beside me.' The royal hand grabbed a chair by its back and dragged it almost up against his large one. He took Mary's hand and bid her sit, and he did not let go of that hand. 'Tell me how your studies have been. Do you know your Latin?'

'Of course. And French. And Greek.' She was prudent and didn't mention Spanish, though I knew she could speak it like a native. 'And . . . English law,' she said.

He jerked up slightly. 'English law? What does a young woman need of that?'

'If I am to serve the kingdom . . . in whatever capacity Your Majesty would wish it of me . . . I saw it fitting to learn of the laws.'

'I doubt I should call upon you to be a lawyer, my dove.'

'I wish to be ready and eager to help your prince when he comes.'

Shrewd. She learned well from her mother. And her father. She showed Henry that she could still be an heir and know her way around the laws and Parliament . . . but still bow to a male issue should one present itself. I scrunched my nose at her in approval. She bowed her head, but not before I saw her secretly smile.

Henry, for his part, patted her shoulder. 'I know you will. You are an obedient child. And I have missed you.'

'Oh, I have missed *you*, Your Grace. It was my greatest sorrow not to see you in all these years.'

'You are here now.'

'The queen has been gracious and kind to me. She allows me to keep in her court. Such a devoted peacemaker.'

'That she is. I am glad you find her company so appealing.'

'Yes, Your Grace.'

'Tell me what a young woman such as yourself likes. Do you dance? Do you still play?'

'As often as I can.'

'Then play something for us. Will, lend her your cittern.'

'Gladly, Uncle.' And so I grabbed the instrument from the basket it rested upon and handed it to her. She handled it expertly and, as any musician does when given a strange instrument, she tuned it before she began to play.

Yes, she was expert and played a tune writ by Henry himself. Clever girl.

They sang songs together, and what a fine voice she had, blending nicely with Henry's own. After a time, they didn't seem to take note of me, and it was then I managed to escape to leave the two alone to learn of each other again. And it was a good thing too, because Cromwell was striding through the many chambers heading for the king, and I was able to get in the way of it.

'Master Crumbled-Well, wither do you go?'

He tried to shake me off, but I had a strong grip of his sleeve, and with Nosewise also getting in his way, we made a formidable gate.

'I am going to see the king.'

'Not just now, master. He is with the Lady Mary.'

His eyes showed that he knew and had hurried to scuttle the meeting.

'Then I *must* see him.'

'Master.' I dragged him back and signalled Nosewise. He began to bark most prodigiously at Cromwell. 'You see, you've upset the dog.'

'Get your dog to calm, Somers, or I shall set the guards upon it.'

'Not even you could be so cruel as to take your anger out on a mere dog.' I pulled a puppet from my basket. It was of Cromwell. 'I shall call a guard to dispatch that cur!' I said in his voice.

'Oh?' I said. 'Which one? The dog or the jester?'

'Both, by heaven!' I made the puppet say. 'One is a fool and one is foul.'

'He can't be fowl,' I interjected in me own voice. 'He's a dog, not a hen.'

'He'll lay no foul eggs to smell up the king's palace.'

'Master Crumbled-Well, you make no sense—' I was just getting started when Cromwell swatted the puppet aside, turned on his heel, seeing that I meant to keep him from Henry, and stalked out the way he had come.

I wiped my brow with the puppet and slipped it back in the basket. 'Good boy, Nosewise.' I patted him on his head. 'Now that Henry is settled, let us see what we can do about this murder business. Time is wasting.'

TEN

I felt the need to find John Blanke and further talk to him, but he was proving elusive. No one knew where he was. And so I seemed to wander and found myself at the queen's court.

Lady Mary was absent, of course, getting reacquainted with her father. I felt a puff of pride in my chest for that. But then I spied Janie and thought to talk further with her . . . if I could get anything out of that fluff of a brain.

'Jane, my love,' I said, and sat next to her as she sat upon the floor, legs tucked underneath her.

'Will!' Excited each time to see me, she leaned over and gave me an awkward hug. 'You promised to teach me to juggle.'

'I did. But I don't know that you can master it.'

She whipped to her feet. 'I can!'

'Yes,' said Queen Jane. 'Let us see how well our Jane can juggle. A promise is a promise, Master Somers.'

On my feet in an instant, I bowed to the queen. 'Indeed it is, my lady. And so.' I called to Nosewise to bring my basket and dutifully he did. I rummaged inside and found three leather balls of many. 'Shall I begin, Janie? I can throw them to you, as I showed you.'

'I remember,' she said eagerly. Her concentrated gaze was upon me, as her eyes followed the path of the single ball I was tossing from one hand to the other.

'As I told you, dearling, are you watching my throw? My arms are at my sides. I'm not reaching for them, I am merely throwing them into an arc, and the height of the throw is consistent every time. See the top of the arc' – and I threw it just above my head but with a spin so it would land in the other hand – 'and see it land. My arms never leave me sides.'

She clapped in impatience. 'Let me try a ball, Will.'

I tossed her mine and then I retrieved another from the basket.

'Ladies of Queen Jane's court,' I said, tossing the ball back and forth as I walked before them in their seats. 'Who would like to try? Has anyone the courage?'

Anne Herbert, Countess of Pembroke, stood. 'I should like to try, Jester.' Courage was this young woman's name, for certain. She had served Queen Catherine *and* Anne Boleyn and was now one of Queen Jane's ladies.

I watched as she centred herself and I waited until she looked ready. 'Are you ready for my balls, my lady?'

They all tittered at my jest.

'One will do for now,' she said with a smirk.

I tossed it and she caught it. 'Well done, my lady! How does it feel to have my ball in your hand?'

They laughed again, but she cocked her head at me. 'It makes me long to throw it.'

'I see. Well, not everyone can love a Fool's balls like my good wife. Position yourself, my lady, as you see our Janie, here. Arms at your sides, toss it high enough that it is above your head, but towards the other hand. The throw is the most important, for it needs to be at the same place every time. One must always know where one's balls are.'

'Master Somers,' Queen Jane warned.

'My queen, I am only telling the truth. Juggling is all about the throw and where one's balls land.'

She narrowed her eyes at me just that much, before I turned to my pupils once more. Anne Herbert struggled because of her sleeves, but with repetition, she found her way.

'Who is ready for a second ball?'

Janie nodded, and there it all fell apart. She could not manage two, but Anne Herbert did. I could tell that Janie was growing cross. 'I can't.'

'Yes, you can. You need only concentrate.'

But now more ladies from the court wanted to learn. 'I haven't enough balls to go around,' I said. But then I reached down to my codpiece. 'I can find two more . . .'

Some crowed their guffaws and I studiously ignored looking towards the queen.

Janie had enough in any case, and I gave her balls to the other ladies, including Lady Horsman. I looked her over.

She wasn't so much a beauty as a handsome woman with good features. Yes, I could see what John Blanke saw in the lady.

But now Janie was pouting, and it seemed the best time to ask her again. I sidled in close and said quietly, 'Janie, would you like to play a game, just you and me?'

Her face brightened, as I knew it would.

'What, Will?'

'You saw something when Geoffrey Payne died, did you not?'

She sucked on a finger, biting down on it.

'Now, now.' I pulled her hand from her face. 'If you saw something, then that might help find the man who killed him. You would be like a saint of old, helping the ministry of God.'

'I would?'

'Oh, indeed. It was a terrible sin, and you would help to right it.'

'How?' she slowly asked.

'Our game. You and I should tread the same path as our late brother Geoffrey Payne, from here to the places you followed him. Can you do that for me? Only that. It is such a little thing to do.'

She looked back at the queen, but she was preoccupied with laughter, watching her ladies try to master juggling. We could easily slip away.

I took her arm, and we ducked out, leaving Nosewise to entertain as he barked and chased after the lost balls, returning them to whichever woman dropped one. We were out in the passage, and I pulled her against the wall. 'And so, my lovely, Geoffrey was in Queen Jane's chamber with all the rest, correct? Just like now?'

'Yes. He was there.'

'And did he take the brooch from the jewel casket?'

'No. Not then.'

'Oh. I thought you said he tried to take it . . .'

'That was before. The day he . . . he died, the queen gave him something.'

I squeezed my eyes tight, examining that information. 'What did she give him?'

'I don't know. She was pretending that she wasn't giving him
aught. Her arm was extended from her chair like this . . .' And
she stretched out her arm with her whole demeanour as the face
of a wealthy noble, eyes lidded, brows arched, as if she cared
not what others thought of her. She dropped the pantomime as
quickly as she started it. 'And then he took her hand as if to
kiss it, but he took something into his own. I saw it.'

'Indeed. Did anyone else in her court see it?'

She shook her head steadily.

'And then he left?'

'He did.'

'Then lead me on to where he went from here.'

She screwed up her face in thought before she launched
from the wall and headed quickly down the passage.

I followed her mad dash through, around and finally to a
lonely portion. This was said to be a dangerous passage since
there were no windows and few doors. If you took ill there,
it might take some time for someone to find you.

Janie stopped and was looking about. 'What now?' I asked.

'He was here, standing, looking. I hid over there so he wouldn't
see me.' She pointed to an alcove with a flickering oil lamp.

'Then let us go there.'

We betook ourselves into the alcove, and Janie pulled me
in and behind a carved griffin. 'And this is where I stood.'

'And where was he?'

'Over there. And a man came to talk to him.'

'Show me.'

She frowned and shook her head.

'Janie, I didn't know you had seen so much. Why didn't
you say so before?'

As was usual when she didn't wish to answer, she shrugged.

'Take me to where you saw him and the other man.'

After sulking a bit, she finally stepped out of the alcove
and took me across the passage again, by a crossroads of sorts.
'Here.'

'And you didn't see who he was talking to?'

She glanced back to where she had taken me to the alcove
and squinted. 'When something is far, it's a blur. I have to get
closer to see. And it was dark. As it is now.'

It *was* dark. God's teeth. She couldn't have seen anything from where she stood before. Even if it had been John Blanke, if they were in shadow – which they certainly would have been – she wouldn't have been able to tell.

I scanned the area . . . and saw on the wainscoting the brownish spatter of blood that had missed the servant's brush, for surely there had been buckets of it when his throat was slit. So it *was* here that it had happened.

'Now, dearling.' I grabbed her arms and forced her to look at me and nothing else. 'Did you hear them? Did you hear at all what was said?'

'The stranger seemed to be in a long gown . . . or maybe it was a cloak. Yes, a cloak because it was dark and so cold, and he came up to Geoffrey and said something, and Geoffrey laughed. But he wasn't laughing long when the man said something in husky whispers. And then Geoffrey turned away and showed him something and then he . . . I don't know. He did something that made the man very cross, and the man leapt upon Geoffrey and he was brought down.'

I stared once again at the spatters, trying to think. Who could the stranger be? It had to be the killer, for this is where the murder happened and where they found the body.

'You did very well, Janie,' I said absently, still searching the sight for any clues. But, of course, men and servants had gone through here since. 'No ideas who the man could have been?'

She shook her head again furiously.

And that was that. But she had told me much, and I slipped my arm around her thin shoulders. 'We must get back. I don't know that Nosewise knows how to instruct in the art of juggling.'

We returned as quickly as we could and found the ladies still trying to throw their balls and dropping them, whilst a happy Nosewise chased down every wayward one as if chasing after rats.

'Well, now!' I said, looking them all over. 'Who's ready for a second ball?'

'Oh!'

I glanced towards Jane Foole who was sitting on the floor at the jewellery casket again, but her face was as white as a sheet. I slid down to the floor next to her. 'My lovely, what is it?'

With a shaking hand, she brought it from the box. 'It's here,' she whispered.

She opened her palm, and there was a pale lavender gem set in an oval of twisted wire with three droplets of pearls. The lost brooch.

Behind me, the queen stood and appeared as pale as her Fool, her hand at her mouth. For she, too, knew it had been gone, and looked mighty surprised at its strange return.

ELEVEN

I wanted to ask Queen Jane, to talk with her alone, but she hadn't taken to me as Henry's other wives had. She didn't like the bawdiness of my jests and, in truth, seemed out of step with most of court. It seemed crude to release my humour upon her . . . though her ladies did not feel the same.

And . . . it *was* my vocation, after all. Not this finding of murderers. Alas.

My thoughts were interrupted by the return of Lady Mary. She gave me a grateful look and I gave back all my love. It seemed that it had been a fruitful exchange. Oh, I did not think she could convince him to make her an heir again, but some things are more important. The love of a father for his child, for one. It might even make Henry happy.

Our own happy gathering was interrupted by the cocksure arrival of Edward Seymour, Viscount Beauchamp. He stood in the doorway with hands on his hips and feet spread apart. He wore his riding boots, which were spattered with mud, and strode into the room as if he owned it. He gave his sister the queen a cursory bow, before he spoke low to her and indicated with a jerk of his head that he wanted a private conference with her in the withdrawing room.

The queen rose from her chair and led her brother to the other room, leaving us to our own devices. Which for me was to comfort Janie, who was still looking at her favourite brooch with confusion.

I sat cross-legged upon the floor beside her and merely watched her with the necklaces and beads, whilst she clutched the brooch in her other hand.

Softly, I said, 'What is it that bedevils you about that brooch, my dearling?'

'Where had it gone all this time?'

'Aye, that is a mystery. Where do *you* think it had gone?'

'Geoffrey. He took it. I know he took it.'

'You didn't seem so certain before.'

'But I am now. He took it.'

'Even though his friend the trumpeter scolded him for it?'

She held it to her chest, her other fingers still worrying amongst the strings of pearls. 'He had it. The . . .' Here her voice fell to a whisper. 'The queen gave it to him.'

So she believed. Had she? But why? If he had tried to steal it before, why so magnanimous to him afterwards? But hang me in my face, I could not ask the queen that directly. No matter what authority Henry gave me, I could not. She must have had her reasons. And royalty did not have to excuse themselves when they decided to do something.

The noise from the other room reached all our ears at once, and the ladies craned their necks trying to hear the heated conversation between the queen and her brother, though it seemed rather one-sided, with Edward's voice foremost.

Edward. An 'E' name. I rose and, as nonchalantly as I could, made my way to the door which had not been closed tightly and stood slightly ajar. I gestured to Nosewise and he came to me. With my foot, I nudged the door wider and signalled for the dog to slip through, and clever cur that he was, he did so.

I positioned myself at the doorjamb and caught the words from Edward: '. . . doing something so obvious!' I could just see them through the gap, and Viscount Beauchamp grabbed Queen Jane by her upper arms and hissed into her face, 'You stupid girl!'

The queen winced, shying her face down as if awaiting a blow.

Nosewise – the good boy that he was – trotted nearly between them. They fell to silence, and I had no choice but to pretend I was looking for the cur and stuck me head in.

Edward scowled as I made my apologies and scooped up the dog, holding him close to my breast. 'He's a tricksy devil.'

Edward shot a glare at the queen whose face was turned down so that her chin was nearly to her chest. Oh, she was an obedient lass. Perhaps too much so, but she was turned away from him, as she must have been used to all her life.

He pushed past me, bumping me a bit, but then he stopped long enough to lean into me. 'I hope, Fool, you remember well how to hold your tongue.'

'Aye, my lord,' I said, loud enough for the queen's ladies to hear in the next room. 'For I do remember how to treat my betters. That she is no longer merely a sister . . . but the *queen*.'

His scowl deepened and he flicked a last glare at his queen before he made a curt bow to her as he withdrew.

I knew I should have withdrawn as well, but I hesitated. Her breast was heaving and her hands trembled, but she worked at composing herself and cautiously turned towards me as she held both sides of her bonnet, adjusting it.

'You look well,' I said softly to reassure her.

She nodded, pasted a gentle smile to her face, swept her skirts behind her and came through the door again.

I thought but a moment before I put down the dog, excused myself and charged after Viscount Beauchamp.

'My lord!' I called out in the passage. His stride faltered, but he didn't even turn round.

'What is it, Fool?'

'Oh, master.' I came up beside him and walked with him, keeping pace with his long strides. 'I just wondered something. Your shirt, my lord.'

'What about my shirt?'

'Did you possibly lose one?'

'Lose one where?'

'On a rubbish pile. Because it had too much blood on it.'

He stopped, and a blacker expression I never saw on a man. I noted how his hand rested on his dagger hilt. 'You are in very great danger, Jester, of having your own blood down your own shirt.'

'Well . . . I shouldn't like that. But as you know, I am a curious fellow. And the king has charged me—'

He threw back his head in a dreadful laugh. Oh no, there was no merriment in it. And then his laughter stopped, and the black expression returned. He poked me in the chest with his finger so hard it might as well have been his dagger. I walked backwards until I fetched up against the wall with nowhere else to go.

'There's something dangerous about you, Somers. Something . . . I don't care to know. But know you this. You have a loose tongue. And if you don't correct it' – and here he punctuated each word with another sharp jab – 'you might . . . just . . . lose it.' He granted me one last scowl before he quit himself from me . . . and I was glad to see him go.

Christ mend me. I never seem to think ahead of time when I might make an enemy. And it was not even as my place as a jester!

Methought, though, that I frightened Edward Seymour just that much. And perhaps that might spark something. Hopefully, not my demise.

Trumpets. Off in the distance.

Oh! Madam Elizabeth was supposed to arrive today. I sprinted forth down the passages to the main gate and, as it was, so had everyone else at court. We filed out to the courtyard, and though I wasn't in a cloak, I was warmed well enough by the chance of seeing my Bess again . . . as well as the warm press of bodies surrounding me.

I jumped, looking above the courtiers in front of me. I wanted to catch a glimpse of her. There! The procession. Horses in colourful caparisons. A covered cart with the little lady herself waving from it. Garlands festooned all around her. Boots and horses trampled the snowy courtyard.

I couldn't help m'self. I pushed those before me aside and squeezed through. An anxious guard lowered his pike towards me before he raised it again, recognizing my silly face.

I ran up to the cart and hung on the window. 'My Bess!' I said to the lovely pink-cheeked child. Three years old, she was, and just as bright and alight with curiosity as a child far older. 'You remember your Will, don't you? You said I was to marry you.'

'Wiw!' she cried, still not yet able to pronounce all her L's. She raised her arms to me and I embraced her, skipping along with the cart.

'That's enough there, Somers,' said a guard. 'Let the little madam enter court first.'

I reluctantly released her and whispered promises to play with her later when it was allowed. She sat back, her expression becoming mild as she was taught. Like a queen, she was. She would have made a good one.

I entered back into the palace with the throng but pushed my way to the forefront. The trumpeting continued, and there, in the watching chamber, the trumpeters had assembled, and I don't mind saying that the sound of them – strong, regal, melodious – filling the chamber with their echoes, made my chest burst with pride and awe at the majesty before us. Henry and Jane arrived together and sat on their thrones set up on a dais under the canopy of state, and the courtiers took their places, highest closest to the throne, throng in the outer regions.

And I, the jester to King Henry, was allowed to stride forward before all these nobles and take *my* place. I could have sat at Henry's feet, but I thought it best to stand beside him to encourage him to greet Bess with proper fatherly affection.

Lady Mary stood beside Queen Jane. Her face was marble.

Bess was marched down a long passage between courtiers. If she had still been a princess, they would have bowed, but as it was, they didn't quite seem to know what to do. Cheer? Give a nod only? It was difficult to know.

Her minders stepped back and bowed low to the king, and Bess strode forward on her own and curtseyed. 'Your Gwace,' she said in a rather loud voice.

Henry smiled and seemed genuinely pleased with her comportment. He opened his arms to her, and she, such a carefully *tutored* Tudor, instead ran to his arms like any child in the realm. He closed his eyes as he embraced her. *Yes, Harry, you truly do love your children. And look at them. They're beautiful.*

He propped her in his lap as she began to talk, and he listened solicitously to every word she babbled. Then Henry motioned to Queen Jane, and Bess . . . ah, my sweet Bess. The child opened her arms to the queen, and the peacemaker took Henry's child into *her* arms. A beautiful, homely scene that brought a tear to me eye. *Forgive them both, Henry,* I said in my head. They would both make marvellous heirs indeed!

But even as I thought it, I knew he would not relent. He relented enough to bring them to court, mostly to keep them safe and to keep an eye on them, but he would go no further.

Henry looked out to his court. 'We welcome our child, Madam Elizabeth, to court. And may her stay be a happy one.'

The courtiers cheered. I'd pay sixpence to know what went through their minds just then. Mary was the daughter of the queen they had loved well. Elizabeth was the daughter of the queen they loved not. But the latter brought them Protestantism, and the former would bring us back to Catholic ways. If they had to choose, which one would do? If following the law, it would be Mary before Elizabeth, and Mary would be wed and have an heir of her own. Elizabeth would never succeed to the throne.

Fie! Lawyers, lawyers, lawyers. And clerics, too. They often got in the way of good governance.

There were some gifts exchanged – regal, expensive gifts – and then Madam Elizabeth was ushered away to await the feast for later . . . with a royal nap.

I looked at Henry and he flicked a glance at me. 'Oh, very well,' he muttered. 'Go.'

'Thank you, my liege!' I scampered away, remembering at the last minute to bow to him, which he waved away, and I was running after her minders and Lady Mary who was also a reluctant minder.

I laid my head on Lady Mary's shoulder as we walked, and she looked to the side, surprised, until she calmed herself. 'Master Somers, such liberties.'

'"Master Somers"? Oh no, my lady. It shall always be "Will" to you.'

She smiled and continued walking, and I beside her. 'Thank you . . . for what you did today.'

'My princess,' I said so quietly, just for her ears alone. 'I shall never abandon you. I haven't.'

'I know. It is fitting that the court Fool should behave so.'

'Not a bit of it. I am the court's greatest observer. Didn't you know?'

She nodded, her veil rippling behind her as we walked. 'I am beginning to see how much.'

Bess must have heard me, for she whipped her head about and suddenly opened her arms to me.

'I beg your mercy, Lady Mary,' I said quietly, 'but I have another love to go to.'

'Go you must. I also see that your loyalty has no bounds.'

'As indeed it should not.' I bowed to her and made a silly walk to Bess, who laughed. Before her minders could stop me, I grabbed her and spun her in the air. Her full-throated laughter filled the space, and I promptly raised her on to my back.

'Master Somers!' complained one of the ladies.

'She wants it, my lady, and I must obey.'

The minders scoffed and looked at each other in concern. As if I would drop such precious cargo!

I trotted like a horse whilst Bess laughed and laughed. We finally got to her chamber whereupon her retinue entered and I with them.

'Please, Master Somers,' said one of her ladies. 'Madam Elizabeth must rest now. She had a long journey.'

I tugged her from my neck and bounced her on the bed. 'You must be tired, my love.'

'I'm not tired. They want me at aw times to nap but I want to run and dance.'

'Now, now, my Bess. You need to rest. Tomorrow is a great banquet. Always remember that one must never turn down good food. And I'll be there. And Jane Foole, too.'

That seemed to cheer her, and I stood aside as the ladies undressed her and left her in her shift, but it was I who tucked her in. 'Rest now. Tomorrow is Christmas Day and there will be more feasting. Dream of music and juggling and your Will right in the centre of it. Will you do that for me?'

She rolled her eyes – the little princess – and settled in. 'Vewy wew.' She sighed, but by now I could tell she was sleepy, for her lids were heavy and she made no more fuss when the soft pillow was under her head, and the smooth sheets and warm blankets covered her. I kissed her forehead – just about the only one at court allowed to do so – and said my farewells as I tiptoed away.

Her ladies eyed me with disdain, but I strode off, satisfied that I had seen to her at last.

* * *

It was Christmas Eve. The Yule Log was brought in and set aflame, to burn throughout the Twelve Days. There were entertainments to come, but this night most of court was to go to the chapel for the midnight mass, and even Marion went with me, though I was close to Henry during the long prayers and song this evening.

I'm afraid my mind was not on it. I had preparations to make. Though the Lord of Misrule would do most of the work, I still had my place to entertain, and I promised to help him organize events and mummers plays, though all the players were schooled well in their jobs and hardly needed me. Marion helped me with the costumes I would wear leading up to Twelfth Night, the biggest feast of the new year, and I needed to collect all that I would need for the Christmas feast tomorrow.

When the prayers were done and all had been consecrated, we returned to our lodgings, and me with Marion on my arm.

'I forgot to ask. Did you see Madam Elizabeth this day?'

'I did indeed. Tucked her in, too.'

'Oh, Will. I'm glad. I'm so very glad she is here.'

'You can thank the queen for that. For though she lacks in many other ways, she is a good and charitable woman. Despite her kin.'

'Oh?' She was just unpinning and unlacing her clothing and rolled her shoulders. Small, tight work was embroidery on a frame, for I had seen her at it too many times to count, bent over it, straining to see by a single candle's flame.

'Come, my love.' I reached out my hands to her and lifted her to her feet, closing her in an embrace. 'You work too hard with little rest. And you stood a long time through all the prayers this night. Could you not have sat with your father?'

'I am your kin now and must stand with the servants and simple folk. It was nothing.' Though I saw her limp a bit and slip off her slippers. 'But you work hard too. Ever in the king's service, you must be near him, even when you intone your prayers before God.'

'So 'tis a good thing we both enjoy our work.' I kissed her forehead, just as I had done to little Bess.

'But what did you mean about the queen's kin, Will?'

I slowly unwound from her and leaned against the bed post. 'I was witness to Edward Seymour's conduct towards his sister, treating her not as his sovereign but as the sister he abused.'

'Ah. I have seen this too. He is not a subtle man.'

'Indeed. "How can you be so stupid?" he said to her. *And I have learned from Jane Foole that Geoffrey Payne was given the brooch by the queen. And when we discovered it was back in her jewellery casket today, the queen was as surprised as Janie.*'

Marion had been at court all her life, since her father, Yeoman of the Records, lived at court and only sometimes on his estates. She had seen it all and was as jaded as any other courtier one could encounter when strange news came to light. But the look on her face now conveyed not jadedness but shock. 'The queen *gave* him the brooch?'

'Aye.'

'To what end?'

'I think this is the most important question of all, my love.'

'Then, Will, you must find out what that was.'

'I know, sweeting. I know.'

'So what are you doing about it?'

My mouth fell open. 'Dearling! Don't you think I'm trying?'

She wrung her hands and walked from embroidery frame to coffer and back again. 'A shirt with an "E" embroidered by Her Majesty herself, a stolen brooch . . . that was *not* stolen but disappeared and is now returned . . . there is some intrigue here, to be sure. And Edward Seymour . . .' She tapped her lower lip with a finger. 'What does this all signify?'

I was about to answer that I hadn't a clue when she said, 'Have you asked Nicholas Pachett?'

I swallowed a suddenly dry throat. 'Er . . . no, I have not.'

'Blessed *Jesu*, why not?'

'Because . . .' I didn't remember sitting on the bed, but there I was, crooked back slumped, suddenly ill at ease with Marion, my long-time love. 'Because . . . I am trying not to see him again.'

All animation left her face. Slowly, she shuffled her feet until she was beside me, and then sat. She was half-clad in her gown, but the bodice had been removed and one sleeve. 'Because of me.'

It wasn't a question in her mind and was not framed that way. She expected it, desired it, and yet, somewhere in her heart, she knew it was not so, because I could see the worry painting her forehead in a wrinkled 'V' between her eyes.

'Partly. He is becoming important to the king. I don't wish to jeopardize that. And I . . . I have . . . feelings for him.'

'Feelings?'

'I didn't know this was going to happen. It has never happened before.'

'You promised me,' she whispered, and the sound of it was like one's conscience echoing in the corridors of one's heart.

'I know. But I never expected something like this to happen.'

'You promised.' It was much quieter this time.

'Marion, I didn't know.'

There fell a long silence between us. Usually, I would break it with a jest, but this was not the time for it.

'You love him, then.'

I couldn't seem to breathe, and so I sat there, choking on air.

'And does he love you?'

'What does it matter?'

'It matters.'

'Marion, I would never leave you. I love *you*!'

'Your love is unnatural, sirrah. And so you think you can love two at once.'

My eyes stung. Her words were designed to be darts and so they were. 'I know it is unnatural. But it is . . . who I seem to be. And, so it must be said, you knew this when we were lovers.'

'I *know*!' Up she shot and paced the floor. She angrily tore at the laces at her shoulder and yanked the sleeve off. 'It was . . . different then.'

'But it's not. I am still the same man. The same man you . . . you loved.'

'But it's not the same.'

'What shall I say to you, Marion, to make it all right? I am trying, you see. Trying not to see him more so that my mind is only on you.'

'And how is that possible when he is still at court?'

'I don't know.'

She stood at the dark window, and I sat on the bed, and only the dog scratching himself and jangling his collar pierced the silence between us.

'Marion . . .'

'I think you should sleep in the outer room. Or perhaps your old rooms.'

Not both of them. I can't lose both of them. 'Marion, please. I was honest with you. I didn't have to be. I could have lied. But I told you the truth that is in my heart so that . . . so that . . .'

'So that *I* could suffer too?'

Mayhap she was right. I didn't need to tell her and make her life a misery as well. But I thought it would help.

I rose. 'Very well. I will be in my old rooms tonight. But I will be back.'

'Suit yourself.'

I found Nosewise's lead and tied it to his collar and tugged at him. I hesitated in the doorway to our bedchamber. 'Marion. I *will* be back. I belong to you. I always have. I am sorry.' And with that, I left. I walked the quieting passages. It was late. There were the sounds of laughter and arguments behind the closed doors I passed. Others living their lives. I am equally certain there was a fair share of tears behind those oaken guardians as well. For the palace, with its twelve hundred or so inhabitants, was always a city of itself, with workers, lay-abouts, thieves, villains, angels, ordinary folk and nobles. All the mix one needed for a habitation. And my life was no worse, no better than the others, when it came down to it. But, oh, how bitter it seemed to be tonight!

'Come along, Nosewise.' I urged him away from sniffing a wall, probably one on to which he had piddled at one time. Marion had never told me to spend the night elsewhere before. Even before we were married, we spent many a time in my bed. And she had known about my escapades. Even liked hearing about them, so she said. Had that all been a lie, or had I only been fooling myself? She said it was different once we were married, so was it merely a woman's birthright to change her mind?

Footfalls.

Christ mend me. I didn't want to encounter anyone now and pretend to be merry and silly. I wanted to be a shadow and left alone. I grabbed Nosewise and held him close to my chest and shrank into a shadowed alcove, waiting for the person to pass.

It was a man in a long, dark gown. A cleric? Almost. Doctor Edmund Bonner, it was, striding through the passage as though in a hurry, and if I didn't know better, I would say that he was heading for Edward Seymour's chambers. Aye, that's where he was going. He spoke softly to the guard there, and then was allowed to enter. Two of our 'E' names together in the same place. Coincidence? No, nothing that happened in the palace seemed to be a coincidence.

I hugged tight to Nosewise to keep him quiet and to give me comfort, whilst I waited to see when Doctor Bonner exited Beauchamp's quarters.

TWELVE

I changed the weight on my feet several times as I leaned against the alcove's wall, waiting for Bonner to come out. What had he to say to Beauchamp at the hour when most were retired for the night that could not wait till the light of day?

I startled when the door opened, and I clutched the warm body of my dog tighter and stepped back further into the shadows.

Bonner exited but didn't look pleased. He dithered in the corridor and looked back at the guarded door before he decided to move into the passage. Well, there was nothing for it but to follow him.

He was a solid gentleman, sturdy like Henry, only slightly more compacted. I imagined the shirt on him, and it seemed to fit the situation. I tried not to follow too close, but he heard either my steps or my breathing, or the jangle of my dog's collar, and he soon slowed and glanced over his shoulder. He stopped when he recognized me.

'Jester, are you following me?'

'*Me* follow *you*?' I said, my face full of injury. 'Might it have occurred to you that perhaps *you* are merely walking in front of *me*?'

He narrowed his eyes in confusion.

'My lord, to clarify, I was merely making my way through the corridor . . . and noticed that you stopped to pay a call on Viscount Beauchamp, in a most protracted visit.'

'And what business is it of yours?'

'All of court is my business, my lord.' I expanded my arms to take in the whole palace and dropped the dog. He scrambled to his feet and trotted towards Bonner to sniff at him.

'Keep your cur to yourself, Jester.'

'It appears he has his own opinion.' Nosewise got a whiff of Bonner, turned up his nose and trotted beyond him towards my old lodgings, dragging his lead.

Bonner didn't wait any longer. He turned away from me and continued his progress. I hurried to catch up alongside him. 'I seem to be at my wits' end, my lord,' I said conversationally.

'I should think so. How long can your wit last, after all?'

'Oh, very good, my lord! I shall have to use that next with the king. But jests aside, he has commanded that I, of all people, investigate the murder of one of the queen's servants.'

'And what has that to do with me?'

'Well, you see, the miscreant slew the poor man, and because his throat was cut, it made a holy mess of his shirt, getting blood on the front and the sleeves. And I discovered that this shirt was abandoned and sold, and I have seen it. And it seems that the person had this shirt embroidered by the highest hand in the land for such things, and that the man's initials were embroidered at the cuffs. With the initial "E".'

His steps faltered and he stopped again, turning a vicious eye on me. 'And you immediately assume it is me who did this deed by benefit of my *name*?'

'Oh, you misinterpret me, my lord. I am merely asking all the "E" names I know at court who would have such a shirt. To see if they have an opinion on the matter.'

Bonner drew himself up and glowered down at me. 'You pillicock! You carrytale! You cock lorel! Breathe a word of any sort of this defamation and I shall report you to the king! And maybe have you excommunicated to boot!'

'My lord! A simple I-know-not-what-you-are-talking-about would have sufficed. No need to load the cart with more.'

He grunted his reply and stormed away, footfalls disappearing around a corner.

I looked about, and Nosewise was nowhere to be found.

Alone. Alone in the corridor, alone with my thoughts and alone without my wife.

What had I done?

What had I expected? Bonner's confession? He was an important man and cleric. He helped Cromwell secure the king's divorce. Henry was grateful to him and trusted him. Was my word worth more than his?

I found my old lodgings and Nosewise sitting before the door, waiting for me. The old lodgings were used mostly for storage now and to keep many of the toys, puppets, wigs and masks for my silliness. They were my sole rooms before I married Marion and we moved into *her* lodgings that her father had secured for her once we were wed.

They were cold and unlived in. Dusty, with a slight smell of mildew. I didn't have any servant clean for me anymore since I spent so little of my time here . . . but perhaps I should reconsider that. There were only a few sticks and branches to light a meagre fire, reminding me of the old days at my father's farm. He was a bit miserly with fuel and most everything else. He did not keep up the few structures of the place, neither the human nor animal lodgings, and there were always holes in the roof, where rain and snow would enter. I was no good at fixing these things, and he often disparaged me and my abilities until I got a job with Richard Fermor, the Wool Staple of Calais. I didn't prove good there either until I did my usual quips and jests for the other servants and found m'self soon doing them for my master. It was he who gave me to Henry, and I am ever grateful to him for it, for in this exchange I had found my rightful calling.

I hurled m'self on to the bed and was immediately sorry I had as I was enclosed in a cloud of dust. I sneezed several times . . . and Nosewise followed suit.

'Am I really to spend the night here alone?'

A knock on the door frightened me badly. Bonner! He realized I knew his guilt and he had come to kill me! But no. He couldn't have known where I was going. Only Marion knew where I was. And she couldn't be here, changing her mind again. Foolish. She would not be here, but perchance it was Michael our servant, coming to tell me to come back?

With a spark of hope in my heart, I leapt out of the bed and threw open the door.

'Your wife told me you might be here.'

Nicholas walked in, not waiting to be asked.

'What . . . what are you doing here, Lord Hammond?'

'Why has your wife expelled you from your lodgings?'

My outrage awakened me. 'She didn't expel me.'

'Is that why you find yourself in your old lodgings for the night?'

'Is that what she said?'

'I understood her meaning. And her coldness towards me. What happened, Will?'

I walked back into the room and sat on the edge of the bed. 'I told her. How I feel about you.'

His eyes were alight, but I could see how he vainly tried *not* to show his excitement. 'Oh? And how *do* you feel about me?'

'Nicholas.' I turned my face from him. My cheeks were suddenly hot from embarrassment, which was some feat for a man who could seldom *be* embarrassed.

Suddenly, he was kneeling at my feet and taking my hand. He brought it to his lips and pressed a tender kiss to it. 'Do you love me?' He pleaded so with his eyes, like a puppy hoping for treats. 'Is that what you told her?'

'Of course I do. I can't help it.'

'Oh, Will!' He sprang to his feet, dragged me forward into his arms and kissed me proper, arms encircling me, growing tighter.

I murmured to his cheek. 'Nick, it isn't a good thing.'

He drew back and truly studied my face. 'No. I see that it is not.'

'Marion isn't pleased. She . . . she did ask me to sleep elsewhere.'

'I'm sorry, Will. I am selfish. I only saw it as good tidings for me, not the consequences of your wedded life. She . . . she seemed so tolerant.'

'And so she was . . . before we wed. Now . . . well, she is not. And since I promised to love only her . . . How could I know I would fall in love with you? I've never felt that way for a man before. Only as a playmate.'

'I can't be sorry that you love me as I love you.'

'I know. What am I to do, Nick?'

He rose and released me. He walked about the room but saw no wine. There was nothing of comfort here in this desolate chamber. 'You are married to her. She deserves your love and loyalty. And, well, in truth, you need a wife to keep tongues from wagging.'

He was a practical man, was Nick.

'I don't know that anyone at court cares much about the life of a jester. It has proved unimportant to the majority.'

'But you never know.'

'True.'

We gazed at one another a while before he moved away from me. 'I realize you have been trying to stay away from me.'

'And look how well it worked!'

'Forgive me for the intrusion. But I am not a man to give in so easily.'

'I know.'

He put his fists to his hips. 'You truly have not been in this situation before, have you?'

'No, my lord. Christ mend me. I have left many disappointed men in my wake, but no one has affected me . . . like you have. And I still think it a better idea to leave you alone so that you can rise in the ranks under His Majesty.'

'I admit that it might well be the best course. But I am a selfish man.'

'You are not.'

'I feel so inside. It is why I am here, after all.'

'You are here as concerns your cod.'

He smiled. 'That too.' But he placed his hand not on his cod, but on his breast. 'And the heart beneath this doublet.'

'You are a pretty speaker, Nick.'

'I *am* trying to woo you.'

My hands covered my reddening face. Were that he had appeared long before I met Marion!

My fingers wiped down my face and dropped away. 'You must not.'

'Like you . . . I cannot help it.' He was at my back again and I felt his arms reach around me, holding me against him . . . and said cod, which was quite interested despite his protestations. His lips reached my neck and nibbled, kissed and tortured me. When he spun me to kiss me again, I didn't resist. I didn't wish to resist ever again, and I was lost.

He had a way of holding my jaw as he kissed me, as if preventing me from tearing away . . . as if I would! I loved the musky smell of him, his sweat, the fresh air upon his cheek that made that flesh cold, the rose water he used in his hair, the deep scent of his maleness that I could not deny myself. My fingers gripped his doublet's shoulders and I held on mightily to him just as he was doing to me.

We landed on the bed, whereupon another cloud of dust ascended round us. But we paid it no heed. It was only him I cared about. His strong arms, his muscled thighs. Such an Adonis was he, like a marble statue. And hard, but not cold like marble. Aye, he made me feel that I was loved and desired, even after we were spent and lying on the dusty sheets.

'Is it dawn?' I asked sleepily. 'Christmas.'

He rustled about. 'Your bed needs cleaning.' Flapping his hand in the air, he dispersed the cloud of dust.

I scanned the room again. 'It has been abandoned all these years. Must I return to it? What am I to do about Marion?'

'You seem to think that I know aught of women. I can assure you, I do not.'

'But I love *her*.' And to assuage that face he made at me, I reached up and traced my finger along his temple and down to his bearded jaw. 'And I love you, too. I love the both of you, equally.'

'You are a strange man, Will Somers.'

'Aye. I've known that all me life.'

He lay back, gazing up at the cobwebs festooned amongst the rafters. 'I suppose you must convince her that you love her. That *you* will not leave *her*. This is her greatest fear. For it is mine as well.'

'I can't leave either of you. I am a weak and cowardly man.'

'Not so.' He turned to me and stroked my face again.

'Now, Nick . . .'

'Tell her you love her. Make her know it. Surely you must . . . tumble with her, do you not?'

'Of course.'

'And . . . you find joy in this?'

'Yes!'

He studied my face, eyes searching all over it. 'You are a strange man. That you can love a woman and love a man.'

'I think I am the perfect man. For I do as the Lord has told us to do. Love thy neighbour. And I do . . . in abundance.'

He laughed and then shook his head as he gazed fondly at
me. 'That you do. But truly, Will, I am trying to help you.
You must woo your wife.'

Cuds-me. The same advice I gave to Henry for Anne Boleyn.
Mark how well *that* turned out.

'She must know she will not lose you,' he continued.

I sighed. 'You have the right of it, Nick. She fears that.'

He rolled over and rested his bearded chin on his laced
hands. 'And I must know it too. You will not give me up.'

'You know it is better that I do.'

'But you won't.'

He had an overabundance of confidence, did Nick. I couldn't
blame him. He was so very handsome. And young. I have
seen how the women of court looked at him with a covetous
eye. Why did he love such a crooked-back, silly-faced man
as me? Surely he could do better.

'I don't know why you love me,' I said shyly, completely
uncharacteristic from such a lusty man. 'But . . . I am glad
that you do. And no, I see that I cannot give you up. But I
won't give up Marion either.'

He rolled again and faced the ceiling. 'Then you should go
to her now. Be firm. Be loving. Do not take "no" for an answer.'

'You're fond of ordering me about.'

'Yes, I am. Go to, Jester. Woo your wife.'

'When I stink from bedding you?'

'Oh.' He settled his folded hands on his chest. 'Perhaps a
wash first.'

'But there is none here.'

'I suppose you could come to *my* chamber . . .'

'God's teeth, I shall have to. Then get dressed, my lord. I
am about to make this morning stranger still.'

We dressed, casting sly looks at each other, and when we
were both presentable, I took Nosewise and we headed towards
his chamber. I admonished Nick to go ahead of me, whilst I
held back so that we would not be seen together, and he, too,
thought that wise.

I lingered then, loosely holding the dog's lead . . . when of
a sudden, the cur sprinted forward and pulled it from my hand.

'Nosewise!' I hissed. 'What are you doing?'

He tore around the corner, and I had to follow. And saw him charge directly into a private room where the door lay ajar. 'Curse you!' I whispered. 'Nosewise!' I whispered as loud as I dared. 'Come here!' And of course he did not respond.

I listened to what he might be doing, and I heard him growling and harrying a pillow, no doubt. Christ! Whose apartments were these? Whose pillow was he destroying? Alas, I didn't know. *Bollocks!* I'd have to go in after him.

I checked the corridor once more before I dared open the door wider and peered into the darkness. 'Nosewise!'

There was no candle lit, no curtain drawn open to give me any sort of light . . . but I did hear movement. Was it the dog? Or . . . the room's inhabitant?

'Christ,' I muttered. I decided to drop to the floor and crawl about like my cursed dog and stretched my arms out to feel my way. A table leg. A rug. A chair, perchance? A shoe. Oh! A foot *in* the shoe . . . and . . . an ankle . . .

And then a dagger pressed to my neck!

THIRTEEN

I rose slowly, that sharp pinprick of the point of a dagger still poking into my flesh. 'Have no fear, my lord,' said I, voice all a-tremble. 'It is only the jester, Will Somers.'

'Will sarding Somers!'

A hand closed over my arm, gripping till all the blood drained out of it as if squeezing a sausage, and dragged me from the room. I whirled away from the man until I hit the corridor's wall and spun to face my quarry. I am such a man of peace I never even reached for me own dagger.

'John Blanke!'

'Hush you.' He looked about, still holding his knife and aiming it at me.

'I went in after my dog.'

'You *sent* your dog in.'

'I didn't! On my oath, sir! I called and called, but Nosewise would not come out . . .'

Until the little whoreson did just that to show me up. Head lifted, tail wagging as fast as you please. He came to me and leapt into my arms.

'Ha,' I chuckled blandly. 'I . . . I trained him to do that.'

'As you trained him to go after thieves, eh?'

I stared with widened eyes. 'Are you a thief, after all?'

'Of course not!'

'Then . . . what were you doing in there?'

'I told you, Jester. It is no business of yours.'

'My business is to make merry and make the court laugh.' The dagger gleamed in the light of a single candle in a sconce. 'This does not make me merry.'

John paused but a moment before he looked down at his naked blade . . . and sheathed it. 'I don't want to soil my blade on you, Somers.'

'Then, for the love of Christ, what are you doing, John?'

The trumpeter glanced both ways down the silent passage. 'Come with me.'

I squeezed Nosewise for comfort, but he wriggled out of my arms, and I let him wander off where he pleased, the sound of his claws on the tiled floor clicking into the distance until I could hear it no more. Into the shadows John and I went, he in the lead as I followed, watching the candles in sconces light our way only to fade again as we stepped into dark patches. He lodged near the other musicians in the communal lodgings of the trumpeters. He opened the door carefully, and as my eyes adjusted, I could see many cots in rows. Quietly, he took me through but exited out another door to a walled back garden. Its pavers were dappled with snow, and the two trees in pots were only black sticks in the darkness.

'Why must you be so nosy, Somers?'

I shrugged. 'It is my nature. And my vocation.'

He puffed a deep breath, cascading that foggy exhale into the clear night. 'It is . . . Jane Foole.'

'What is Jane Foole? Hold. You don't mean to tell me you've become enamoured of her?'

'Don't be more of a fool than you already are, man.' He pulled at his tunic. 'She is a friend. And I would see no harm come to her.'

My belly twisted. What was here? Was Jane responsible for Geoffrey's death? Is that what he meant? That she was . . . involved? I moistened my dry lips. 'What mean you?'

'I mean . . .' He stopped, gazed up to the heavens and snorted a breathy laugh, expelling more clouds about his head. 'She's a bit of a magpie, is our Jane. She likes shiny things.'

'Aye. She loves the queen's jewels.'

'And not only the queen's.' He fastened his gaze on me, perhaps hoping I would answer my own question still on the tip of my tongue. Alas, I was as ignorant as when I started.

So he tried again. 'She likes . . . to *take* pretty things. Take them . . . from other courtiers when she entertains in their apartments.'

My jaw dropped and my hand covered my open mouth. 'God's bodikins!' I whispered. 'She's been stealing from the court?'

'Yes. I caught her one day. I told her it was very naughty, and she seemed to repent of it, but later I discovered she had not returned it.'

'John.' Enlightenment finally gripped me. 'Do you mean to say that you have been returning all the stolen goods?'

He nodded, looking ashamed of himself. But I clutched his arm. 'John, you have been her guardian angel. But you have put yourself in peril for her. You cannot continue. Someone will catch you and blame *you* for stealing it.'

He shrugged. 'Better me than her.'

'But they won't do anything to her. The queen, Lady Mary and a host of other courtiers will defend her. The natural fool is protected by their guilelessness. But you! They know you not.'

'Then . . . what shall I do?'

'Quit jabbering and go to bed, you simpletons!' said a harsh voice in the doorway. God's teeth, we had not noticed him come upon us.

John waved him off. 'Go to bed yourself, Dickon. I am talking to Will Somers.'

'I don't care if it's God Himself; we're trying to sleep.'

John looked at me with wilting shoulders and I gave in. 'Good night, John. And to you too, Dickon. But harken to my advice, John.'

I walked through the beds again and exited to the corridor. John did not follow.

Suddenly, I remembered I was to use Nick's washing water and had left him quite a while ago. Off I went in that direction and knocked softly upon his door. He must have been standing near it, for he opened it at once, grabbed my wrist and hauled me in, closing the door after.

'Where have you been?' He gestured towards the basin that had been filled with still steaming water, with a cake of soap sitting beside it on a towel.

'Forgive me, Nicholas. I was waylaid by . . . another problem. But it eliminated a suspect. I hope.'

'Who—'

'I'd rather not say.' I doffed my coat, doublet and shirt. And in the cold of the room, I washed m'self quickly.

'What about . . .' His eyes darted to my nether regions.

'I'd rather not tempt you.'

'Shall I leave you in peace, then?'

I shrugged into my shirt, tucked it around me, before I donned my doublet and laced it up. 'Not necessary. She won't want that sort of homecoming anyway.'

I was dressed again, grateful that he had helped me. Grateful that he . . . he loved me.

'I must go.' We gazed at one another, before I moved in quickly and kissed his cheek. I longed to take his lips, but it was best I did not. 'Good night, Nicholas. And . . . merry Christmas.'

He stepped towards me and took me in his arms faster than I could react and kissed me properly on the lips. 'Merry Christmas, my love.'

It made me squirm for some reason. I hastened out of there quick-like and hurried back to my lodgings with Marion.

The door was locked, and when I reached for my key, it abruptly opened. Michael stood there, merely staring at me. The longer he stood *not* letting me pass, the greater my agitation.

'Michael. Good ev'ning. Or should I say "good morn"? Shouldn't you be . . . er . . . stepping aside?'

'My mistress does not wish you here tonight.'

I drew myself up indignantly. 'Who is the master here? Her or me?' Verily, I did not know the answer to that m'self.

Michael's face showed all the levels of his concern. After all, he was her servant first, but 'tis true that I was the man, and he must yield to me. And so he did, head down, drawing himself aside to let me pass.

I yanked at my coat as I postured and stomped towards the bedchamber. I tried the door. 'Twas locked.

I knocked gently. 'Marion?' I said softly.

'Go away, Will Somers.'

The *two* names. Christ mend me. 'Marion. My sweet. My love. On this early Christmas morn, a most holy day, is there no charity in you to merely talk to your husband?'

There was no sound from the other side of the door, but I well imagined the many perturbed faces she was making.

The bolt was thrown back. Timidly, I opened the door. I looked back at Michael standing near his cot but not yet getting in it. 'That will be all, Michael,' I said sternly. It wasn't his fault. He was only doing his appointed task. It was not easy being a servant. I gently closed the door behind me and leaned against it.

Marion was in her nightshift and sitting by the fire. When I glanced at the bed, I noticed she had not been in it. 'Do you come directly from *him*?'

Was honesty best? I have always tried to be honest in the dealings with my friends, for honesty was one of those commodities at court that was not always available on the shelf. In the end, I decided to use it. 'N–not at first. I mean, I headed to my old lodgings. But . . . Lord Hammond found me.'

'I see.' Her speech was tight, defensive. Of course it was.

'But then I left him and encountered John Blanke, and the varlet had the nerve to put a dagger to me neck.' I touched the spot and imagined a gaping hole where none was.

That stirred her somewhat. She glanced over her shoulder at me but didn't quite meet my eyes. 'Did he hurt you?'

Did I detect something hopeful in that question?

'Marion! Shame on you for wishing harm to me. He didn't, as it happens. But his creeping about at night in other people's rooms was a precious mission of his. He was returning pieces of jewellery that . . . that Jane Foole had been stealing.'

She turned fully then. 'The jester?'

'Aye. John said she is likened to a magpie, devoted to shiny things, even when they weren't hers to take.'

'Blessed *Jesu*.'

'Indeed. And even at risk to himself, he did it for her sake.' I shook my head at it. 'That is a friend indeed. But I told him that he must stop this practice. Those who were stolen from would not thank him . . . or believe him.'

'Oh, Will.'

'So you see, it took some time for me to return to you. I had hoped . . .' I rose but only to stand beside her. 'I had hoped that your anger would have cooled.'

'Was this a farewell to Lord Hammond?' She sat on her chair, looking away from me and fiddling with the loose ends of her plait.

I wanted to lie, to ease her mind. But in the end, I could not. I straightened. 'No, Marion. I love him. I love him as I love you. My love for you has never wavered. It has not diminished by this other love. It is not a matter of choosing whom I love more, for I love you both equally. Marion, I seem to be another kind of creature not dreamed of in the words of scripture. But you know that I am as guileless as any natural fool. I mean no harm or menace to anyone. Not to you and not to Nicholas. You and I are husband and wife under the eyes of God, but to him, I am just as devoted. And I will not give him up. If you cannot live with this, then . . . then . . . oh, Christ help me, Marion. I do not know what I am going to do. I do not want to be without you. But I will understand as no husband has ever understood . . . if you cannot bear it.'

I got down on my knees to her. She tried not to look, but her eyes betrayed her. 'Marion . . . I love you. Nothing will change that. You will always have the best of me.'

Her eyes were wet, and it stabbed me directly in the heart to see it. 'I thought when we married, I would be the only one. Fool that I am.'

I took her small hand in mine. Such a delicate hand as only a woman could have. I craved its touch just as I craved the touch of a man. But this hand was thrifty and crafty in its talents of embroidery. And . . . other such ways in the marriage bed. 'There's only room in the family for one fool. And as far as women are concerned, you *are* the only one. My only wife, that is.'

'They told me not to marry the jester,' she said, almost to herself. 'My father, my friends. They said it would be as foolish a life as the man himself. That I would regret it.'

I swallowed hard in my suddenly thickened throat. '*Do* you regret it?'

'Sometimes. The damnable thing of it is . . . I *like* Nicholas Pachett.' She looked at me then, perhaps trying to see *into* me, into the deep places in my mind that could sort out man from woman and back again. 'For me to have you, he must be in our lives. Is that what you are saying?'

'Until he sees the sense in it and gives *me* up.'

'And once having had you, who would be such a simpleton as to do that?' She raised her other hand, the one I had not captured, and laid it to my cheek. 'Dear, sweet Will. Whoever thought that there would be this kind of trouble from marrying a jester.'

'It's . . . my gift.'

She couldn't help herself and laughed through her tears. 'Such a gift, Master Jester.' She wiped her wet cheeks with the back of her hand.

I laid my head in her lap. 'Don't give up on me, Marion. Even I don't understand it. But if you can tolerate me, I shall not let you regret it. Not ever.'

She caressed my short hair, and thus we sat, until the weak dawn broke into the crystal cold sky.

Early in the morn, with naught but a moment or two of sleep for me, we got word that Robert Aske, leader of the Pilgrimage of Grace, would arrive today. Christmas Day.

FOURTEEN

There was already so much to do. So many preparations to make for the Christmas feast and entertainments after the morning mass. The court did not need Robert Aske to barge into our merry-making.

Alas. We must accede to the politics around us. Henry invited him; therefore, the rest of us had naught to say on the matter. But I worried. How would Aske *leave* the court? Wrapped in a winding sheet? Or on his own two feet?

It wasn't long till the court was in its finery and the king was being readied – he shooed me out of his chamber with all the other fussing going on round him – and John Blanke and the other trumpeters were readying in their places on the frigid battlements to announce him.

There was a trumpet call in the distance from the road to the palace, and by that we were alerted that Aske's arrival was imminent. Henry's ministers had wanted the king to be situated outside to greet his subject, but Henry put his foot down. He would await Aske in the watching chamber on his throne under his cloth of state like some Pharoah of old whilst Aske would enter into the king's presence like Moses imploring the Pharoah to 'let his people go'. Indeed, the metaphor was apt, for surely the Pharoah thought Moses an upstart and traitor for daring to plead for something as momentous, and Aske, too, dared to do such. It was in his name, after all. It must have raised his spirits indeed to be so invited to court . . . and raised Henry's hackles. It made my heart hurt to think about it.

Henry was in a white doublet sparkling with gold and jewels, with ermine trimming his coat. He made himself as regal as possible, even to wearing a crown, though he never needed one, for he was magnificent in his elegance, his flaming red hair and beard, his mighty stature, his *presence*. I stood beside and a little behind his throne, proud I was to be able to be there with my king.

The queen was also regal in her golds and velvets. She was reminiscent of the Holy Mother, even down to the pale of her cheek that seemed somewhat paler today. To my trained eye, she looked concerned, and I was reminded that she had *given* her brooch to Geoffrey Payne, and that I ought not forget that. Because it finally made me wonder in the forefront of my mind just *why* she would do such a thing. Surely not as a reward for good work. Coins were best for that. Small tokens of jewellery perhaps, but not that behemoth of a brooch. Why would she sacrifice such bounty to a servant? I had to think on it. And I had to question Jane Foole once more, for there may be more she knew that she had not said, that with time she *could* say. In any case, I needed to stop her from stealing further from courtiers. If she became too much of a nuisance, the queen would be forced to send her away, and I didn't want that.

The trumpets sounded from the battlements. Robert Aske and his men had arrived!

I hadn't noticed that I was clutching at the back of Henry's throne with tight fingers. But I couldn't let go. It was as if by some sorcery – as long as I kept hold of his throne – he would do no harm. Foolish, I know, but that was how it felt.

There was noise and movement down the corridors. I noted that Lady Mary and Madam Elizabeth were not present. There was fear that they might be used as hostages, and so they were kept deep in the palace and under guard.

And then the procession arrived. Since all of court knew who he was and his mission, there was nothing by way of cheering, just polite attention. He was dressed in what he must have considered his best. Indeed, he had travelled all over the north country, the captain of this pilgrimage, and had only the clothes of a lawyer, and a slightly mud-spattered one at that. He was garbed in a black coat with black fur . . . looking a bit like Cromwell, come to think of it. He was a small man. Oh, I do not mean short, but a man who looked so very . . . ordinary. He was said to be nearly forty with no family, and already with side whiskers of grey as testament to his years.

Then the tall, brawny Gentleman of the Privy Chamber Peter Meutas stepped forward. A long, well-trimmed beard of chestnut brown covered his chin, and he bowed low to the king.

He was the king's expert on the arquebus – a loud shooting weapon – and perhaps when Henry thought to send him to fetch Aske, if he failed to bring him peaceably, he would shoot him like any assassin instead. But here he was with his quarry. I did not know the man well, but I didn't much like his secretive ways. Though he was fiercely loyal to Henry, and in that he had my hand in friendship.

'Your Majesty,' said Meutas, with an elegant bow. 'May I present Master Robert Aske, barrister of Gray's Inn and captain of the Pilgrimage of Grace. He has come to pay you homage.'

Aske swept off his hat and bowed low to the king, and Henry acknowledged him with a magnanimous nod.

'Your Majesty,' said the man with humility and grace. He said only those two words, but for some reason, I liked him instantly. He was not a preening peacock, but a simple man whose heart was sore for his religion. I saw no treason in him. He did not want the death of my Henry, for if he had, I should take my dagger to him myself. No, I began to think that he would make a good minister for Henry. He'd advise with simple language and with simple deeds. I wanted to tell Henry, whisper in his ear, 'This is not a man to be spurned or gaoled. Not like Cromwell. This is a man with sense. You should listen to him, Harry.' But I had no place in this ritual. I would talk to Henry later. I would tell him my thoughts. He listened to his Will more often than not.

'Master Aske,' said Henry in his regal voice that could be heard in the outer reaches of the hall. 'We welcome you most heartily to court. I have declared,' he seemed to be saying to the court more than to Aske, 'that I shall confer full pardons for all those in your pilgrimage who lay down their arms. I am not insensitive to your woes, sir.'

Aske bowed again. 'You are a gracious lord in this, sire. My northern countrymen mean no harm.' Ah yes, his York accent was strong, but we could understand him well enough. 'We only seek to follow God as He has commanded us. And you, my liege, for leading us to the way.'

Henry nodded again, ever the lord. 'Yorkshire is a proud country. I wish to hold my next Parliament at York, and my queen . . .' He turned to gaze at Jane and held his bejewelled hand out for her, which she took graciously. She conferred a smile on Aske. 'We further intend to crown our beloved wife and queen in York in the spring. You see, I hold no ill will for your holy pilgrimage, and we tender to all our subjects our mercy from our heart. Our only desire is to hold all our subjects in our hands as one people.'

'I so desire that, too, Your Grace.'

Henry signalled to someone amongst his men who stepped forward, some red material draped over his hands. 'A token of our love, Master Aske. A jacket of crimson satin.'

The court gave a low gasp. Such an expensive gift for one Henry had considered a traitor? I could almost hear the wheels turning in their heads.

'A gracious gift this is, Your Grace. I am unworthy of such beneficence.'

'Nonsense. You shall be worthy of it, when you take the message of mercy back to the people of the north.' He nodded to Meutas who stepped forward again.

'His Majesty wishes to convey his benevolence and to enjoin you to partake in the Christmas festivities. My men will conduct you to your lodgings to ready yourself for them.' He gestured for Aske to follow the men he indicated – more of Henry's privy gentlemen – and Aske bowed again to the king and queen and was hastened away.

I saw Henry cast an eye towards Cromwell and a look pass between them that gave me a chill.

How I longed to talk to Aske alone. Alas, I would most certainly never be allowed to do so. Instead, I sought to keep nigh Henry. I wanted at least a moment with him alone, and I'd never find that opportunity unless I pressed close to his person. He must have been surprised that I was present and yet so quiet, for I did not quip or rhyme or waste his time with jests. I looked only for my opportunity . . . and then it came.

He dismissed his privy council with only a few Gentlemen Ushers remaining. Henry was readying to be entertained by the Lord of Misrule's beguilements, and his ushers were undressing him for to don yet another sumptuous doublet and coat.

I sat on his table with my feet in the chair Henry had just vacated whilst one usher unpinned each slash in his doublet and another divested him of his ermine-trimmed coat. 'I must say, Harry, I was impressed with Master Aske.'

'Oh?' he said, sparing me an eye and an arched brow.

'Oh, indeed. Very impressed. Such a simple man. An ordinary man. You might even say he is the model subject of the realm.'

'Model? Hmpf!'

The bejewelled doublet was unlaced and lifted from the royal body.

'Aye, Uncle. Think on it. He's a simple barrister and hears grievances all the time. Perhaps even more than you do, what with the sieve of ministers about you.'

Henry eyed his attendants as they worked and said nothing.

'And he was sincere. I could see it on his face and hear it in his voice. Seldom am I deceived such, for I do observe carefully for to cast my jests upon our courtiers.'

'You think he is sincere. Indeed. I have seen their requests. They would have the monasteries restored and the monks and nuns returned to them. By violence, they had done that very thing in the north – seized certain monasteries I myself have gifted to my worthy servants, and thrust the monks back into their places against my command!'

'Well . . . they are zealous pilgrims at that. But, Harry, you must look at it from their point of view.'

'Why? *My* point of view is foremost.'

'But, Uncle, so many lost their income. So many worked for the monasteries and suddenly they have been cut off. Overnight, they were made into poor men. And the mills. Many of the flour mills were owned and serviced by the monks. Now no more. The people must travel great distances just to have their bread. It is sad, Uncle, and they have no recourse.'

'They demand that the monastery visitors, including my Chancellor of the Exchequer, be executed for their part in it, when they were only following my commands.'

The execution of Cromwell? I might rejoice but I wouldn't speak *that* aloud. 'They were the instigators, though. Was it

not Master Crumbled-Well who devoted some time to disman-
tling your monasteries?'

'Somers, you'd be wise not to speak of things about which
you are ignorant.'

'Oh, if only I could, Uncle. But it is my vocation to add
verbiage to my thoughts. Whenever a thought comes to me.'

'Well, curb it! I have told you before, you will not meddle
in my policies.'

'Even when your policies stink like yesterday's fish?'

He kicked the chair out from under me and I fell to the
floor. 'You're a nuisance, Somers. Get out.'

'But, Harry,' said I, rubbing my bum, 'this is a momentous
occasion. Never before has a king listened so diligently to a
subject who brings unpleasant requests. You are truly magnanimous in this.'

He gazed at me with narrowed eyes as his new scarlet doublet
was laced about him. There were more jewels on that as well,
and a fox-trimmed coat was adjusted over his padded shoulders.

'I can see it now,' I pressed. 'Aske returns from court, so
amazed, so awed by your magnificence. He tells all nine
thousand of his followers that the king requests they put down
their arms and all will be forgiven. He explains how gracious,
how sensible you were. You've . . . *instructed* like the kings
of old. And then, suddenly, this rebellion is done.'

Henry had not stopped looking at me as I talked, and I
could see the mill wheel turning in his mind. *Could this be*,
he must be thinking, *that my generosity actually worked to
change their minds?*

Believe it, Harry, I longed to say aloud. But it was best that
he worked it out for himself . . . so that he could claim it was
his idea.

Once Henry was dressed again, he, his wife, his retinue and
I travelled back to the watching chamber to enjoy the Christmas
entertainments and so that the king could confer gifts on his
most loyal. I was proud to receive a small pouch of gold coins
which Henry presented to me himself. 'With my love and my
thanks, Will,' he said with a tender smile.

The servant Lionel took to his duties as the Lord of Misrule,
and conducted the mystery play with smoke, and bells, and

the sound of thunder. I did not know how he accomplished it, but we were all very entertained by it, even as jugglers and tumblers entered in and performed for the court.

Robert Aske was there amongst the court with a few of his men, surrounded by Yeoman Guards and under the watchful eye of Peter Meutas. It was only then that Lady Mary and Madam Elizabeth were allowed to the crowds . . . with guards stationed directly behind their seats.

Naturally, I sidled over towards Meutas, who looked on me with suspicion. 'Why so unhappy, my lord?' I said, venturing no nearer to Aske as Meutas would allow. 'Is this not a holy day, a momentous day? You performed your duties admirably.'

He moved not a muscle, still wary.

'Never need to be cautious of me. I am but the jester, as you well know.'

'I know you,' was all he said, stone-faced.

I arched a brow. 'Well . . . you look to be having as merry a time as you are able.' I left him alone with his tart face. Curse it, I could get no closer to Aske unless I wished to be set upon by the king's guards.

And just where was Meutas, I wondered, a fortnight ago when Geoffrey Payne was being murdered? Likely already gone on his mission to find Robert Aske. He was sour enough to commit murder, or so it looked to me. But he was a 'P' name, not an 'E' one. Alas.

And just as I looked across the room, whom should I spy but Edmund Bonner, a distinctly 'E' name. I made my way across the hall. Groups of people made way for me . . . like a leper. One didn't wish to tangle with the Fool who could easily make a fool out of them.

'My lord!' I greeted, as if we were old friends. I even slapped him heartily on the back. He lurched forward, then turned an acid glare on me. 'So good to see you . . . in the light of day.'

He seemed to want to come back with a rejoinder. 'It was not *me* skulking about in the mid of night,' he might wish to say, but he'd have to admit to skulking as much as I had. He bit his tongue on it instead and said nothing.

'Come, come, my lord. You and I are old friends, are we not? Spying our way through the palace passages and such, eh?' Others around us pressed their lips together, keeping close their titters. 'It's great fun, isn't it?'

'Somers,' he said, low and dark, 'if you do not get your hands from me immediately, I will make your life difficult.'

'Make my life difficult?' I said at the top of my voice. 'Oh dear, dear, dear. Well, if you must know, a jester's life is not an easy one. Oh no. It looks to be all merriment from sunrise to sunset, but I can assure you, sir, that it is not. There is my wife to worry over. My dog, who is . . . somewhere, likely making mischief. And the quips and jests I must come up with every day is work, work, work. I must please the king! Oh, such work is that, but most pleasant. So, I don't see how you could make my life *more* difficult.'

'Pillicock,' he hissed, and melded into the crowd.

Aye, I liked him very much for a murderer, for I did not much like the man at all.

'Why do you harry Doctor Bonner?' asked one of the king's Gentlemen Ushers, Thomas Giffard. He had a handsome face, windblown with his usual swarthy complexion fading from winter's clouds. A dark beard kept short, but usually a wry smile at my many jests. I liked this man who was loyal to Henry, though still secretly Catholic. I think even Henry knew but said nothing, for he trusted the Giffards from their long-time service with never a sour word about them from any man.

'Because he is an unpleasant fellow. Surely you must feel the same.'

He sighed and lifted his chin to peer through the crowd at Bonner's retreating back. 'He is damned unpleasant. Even as he—' But he cut himself off from saying what he seemed to suddenly realize he shouldn't.

But that was the chink in the armour I was looking for! 'Even as he services donkeys? Lies down with sheep? Performs unnatural acts with swine?'

Thomas laughed and covered it with his hand. 'Somers, I like you best of all men in this kingdom, save for His Grace, of course.'

'Of course. And I thank you for that fine compliment, Lord Giffard. But . . . what was it you were going to say, sir?'

'Treason, I expect,' he said so low I barely caught it.

A flash of an idea crossed my mind. Bonner was Bishop of London at one time in those early days. Surely . . . *surely* he was not *still* secretly Catholic like Thomas? 'You mean because of the faith he still covertly practises . . . much like you.'

Thomas shot me a look that chilled me. I made light of it, but it was no light thing to admit. For Thomas was right: it was treason to practise the Roman faith as he and his family did.

'Be at ease, my lord,' I said in quiet tones. 'I would never betray a courtier as loyal to Henry as you are. You must know that by now.'

His muscles seemed to unwind, and he squared his shoulders under their broad fur collar. 'You are a wily fellow, are you not? But there are layers to you that most of court completely misses. Yes, you do know me. And you seem to know Doctor Bonner. He is a fierce Catholic.' He said the last very quietly.

'But he worked with Wolsey to break with Rome.'

'There are such men who can . . . categorize their morality. He put his principles aside to serve his king, unlike Thomas More, who would not surrender them even to his detriment.'

One's head on a pike. I'd say that was detriment.

'But, as you must surely know, Somers, there are many men at court who blow with the wind one day here, one day there.'

'Not you.'

'I try mightily to keep to the principles that I can do. I only hope that God in His mercy will remember me.'

'I'm certain He will, my lord. God can afford to be magnanimous. A king cannot.'

He shook his head and chuckled. 'You are a devil of a man, Somers.'

'Sometimes, my lord.'

'You must realize that Doctor Bonner agrees with this pilgrimage. I know he has tried to support them by sending them funds or asking that others of high rank send aid. He even asked me.'

'And did you?'

He studied me, trying to discern if I could be so trusted. 'I would not have risked it. Not the king's wrath, nor the headsman.'

'But others risk it,' I said, more to myself.

'That they do.' He shook his head again. 'God's wounds, Somers. You are a sorcerer to pull such confessions from me. You realize my life is in your hands.'

And he did suddenly look concerned. I pressed my hand to his arm. 'My lord, I am no man's enemy . . . save Cromwell's. Do not fear me. I swear to you. I will make any oath you wish of me.'

'No need, Will. I know you in this. But I had better learn to curb my tongue when I am nigh you.'

'I suppose that is always best.'

He shook my hand and wished me and my wife a merry Christmas before he moved into the crowd again. A good man was Thomas Giffard. And such an invaluable servant to His Majesty. Unlike Doctor Bonner. So, another trimmer in Henry's court, bowing to the direction of the wind.

And collecting funds to support Robert Aske and his compatriots? What can I learn from that?

FIFTEEN

The merriments continued, and I the Fool was decidedly not needed under the onslaught of so many festivities prepared by others. And so I had time to ponder these facts that had suddenly come to light. They grew in my mind like a tide, and I looked round desperately for Marion so that I might discuss them with her. She could always clarify what was jumbled in my head. Where, by the Rood, was she?

In my ear a most pleasant voice whispered. 'I am disappointed that you are not Lord of Misrule, Will,' said Nicholas. When I pulled away, he was smiling.

'I am Lord of Misrule all the rest of the time, my lord. This is the time for someone else to perform as such, and my good friend Lionel is doing the job admirably. In fact, I might have to take him to the law courts for impersonating me. I recall some of those japes most distinctly.'

'No doubt.' The people were many at court and the crowd pressed close to watch the performances of jugglers and tumblers. So it was nothing that he sidled closer and spoke to my ear where I indulged in those deep tones. 'I missed you this morn.'

'You already spent time with me early this morn.'

'I know. And it was lovely.'

'Hush, my lord.'

'I long to touch you.'

'That would be foolish indeed.'

'Which is why I will not . . . and leave you to your own devices.'

But he did manage, in the press of bodies all round us, to caress my hand once before he left me.

Cuds-me. I loved the man. But then my heart heaved and filled with the warmth that was my love for Marion . . . and then I saw her. Whenever I saw her from afar, I could not believe my good fortune in her finding a life with this crook-backed jester. What a marvel it was, and she so beautiful.

She was dressed in her finery, with broad embroidered ribbons trimming her sleeves from her days before she wed me, a gift from her father. She was not bejewelled as courtiers were, but she decorated her bodices with embroidery that looked so fine as to be made from the costliest of fabrics. She had to be careful, of course, because of the sumptuary laws. Those of low status such as Marion and I were not allowed velvets or furs or certain colours reserved for the king and queen alone. We must look fit for our places but not too low as to offend the sensibilities of court. Of course, for me, it was easy. I would never wear fur or velvets unless the king conferred them upon me personally, but Marion . . . well, women loved their finery, and she made do with what she could devise.

Gazing at her bright eyes and glowing cheeks, I fell in love all over again.

Verily, I know this is hard to follow – the loves of Will Somers, which would make a very interesting tapestry – but 'twas true. I loved them both.

I pushed my way through, for the Christmas feast day was the one day a year that I was little needed, and therefore I could attend to my wife. I reached her at last right under the Kissing Bough.

She startled when I grabbed her, perhaps thinking some other swain had ungallantly approached her, but I could see the relief on her face when she saw it was me . . . until she remembered she was cross with me.

'Now, Marion,' I said, hastening to stop those thoughts. 'It is Christmas, and we find ourselves under the Kissing Bough.' I looked up and her glance followed mine. Above us in the arch of the doorway was the decoration – a series of hoops wired together to look like an open sphere, each hoop being wrapped with ivy, with red apples hanging within it by red ribbons. Below it hung a sprig of mistletoe.

She hesitated only a moment before she leaned in and tried to impart a chaste kiss. But I encased her shoulders in an embrace and kissed her proper as lovers did, not as long-time husbands and wives.

There were cheers all round when we pulled apart. Our

audience of courtiers and servants applauded us, whereupon I promptly bowed and, to my surprise, so did Marion, flushed pink from embarrassment . . . and perhaps from the love of the kiss.

I waved to my audience as I led her away out into the corridor. 'Marion, an idea is stirring in my head, and we must find Jane Foole so that I may question her again. She may know more than she is telling, or is capable of telling. Perhaps the two of us can coax it fully out of her.'

'About the murder, you mean?'

'Aye. It is troubling me. I feel I am closer to an answer than I imagined.'

We returned to the hall and began to search for her. 'I liked Doctor Bonner for the murderer because he is so odious a man,' I rambled, tugging her with me by her small hand, 'but that does not necessarily a murderer make.'

'He is a foul man,' she agreed. 'When he was Bishop of London, he sought all sorts of rules to punish people for various grievances against Church law. At first I thought he might explode like a pudding when the king declared himself the head of the Church, but like most hypocritical men, he bowed to the new order.'

'He didn't bow very far,' I said close to her ear. 'I was told by a reliable source that he is still a covert Catholic.'

'Which reliable source?'

I touched my finger to my lips.

'Will Somers, are you telling tales?'

'On my honour, my love. But I promised this source that I would not reveal his name.'

She pressed her lips together – such delectable lips! – whilst she thought on it. 'I will never understand why people tell you things as if you are their confessor.'

'Because I am the most trustworthy man at court. I have a kind face.'

She laughed. '*Some* kind of face.'

'Here now! It is the only face I've got. And you said you loved it.'

She offered a mild gaze and laid a hand to my cheek. 'And so I do.'

'Well, then. You must certainly see how the honesty just bursts forth from this visage. Everyone thinks so.'

She laughed again, and this time nodded her agreement. She soon sobered and continued her thoughts aloud as I'd hoped she would. 'So what does Bonner's Catholic faith have to do with this murder? Had the man blasphemed in front of him and he took his revenge for God?'

'It's possible. But the main thing on my mind is why did the queen give the brooch to Geoffrey in the first place? Is it possible that Bonner saw it and thought the man stole it? But if that were the case, why has it just been returned to the queen's jewel casket? Why not weeks ago when the man was killed?'

'And why was he dug up only a few days ago?'

'Right, Marion! Why murder the man a fortnight ago and then wait to dig him up, when he was surely at his worst?' I shuddered. 'What a ghastly intent.'

'So strange.' She shook her head at it as did I. 'Look!' she said suddenly with her arm outstretched to point. 'There she is.'

We wove through the crush of people and finally reached Janie, entertaining some of the children with puppets.

'It's Will Somers!' cried one of the children, and the others took up the call. Ah, how they loved me and how I loved them! The wee ones of court, the little ladies and gentlemen who would someday grow up and rule us all. I opened my arms wide and took them in, and they rose and rushed forward to be compassed by me.

'My lords and ladies,' I told them, and they loved to be called so. 'I did not mean to interrupt your merriment from our Janie here, but if you will pardon us, I must speak with her and then I promise to return her to you anon.'

There were some pouty faces, until I did a little tumbling that made them laugh, and then I quickly grabbed a confused Janie and stole away with her.

'Will!' she said impatiently as Marion took her other arm and led her to a far and lonely corner. 'And Madam Will. What do you want of me?'

'Janie,' I said in placating tones, 'I need you to remember more about poor Geoffrey.'

She raised her lip in a sneer of discomfort. 'I don't want to think of him. It's Christmas.'

'And what a time it is. Fun all the day and feasting tonight. But, Janie, I must know more, and I think you *do* know more than you have said. After all, you are very observant.'

She postured, raising her chin. The strap of her cap seemed to cut deep under her jawline. 'I see everything.'

'As I knew you did. Won't you tell us about this brooch you saw the queen give to Geoffrey? Can you tell us why you think the queen would have given him such a gift?'

She sighed like a petulant child. 'I do not know.'

Marion moved in then and gently took Janie's hand. The Fool smiled up at my wife. 'You're pretty,' she said, charmed by Marion as I was.

'Thank you very much,' said Marion. 'And I think you are pretty too. Is that a new headdress?'

Janie liked her Dutch bonnets, and Queen Jane gave her the new one she was wearing, made of white brushed fur. Janie's hands flew to it and petted the carefully trimmed pelt. 'My beloved queen gave it me this morn. It is beautiful.' She posed as if she were a great lady sitting before Master Holbein.

'It is indeed beautiful,' said Marion. 'More so than my old headdress.'

'But you made yours, did you not?' Janie reached out to touch it with questing fingers. 'I could never make anything so beautiful. And you embroidered it.'

'I could teach you how.'

She shook her head and scrunched up her eyes. She wiggled her fingers before her face. 'I can't make them sew.'

Marion smiled indulgently. She should have made a wonderful mother. Alas. 'I will teach you something simple. And if you take to it, we can try other things. Wouldn't you like to decorate your bonnet with a bead or two?'

With eyes wide in awe and mouth agape, Janie was completely won over by my clever wife.

'But for now,' Marion continued, 'I wonder if you can think hard. Think very hard indeed and see if you can remember the queen talking to anyone recently. Maybe they asked something that she did not wish to do at first but might have been talked into.'

Oh, very good Marion! I hadn't got that far in thinking it through.

Janie stuck the knuckle of one finger into her mouth as those slow mill wheels churned in her mind. Janie's thoughts were like patches on a poor man's cloak: random, awkward and sometimes not well sewn in.

'The queen is always talking to someone,' she said slowly. 'Mostly her brother, Viscount Beauchamp.' She leaned in and put her hand to the side of her mouth and said quietly, 'He yells at her. Like a brother. She *hates* him.'

'She does?' asked Marion, every bit as solicitous as a nun. 'Why does she hate him? That seems uncharacteristic of our loving queen.'

Janie's attention was taken by a procession of dancers garbed with streamers on their doublets, and she watched that as she tried to answer. 'He treats her like a younger sister instead of a queen.'

'I have seen this for myself,' I added.

She nodded at me. 'And my lady does not like that. She said to me when we were alone . . .' She trailed off as another set of jugglers came walking through and entranced her.

'When you were alone?' I urged and turned her away from them and back to Marion and me.

'Yes, we were alone, and she sighed a lot, and then she bid me sit on her footstool so she could stroke my shoulder. "Aye me," she said. "My brother needs his sister to do his bidding even now. Especially now," or some such, she said. "And I a queen." And she seemed sad, but I could tell she was angry, for she clutched her kerchief in her other hand as if to strangle it. And then *I* said, "But you are the queen. Can you not do what you like?" And she shook her head. "He *made* me queen," she said, "so that I could do *his* bidding." And then she looked at me, sad-like, like she does, and said, "Wouldn't you like to pray to the Virgin again? And go to mass, and see the relics?" You know how I liked the incense and bells, Will.'

'I remember.'

Marion edged closer. 'And so Viscount Beauchamp wanted the queen to talk the king back into our Catholic religion?'

'He said it needed to be funded. He said it to the queen. What does "funded" mean, Will?'

'It means money, my sugar sweetie. Someone needs money to make it happen. To bring back our old religion.'

She turned to Marion again, as if forgetting for a while that she was there. She smiled at my wife's beautiful face. 'Do we want to be Catholic again?'

'The king will not permit it.' My diplomatic wife.

'Oh.' The wet finger returned to her mouth but for a moment. 'Then why did the queen give the brooch to Geoffrey to take to the north?'

My heart stopped. When I looked at Marion, hers must have stopped too. 'The . . . the north?' I asked. 'Is that why she gave Geoffrey the brooch, to give it to the people of the north? You heard her say that?'

'She said, "Take this to the pilgrims in the north for I wish for them to succeed."'

Marion and I were silenced again. Until I queried, 'Did Beauchamp ask her to do this?'

'Oh aye,' she said, distracted by the musicians who began to play a merry tune. She watched them as she tried to answer me. '"Sell one of your trinkets!" he said, rather nastily.' She sneered. 'I don't like him very much when he does that to my beloved lady. Geoffrey took it and left to do it for the queen, because he loved her too. We all would have done it because we love her. *I* love her. She is like the Holy Mother to me.'

'Is there aught else you recall?' said Marion.

She shook her head. I was certain the mill wheels had come to a halt as she watched the dancers perform. That was the terminus of what our wheedling could get out of her. At least for now. And it was plenty.

We thanked her even though she paid us no mind, and I pulled Marion along to another secluded part of the corridor. 'Marion, did you hear her?'

'I did. And can scarce believe it.'

'Did she not say that the queen's brother, Edward Seymour,

told her to sell her jewels to fund the Pilgrimage of Grace? Did he tell his sister the queen to . . . to commit treason?'

She was breathing quickly with a hastening fall and rise of her bosom. She licked her lips, eyes darting for to seek any wide-open ears, and, finding none, said breathlessly, 'He did.'

SIXTEEN

'God's eyes, Marion,' I said, slumping against the wainscoting of the corridor, just inside the arch that led to the watching chamber where all of court was enjoying the Christmas entertainments. 'I cannot bear it. I cannot bear another treason trial for a queen.'

Marion wrung her hands. 'Maybe . . . maybe it is not as bad as it sounds.'

'Not as bad as it sounds?'

'Lower your voice, husband. Do you want all of court to hear you?'

'Sorry, sorry.' Now *I* gnawed on a finger.

She stood close to me so that we could talk quietly. 'I say this because . . . it was not accomplished. Geoffrey was murdered instead.'

'And the brooch returned to the jewel casket.'

'So who knew what Geoffrey was about? Who heard the queen ask him to do this task? And who thought it the best course to kill him?'

'That is the question, Marion. Was Geoffrey a secret Catholic?'

'That sounds like an enquiry *you* should be making of his friends and fellow servants.'

'But don't you see, Marion? We are quickly running out of "E" names. Edmund Bonner is also a secret Catholic. He would not have stopped Geoffrey on his course. Edward Seymour *requested* this venture from the queen, and so he would not have murdered the man.'

Marion pointed a finger at me. 'Unless Geoffrey refused to do this service for the queen. For he must surely have realized it was treason.'

'And to be caught with the jewel would have been evidence to send him to the gallows. Oh, Marion! What a tangled weave this is. Then we cannot eliminate Edward Seymour from our "E" list at all.'

'Not yet. Not until there is further evidence.'

I thought hard. These puzzles without all the pieces were impossible! 'But then . . . why would Edward Seymour return it to her jewel box? Surely he would keep it and give it to his own man to do the deed and travel to the north.'

'That *is* strange.'

'We are walking in circles within circles.'

'Will, maybe Geoffrey returned it.'

'No, that could not be it. Because Geoffrey was killed a fortnight ago, and the brooch was returned only a few days back. Where was it all this time?'

'Christ mend me,' she muttered. Dear me. She was picking up *my* way of speaking. And it unaccountably heartened me, for when married couples are long together, they do tend to speak the same way. It gladdened my heart . . . for only a moment, because the seriousness of the rest of it wiped away all cheer.

'Marion, something damnable is happening.'

'I don't like it, Will. I don't like that you are getting close to it. The last time with Queen Anne was bad enough . . .'

I recalled it well. Was this the hand of Cromwell? No, he couldn't have known. Not if Edward Seymour was keeping it a secret, and a close secret it needed to be. For his brother-in-law the king would not look kindly on this treason, and Seymour would last as long as a crust of bread amongst beggars if Cromwell got wind of it.

'We . . . We'd best get back to the festival,' said I.

She glanced over her shoulder through the arch to the merry-making. The feast was coming on apace. I wondered how much I could do when all the servants were as busy as bees in a skep. 'This is intolerable,' I muttered.

'It's impossible,' she said, but took my arm anyway as we returned to the throng like proper courtiers.

Janie had returned to entertaining the children. I didn't like Aske very well in that instance. For more deaths could be attributed to these rebels. I knew they meant no harm, but they had violently returned some of the monks to their monasteries in the north. And Geoffrey was killed and our queen put in peril. No, I began to see what Henry saw. When a king declares something, it ought to be obeyed or there is chaos in the entire kingdom. These conspiracies in shadows of court were driving me mad. I could not believe I was coming to see Henry's point of view, but there it was. He had a great burden on his shoulders, and now that burden was laid on the delicate shoulders of the queen. For Henry had started all of this because he needed a male heir. He reformed a religion he had defended only a decade or so earlier. He had loved the veneration of saints' relics, but had them all removed and destroyed as idolatry. He gave up a wife he had loved for nearly twenty-five years to marry another that he thought he loved . . . and had her put to the block. And now if Jane Seymour does not give Henry the son he so desires, there is treason blowing under the clouds that Cromwell can surely use to bring yet another queen to the block. God help us all.

It was up to me . . . and Marion and Nicholas . . . to stop this. To keep it secret. To not allow my beloveds to become entangled in treason.

And Doctor Bonner wanted to make my life difficult! *I can do that very well enough on me own, sirrah!*

There was no finding the servants I needed to talk to. All servants are usually harried, but there are schedules to adhere to, and I can usually find them when I needed them, knowing how the court runs day to day. Today was an exception. Everyone was everywhere! It was useless trying to find their trails. And in any case, the feasting was about to begin.

The boar's head was brought in to great ceremony. Delicacies of cake and sugar built into the form of Greenwich Palace drew the applause of the court. Sweetmeats, leeks in butter, apple tarts, cheese tarts flavoured with elderflower, marrow fryture with a chestnut sauce . . . and the most magnificent of all, a deboned roast goose with feathers and head, stuffed with a pullet, which itself was stuffed with a duck and itself stuffed with a pigeon. A boneless feast for the eyes as well as the tongue – all paraded through, tempting the most recalcitrant diners.

Robert Aske and his men were seated near the king (as much as to keep an eye on them) several seats down the row

after Charles Brandon, Nicholas Carew and Cromwell. In fact,
Cromwell – whom one might think would ignore the man –
was deep in conversation with him, nodding solicitously,
offering comment, and I could see how cheered Aske was at
the attention. Foolish, foolish man! *Your march south was a
day at the fair compared to the pit of vipers you have been
thrust into. Watch your step*, I longed to tell him, *and your
tongue, sir!*

I sat in my usual place before Henry, who had clearly
pasted a mask of a smile on his face, for I could tell that
Christmas was ruined for him by the presence of the rebel
leader. He loved his entertainments. So did we all, but now
politics was interfering, as it does during even the most
pleasant of diversions.

But Henry was trying to play his part – as must we all as
well – and he seized every opportunity to speak to his men
about this pilgrimage *around* Aske. They were polite and
politic, and they gave no offence. Meanwhile, Cromwell sat
quietly and without comment as his fellow courtiers gave this
opinion or that, always skirting away from words like 'treason'
or 'rebellion'.

Until my own Nicholas Pachett, Lord Hammond, my lover
of some months, who was sitting at table again with Henry,
piped up with, 'Perhaps Master Aske can justify his defying
his king so publicly and so violently.'

The room, in all its bustle, music and clattering of cups and
plates . . . fell to silence.

I wanted to sink into the tiles.

Henry turned to him. He gave Nick his fiercest glare, but
I knew it was all for show. It was something Henry had
wanted to ask for himself. He was secretly pleased by this
upstart lord.

Nicholas, for his part, held his ground, never averting his
eyes from the king, nor lowering his chin which was held high.

Aske adjusted himself in his seat. 'My lord,' he said in that
soft way he had. Little wonder how he inspired followers to his
cause. 'And Your Majesty. It was the farthest thing from our
minds to give offence to you. We followed our hearts and the
urging of the Almighty for our authority. The people love you,

sire. And it breaks our hearts that we are compelled to march, but our banner is not that of a lord or a county or a knight, but that of God, whom we seek to please. Nothing more than that.'

Silence. The hall fairly rang with it.

Aske fussed with his plate and goblet. 'His Majesty invited me here to speak with him sincerely and I accepted in all humility. The people hunger for the familiar. For their faith. Their souls cry out to do what is right.'

I leaned over the table towards Aske. 'Master Aske, the court fears that once we are done with what is *right*,' and I gestured with my right hand and then with the other, 'there will be nothing *left*.'

A few titters filtered throughout the hall, and then I glanced at Henry. His smile was growing, and then he laughed, and the court felt free to let loose with their own relieved guffaws. 'Wisdom at last . . . from the court Fool,' said he.

'Uncle,' I acknowledged with a bow.

'This is your Fool?' said Aske. 'Even in the north, we have heard of the wisdom of Will Somers.'

I was aghast. Never before had I heard even a hint that my antics reached farther than the intimates of court. 'Your servant, sir,' I said with a bow and with the wave of a piece of boar hanging from my knife.

'So even you question the veracity of those in the pilgrimage?' He showed no rancour. He was sincere in his question.

'Sir,' I said to him. 'I do not think that anyone here naysays your sincerity – though, by my life, I am uncertain of *all* of court on the matter.' Here I swept my gaze over Henry's side of the head table. 'But I know of the deprivations of those who worked for the monasteries and how difficult it has been. Perhaps . . .' I turned to Henry. 'Uncle, could nothing be done in relief for those poor souls who had no argument with your right to supremacy over the Church in England, but find themselves innocent victims of its consequences? I am speaking of those who relied on work from the many monasteries speckling the kingdom, sire.'

Henry did not like this question. I saw it burn in his eyes. But still. It was necessary to say again, to make him see the unintentional hurt he had caused.

He must have considered my words, for it took but a moment for him to relent. 'If what you say is true, Somers, then we will investigate it. I should not like to have paupered my innocent subjects.'

'There, you see, Master Aske? The king only wishes for good for his subjects. Any reasonable man can see that.'

'I thank you, Master Somers, for putting it so succinctly.'

'I am here to serve, master. Sometimes wisdom comes from the most unlikely source. Which reminds me.' I set my eating knife aside. 'A famous doctor was in the midst of a tumble with his maidservant when he was caught by his wife. The lady shrieked with shocked surprise and angrily asked her husband, "What of the scandal? Where now is that precious wisdom you are always spouting?" "Here in this hole," he replied hastily, "and I must return to it forthwith, for I have a mind to become wiser and wiser!"'

Aske laughed and so did the king. And any harsh thoughts were soon forgot.

The rest of the meal was too busy with entertainments from Lionel our Lord of Misrule, who took his pleasure rapping the heads of gentlemen with his rod; gentlemen in his capacity as a servant he usually obeyed with all subservience.

I shot a covert glance at Nicholas, but he was ruminating in his goblet, face slightly flushed. I reckoned he thought he fell into disfavour, but I knew Henry well. He *did* the king a favour by saying what Henry could not, which enabled me to broach a subject near to my heart with Henry in defence of Robert Aske.

I next slid my gaze towards Cromwell. Cuds-me! He was not measuring Henry, or Lord Pachett, or even Aske.

It was *me* he was studying with those reptilian eyes.

It was a most unusual feast, one unlike any other. I don't know that there was a single man there who was not glad that it was over.

Aske and his men were escorted to their chambers for the night, whilst Henry and his privy gentlemen retired to his sleeping chamber, to which I was *not* invited. Well! And with all the ice I broke today amongst him and his rebel. That's thanks for you!

I wanted to talk to Nicholas, but I thought it wise to attend to my wife. There had been no chance to question any servants, and I had to content myself with getting at it in the morning.

Marion was thoughtful as we both undressed and got ourselves into our sleeping shifts.

'That was very incautious of your Nicholas Pachett to have provoked the king,' she said, plaiting her hair and tucking it under her cap.

'Oh, not so, Marion.' I pulled the bedding aside and slid on to the cold sheets, fluffing my pillow behind me. 'Henry had wanted to ask that very thing but had been held back by his ministers. I can't help but think he will knight Nicholas for that.'

'But the king looked so angry.'

'He was angry at his privy council for insisting he pursue this deception.'

Marion slipped under the blankets and shivered as she nestled in. I wondered whether my advances might be welcomed when she slid over nigh me and snuggled against my chest. My heart soared. 'What a world we live in when deception is the order of the day over truth and trustworthiness.'

'That is the game of politics, my love. I don't like it either. Should we trust our fellow man and have done with all this playacting?'

'I reckon it is because wily men always wish to win. And that means someone must lose. This rebel, of course. No matter how sound his argument, he rebelled against the king and he must lose. Why does he not realize this?'

'Because, Marion, he is an honest but naïve man who has not had dealings with the court. He doesn't realize his danger because, like an innocent lamb, he trusts too much in the good nature of men.'

We lay silently for a time under the single candle flame at my bedside. I leaned up and blew it out. 'Marion . . .'

'Yes, Will?'

'Are you still angry with me?'

'No. I suppose not.'

'I love you.'

'I know.'

I held her tight and rubbed my cheek against the top of her cap-covered head. 'You surely must realize what a strange and extraordinary person I am.'

She snorted. 'Is that what you are?'

'Indeed. Who else could hold the King of England in the palm of his hand?'

'Don't be so cocksure. He could easily upend his palm someday.'

'Aye, I do think about that. But, ever the dreamer, I have never planned for that eventuality.'

'Mayhap you should. Sometimes, Will Somers, I fear your quips will be the end of you.'

Cuds-me. So did I.

It took me a long time to fall asleep. I wasn't even certain that I had, except for the wetness at the side of my mouth that meant I had drooled on my pillow. I thought about all I learned yesterday, and the facts swirled in me head: Edward Seymour *told* his sister the queen to send the brooch to Aske. But someone killed Geoffrey before he could do so. And stranger still, Geoffrey was dug up two weeks later and disembowelled for what reason we know not. Then the brooch, long lost, all of a sudden returns and is found in the jewel casket where, only a day ago, it decidedly was not. Round and round in my head it whirled. And all through, I knew I was missing something. Not an unknown something. For I think I had already discovered this something that loomed important, but that I could not put my finger on. It was there before me like a dream, but very like most dreams simply slipped away before the dreamer could reach out and grasp it.

But then I realized what woke me, for it was still night. No light shone from between the curtains, but only darkness was there. It was the pounding on our door and the shifting of feet and voices that took me from slumber.

Soon, someone rapped on our bedchamber door. I rose quickly, donned my dressing gown and spoke in hushed whispers to Michael through the small gap in the door. 'What's amiss?'

'Master Will, I do not wish to bestir your slumber, but the king wants you.'

'Now?'

'Yes, master.'

I nodded to Michael who closed the door, and I heard him speak quietly to the guard who seemed to be waiting for me. I cast off the dressing gown and donned my doublet, hose and breeches.

'What is it?' asked my sleepy wife.

'Just the king. I must go.'

'So early?'

'Go back to sleep, my love. I'll probably be back before first cock crow.'

Once dressed in haste, I left our chamber with Andrew the guard.

'Hurry you now, Will.'

'Do you know why—'

'The king bellowed for you. I need no why.'

Indeed not. I hurried to keep up with Andrew's long strides and finally arrived through the many chambers of the king to his private bedchamber.

Henry, in his own resplendent dressing gown of the costliest silk lined with fur, paced before the fire. He turned at my step and relief flooded his face. 'Thank God, Will.'

I hurried in. He was all afret with something.

'Harry, what ails you? Are you well?'

'How can I be well when I have such dreams?'

'Ah, a nightmare, then? Tell me. Sit yourself down first. In the chair by the fire. That's it. Your Will is here, Uncle. Let me get the fur.' I took up the fur discarded from his bed, and laid it gently over his chest and legs, making sure it was tucked all round him like a child. 'There you are. All comfortable and warm. Now, can you tell me?'

'Bring me wine.'

'Of course, Harry.' I hastened to his sideboard and poured a generous portion into his favourite silver goblet. I put it into his hand, and he did not hesitate to take a long draught. He licked his lips and held the goblet to his chest.

'Tell me.'

'I . . . I dreamed . . . of Anne Boleyn.'

'Again?' He had such dreams often. Methought it was his conscience niggling at him. There was such terror in his eyes.

'She accused me again, Will. She haunts my dreams. I heard from some of the guards that in truth she haunts the Tower.'

'They *told* you such?'

'No, of course not. I heard them talking.'

'Fie on them! They should not have said.'

'Do you think it true?'

'I . . . I know not of such shades and spirits.'

'But what of my dreams, Will?'

'What was it? Did she speak?'

'Aye, she spoke. She blamed *me*. Accused *me*. Told me again that she was innocent.'

'Did you . . . speak to her?'

'I could not. In the dream, my tongue was frozen. I could only stand and listen to her berate me. And it was terrible, Will. There was so much cold and darkness surrounding her. She was pale as death. Very pale. And I could see – God help me – whenever she turned her head, the . . . the awful *seam* where neck met head, that the swordsman had made.'

He dropped his face into his hand.

Ghastly. I was certain it was Anne, having her final revenge, her final say. But this I could not tell His Majesty. It would not ease him or change him.

'Oh, Harry. Wouldn't you rather have a priest here with you?'

'No,' he cried and shot out a hand to grasp my wrist. 'I wanted you!'

But what could I tell him? The shade of Anne Boleyn spoke the truth to him? That it was his fault and his alone? A truth even *he* knew to be true, but only in his dreams?

'Will she always haunt me?' he said in a small voice I have never heard him express before.

'I know not, Harry. It was . . .' *Tread carefully, Will.* 'It was a cruelty that was done to your wife. Your queen. Perhaps seeing Madam Elizabeth again has stirred up the memories, this dream.'

'Maybe so.' He slowly spun the goblet's stem with trembling fingers. He had not released my wrist with his other hand. 'But Bess is so sweet. So like me. And . . . her.'

'She is your daughter through and through.'

'But it cannot be true what the shade of Anne said to me. It cannot. There was such evidence . . .'

'You should pray on it, Harry. Say your prayers and ask her for forgiveness.'

'*Me?*' He raised his head with its sleeping cap askew. 'Ask *her* for forgiveness when *she* committed treason against her king and husband?'

I patted his shoulder with the hand captured at the wrist and he slowly unwound his fingers from me. 'Your mind is on treason. Are you certain it was Nan you saw in your dream . . . and not Robert Aske?'

His ginger brows lowered over his eyes as he searched his mind. 'It was Anne . . . but maybe Aske was there, pushing her to say these words to me.'

Oh aye. I knew if I could turn his fear to anger, then he would be appeased. And I was sorry that I used Aske so.

'Yes,' he muttered. 'That must be it.' He drank down the rest of his wine. 'Do you know, Will, that sometimes . . . only sometimes . . . I find myself *missing* Anne? She was, after all, a lusty partner, full of adventure.' He breathed in long huffs, holding the empty goblet to his chest, eyes darting here and there into the shadows as he sought the good memories. 'She could be a shrew, though. And she committed adultery against me. That . . . that hurt me, Will.'

There was little to be gained in arguing the point now that Nan *had* been innocent. He would rather convince himself of her guilt than entertain the notion that Cromwell had manufactured the lies to quit him legally of her. Poor thing. Poor Nan.

I said nothing more. And so I began to sing a soft song to lull him to sleep. He was still in his chair, his feet resting on his footstool and his furs wrapped about him. He was a child still, that little boy. So unloved by a distant father, or so it was said. And befriended by boys grown to men who only wanted what they could get from him. I almost caressed that worried brow, but refrained. He had not called for his wife, his friends, his priest. He had called for me. And always I would remember that.

Soon, he snored, relaxed at last, and I tiptoed out of his chamber and returned to my own.

'What of the king?' asked Marion as I undressed again.

'He had a nightmare. About Anne Boleyn.'

'Again?'

'I fear he shall have them the rest of his life.'

Weak pre-dawn light crept about the edges of the curtains. It was early morn, but I tried to get back to sleep if for but an hour more. St Stephen's Day, the day of the first martyr for Christ. The day of forgiveness and for giving. If only St Stephen could give Henry relief from his shadows, and me a clue as to what next to do.

SEVENTEEN

S t Stephen's Day, the day following Christmas, was the time for cracking open alms boxes and paying out to the poor. Queen Jane fulfilled that duty at the chapel in the palace, but bishops and priests all across the country were doing the same, in big parishes in cities and in small ones in villages. I always gave to the alms boxes, for I was grateful for my place at court, but always conscious – as Marion often reminded me – that it could all turn on the head of a pin . . . or on Henry's whim, and Marion and I could find ourselves on the receiving end of the alms to the poor. Nothing in life was sure but death.

Henry did not wish me to entertain for the day, for he was instead deep in conversations with Robert Aske. Alas, my chance to speak with the man did not now seem likely. It was just as well. What had begun could not now be stopped. I did not think that Aske was a man who would shy from his duty. He must have known the consequences but trusted in God to save him. Christ mend me.

But it was now time that I could question the servants close to the queen to determine just who knew what when.

Having eliminated Edmund Bonner – more's the pity – and John Blanke – and thankful was I for that – there were still more in the game. There was still Edward Seymour who was not yet eliminated in my eyes. And then there was Eustace Edgar, Viscount FitzAllen, the man who oversees the queen's purse, and Doctor Ellis Dawlish, envoy to the queen's charities. More and more did these two seem to the point of these investigations. For the queen's purse was surely directly linked to her charities.

And what of Lady Margery Horsman, the Keeper of the Queen's Jewels? Was there something there? More than the attentions of John Blanke? I should talk to her next, see if talk of the brooch sparks something in her eyes.

Still, FitzAllen and Dawlish. Why would either man have cause to kill Geoffrey? Or to have their shirts embroidered by Queen Jane?

Marion had her duties to the queen. I tried to reason with myself that I needed to talk to Nicholas, but was it true? *Did* I need to talk with him about this murder? Or was it because I merely *wanted* to?

I stifled the voices arguing in me head and sought him out anyway. Making my way down the corridor, I noticed him in a gathering of young courtiers. They appeared to be congratulating him on his good fortune with the king, and I finally realized that this is where he belonged: with those of his own social status, forging relationships that would carry him into his seniority. *Suum cuique*, I thought. It was time for him to receive 'his own' and not be deprived of it.

He hadn't yet seen me, so I backed into the shadows and stayed there, watching him for a time, before I slipped away down the passage.

I was alone, then. I would have to seek out these 'E'-named men myself. Now, where the hell would they be?

I took m'self to where the queen's court was and peered into the doorway without going in. Jane Foole was holding court with her antics, and I didn't wish to disturb them at this time. So I pulled me head back out and faced the Yeoman Guards. My old friends from Queen Anne's days, John Bromefeld and Adam Holland.

'Greetings, my fine fellows.'

Bromefeld nodded to me. 'Somers.'

'I hope you enjoyed the Christmas Day celebrations, and we can all now look forward to the Twelve Days. Oh! Or were you preoccupied with guard duty? A poor fellow am I that does not know how his friends fare during these most holy of days.'

'We have no rest from our service to the king,' he said.

'Of course not. For the same is true for me. I might think that I am free for an afternoon until the king changes his mind . . . or the queen calls for me, though she seems to prefer the less vulgar attentions of Jane Foole.'

Holland looked back through the archway and shrugged. 'She prefers the company of women about her, 'tis true.'

'Today I am at my wits' end. The king doesn't need me what with Robert Aske here, and the queen does not with her female Fool. And so I languish.'

Holland chuckled. 'You? Languish?'

'Verily, I *can* find things to occupy me. For instance, I have need to speak with Viscount FitzAllen and Doctor Ellis Dawlish, but I haven't a clue as to where those worthies spend their time.'

Holland exchanged glances with Bromefeld. 'You can find the queen's purse in those lodgings.' He pointed across the passage to a set of doors. 'And Doctor Ellis has his lodgings in town, on Fenchurch at Lime.'

'Thank you, gentlemen,' I said with a bow. 'I knew I could count on you two.'

FitzAllen was across the passage, whilst Dawlish was an hour into London . . . on horseback. I chose the closer course, strode across the corridor and knocked upon the door.

A servant opened the entry and peered at me. I wasn't familiar with him. I bowed. 'Good sir, I am Will Somers, the king's jester, and I come to inquire if my lord FitzAllen is in.'

'He needs no jester,' came the curt reply.

'Oh, but, good sir, in this instance, I am no Fool to prat about. I come to your lord because of my orders from the king on an entirely different matter.'

He looked at me askance, for I was either a liar or natural fool.

'Master,' I said, sidling closer. 'The king has charged me with the unusual task of investigating the murder of a servant, and who better to do such a deed *than* a servant – myself?'

'Why would the king—'

'It is not our part to put reason to it, only to obey.' I stretched my hand out to examine my nails, well-cared-for and clean. 'I may have some facility with such, you see.' It was not boasting. It was true that I had solved two strange murders before this.

He considered a moment more before he reluctantly let me pass through the portal. 'Wait here,' he said and pointed to a spot on the floor in the anteroom. I dutifully stood there and positioned m'self like a courtier, hand on hip, opposing foot stretched out to make a nice leg.

He left me to enquire of his master whether he would receive the Fool looking to investigate a murder. I would have liked to have heard just how he put it, but then I heard the master shout. However he put it, it was not received well.

The servant came rushing out, breathing hard and quick with a reddened face. 'My master has instructed me to toss you out.'

'And well you should, master,' I hurried to say. 'It's just that the king himself – in the company of all of court – commanded that I do this. Would his grace the viscount wish for me to tell the king that he would not assist in my appointed task?'

He'd screwed up his mouth in a most unbecoming way, before he stiffly turned on his heel and returned through the door. There was more shouting, the soft tones of the servant pleading, a bit more shouting and then the calm of an ocean after a storm.

The servant emerged again and stood beside the door, face still flushed. 'His grace will see you now.'

I bowed to the man. I knew, as a servant m'self, how much we must take from our betters. Some have kind masters, some have cruel masters, and some – like me – had strange and changeable masters. It was our lot.

I strode past him and entered the outer chamber where the viscount was seated at a great table, parchments and rolls spread out before him. He was not pleased to have been disturbed and it, too, showed on his bearded face, flushed with his impatience.

'What do you want, Somers?'

'My lord,' said I, sweeping nearly to the floor with my bow. 'Greetings from the king. You must surely have known that His Majesty was sore upset that a servant, so close to the queen, was killed in these very corridors. Why, it could not have been too many steps from your own lodgings.'

'And what of it?'

'Well! I have come to understand that this man, Geoffrey Payne of recent memory, was given an object of great price to sell or to present to another worthy, and this was why he was slain. Know you anything of that?'

'I did not know the man at all.'

'True, it is easy to disregard servants, even close ones. Can you, for example, name the colour of the servant's eyes that serve you here in these rooms? The one who just left you.'

'The colour of his eyes? What nonsense is this?'

'Just so, your grace. What is the colour of your servant's eyes?'

He stared at me a long moment, neither moving nor breathing overmuch when he of a sudden sat back. 'By the Rood,' he muttered. 'You are wily indeed, Somers, for I cannot say with any accuracy what is the colour of his eyes.'

'They are grey, your grace. You see, I am used to looking men in the eye, even the lowly servant.'

He laced his fingers over his stomach and regarded me more kindly. 'You have taught me a valuable lesson, Jester. It must be, as you have the ability to grasp jests out of thin air.'

'Oh, indeed! It comes in handily enough. Now. About this Geoffrey Payne . . .'

'Yes, as I said, I do not know him. And I am curious about his being given an object of great price.'

'I daren't mention who gave it to him, only that it was a courtier of high status, and as a servant, he would not question it. But I believe that he was killed *because* of it.'

'Because of possessing it . . . or what he was to do with it?'

'Now *that* is an interesting point, your grace. You see? I knew talking to you would be useful.'

'And this object,' he said. I measured him. He might be a wonder at pretending, for he did not look as if he were playing a role. He seemed genuinely interested . . . and confused. 'From whence did it come?'

'This is the tricky part. All I can say is, it was a brooch that came from the queen's own coffers.'

'And this is why you come to me?'

'Partly.'

'Oh? What is the other part?'

'Let us first understand why such a thing was given and used.'

'A valuable brooch could be sold for a great sum of coin. Was it a charity the, er, giver was inclined to? And if so, would not Doctor Ellis Dawlish be the proper man to query?'

'He's next. But I am asking you.'

Looking down at his desk with all the work lying ahead for him, he shook his head. 'I do not know if I can enlighten you.'

'Then let me ask this. Did the queen embroider the cuffs of your shirt? With your initial?'

His eyes narrowed with confusion. 'My shirt? My cuffs?' He looked down at his sleeve, his cuff now visible under the dark fur. There was embroidered blackwork, but no initial. 'Why would the queen embroider *my* shirts?'

'Oh . . . it was merely my own curiosity. I shall trouble you no more, sir.'

'Wait! This brooch. Are you saying that it was taken from the queen's jewels and given to this servant to sell?'

'I can say no more. And I urge you, my lord, not to speak of this to anyone. It is the king's mandate.' Well, the last was a lie, but it was a lie to save the queen.

He nodded, but his face betrayed that he was continuing to work on the problem even as I left him.

When I stood in the corridor again, I began to wonder if I were not asking the right question. The shirt. The shirt was the all-important clue. I should be foremost asking about the shirt.

And so . . . it was time for me to hire a horse.

EIGHTEEN

Before I ventured to the stables, I made certain that Doctor Ellis Dawlish was not at court but in his London home, so I wouldn't waste my time. I bundled into my best jacket with a fleece-lined hood and set out.

London was cold. The Thames that had frozen over when we first ventured to Greenwich was still covered in slow-moving ice, with the cracking and popping sounding like a gun's report jarring the stillness. Snow patches lay everywhere along the road, like sugar icing on a pastry. I hoped that Henry was occupied as he had said and was not shouting for me. I didn't wish to explain where I was or any of the details, lest he use it against his wife somehow. I prayed as I rode that she would soon swell with child and a boy at that. Naught else would save her from his insatiable need for a male heir, for he did not have much love for her.

There were few on the streets as the population were either at their many parish churches or at home or taverns for their own celebrations. The Twelve Days were a lingering feast of entertainments, exchanging of gifts and travelling to meet with friends and kin. I had never trekked thus myself, and today was a lonely road I travelled indeed. I suddenly realized that I had told no one where I was going. If Doctor Ellis was the murderer and understood what I was getting at with my questions, I might never reach home again. 'You foolish idiot,' I admonished myself. The horse turned his bristly snout to look at me over his withers, as if to say, *And so you are!*

'Aye, even the horse thinks I'm a fool. I should have told Marion. I could have told Michael at the very least. Why had I rushed off?' I looked back, but the palace was too far away now. I would have to follow the river and cross at the bridge, for I could see no ferrymen.

London was stark, with its patches of white upon the muddy ground and the look of the pale sky and unmoving clouds as if they were set in amber. It felt like an eternity as the horse plodded along in the slushy mud, utterly alone and unchecked. And then I wondered if a horse's foot could *get* cold. Their hooves were like mighty shoes that spared them from the weather . . . or so I assumed. Such thoughts and more did run through my head until I finally reached London Bridge, paid my toll and rode down its centre of houses and shops, all shut up for the holidays. The bridge served as its own parish complete with a chapel, all jettied out over the usually rushing Thames. But it was fairly quiet and still, and I wondered if anyone but the toll-taker existed on the white, snowy street under a wintry, cloud-swept sky.

When I passed through the gate on the other side, I followed Bridge Street until it became Gracechurch and turned left once I came to Fenchurch where it crossed Lime. And now I had to choose, for I did not know which house it was. I supposed it was the grandest one there, the one with a gatehouse arch that wandered into a courtyard. When a man came to me and held my reins and asked me who I was, I told him 'Will Somers, come by order of the king. Is this the house of Doctor Dawlish?'

He looked at me oddly. Perhaps he knew the name Will Somers. Or perhaps he did not believe me about being ordered by the king since I wore no tabard with the king's colours. But he gestured that I should dismount anyway, which I did. He had not let go of the horse's lead and asked that I follow him to the house. Snow had blown against the inside corners and wall surrounding it, with spindles of trees standing bravely and naked against the stone and lime-washed daub.

A boy ran forth from the stable and took the horse from the man, who continued to lead me to the front entrance. He knocked and told the porter who I was. This elicited a minor response of an arched brow, and I saw him scan the snowy courtyard for other men or guards. He then studied me, this lone envoy, and noted the one shoulder higher than the other, even with my fleeced lapels and collar, and stepped aside for me to enter.

I was usually at home anywhere I went. I could frolic in a meadow with my tumbling and jests, or in any withdrawing room or banqueting hall to act the silly arse, but coming to

the home of a man I did not know well for a purpose beyond
my jestering abilities felt odd and uncomfortable, as if I had
put my arm into the wrong sleeve of me own jacket.

I was led to a parlour and asked to wait. The servant retreated
to the place where the master was – no doubt, spending time
with his family, not expecting a stranger to come to his home
and accuse him of murder. *Steady, Will,* I told myself. *Simply
ask about the shirt. For he will tell you nothing about the
queen's charities even if he knew she was donating to a trea-
sonous pilgrimage.*

The servant returned and led me to yet another room, with
a table, two chairs and shelves of parchment rolls and books.
We had passed a door through which I could hear music and
talking and laughter, and I knew that his family must be
together there enjoying themselves, *being* themselves, far from
the eye of court, not performing a version of oneself as one
must do under the glaring eyes of courtiers.

I did not sit as I had not been bid to, but I waited, nervous
and fidgety, with only the fleece of my coat to toy with. The
door opened again and a man I could only presume was Doctor
Ellis hastened through. He wore a long, dark gown with a gold
chain swagged across his chest. A dark cap covered his ears,
and as I stood in the cold room, I wished I had one similar.

He looked at me carefully as he sat. 'Are you not . . . the
king's jester? Did I hear your name aright?'

I bowed. 'Aye, my lord. The king's jester on an unusual
errand. And therefore here to ask you unusual questions.'

'*Today?* On this holy feast day of St Stephen?'

'I am afraid so, my lord. You see, the king has sent me on
a particular task, and obey I must.'

'Of course. His Majesty must always be served with cheerful
mindfulness.'

I juggled that thought, tossing it back and forth, and then
discarded it. Instead, I ventured, 'Sir, has the queen ever had
occasion to embroider shirts for you?'

As expected, he stared at me blankly. 'What?'

'Your, erm, shirts, sir. You see . . .' I pulled my cuff from
my warm sleeve. 'The blackwork and my initials.' Mine had
a W and an S with a small Fool's hood. 'The queen most

graciously did this for me.' It was a lie, of course. My own Marion had done all my shirts.

He pulled his own sleeve from his coat and showed me the blackwork on his cuff. No initials at all. 'There has never been any occasion where Queen Jane offered to embroider them, and never would I have had the gall to ask it of her. My own wife, though not as proficient with embroidery, could have had them done by another, but neither of us could find a reason to do so.'

'And so none of your shirts were ever so decorated?'

'No. Does my word satisfy, or would you speak to my groom?'

His tone was not sarcastic as I would have expected. He seemed to truly wish to be helpful even as perplexed as he was. It was always a pleasant surprise to meet men of honesty and loyalty at court. By this I knew I did not have my man. 'No, my lord,' I answered with a bow. 'I have interrupted your festivities enough. I shall depart now.'

'You have come all this way to simply ask about my shirts? Come, come, sir. You must at least share a cup of wassail with us.'

It sounded like a good idea to me. I was introduced to his wife and children. One was a youth, almost a man, and the other was a child of ten or so. I instantly went to the boy and played games and rhymes with him, and I think I made them a little merrier than before I arrived.

I left in good spirits, but also with the realization that neither Doctor Ellis Dawlish nor Eustace Edgar, Viscount FitzAllen, were guilty of murder. At least, they seemed to me to have no knowledge of the ghastly affair. And though it confounded my investigation, I was somehow happier these two dedicated men were not involved. At least, they didn't seem so. It wasn't as if I could share the queen's treason with them and hope that they would not tell tales. I could not put her in such danger.

And so I took back my horse and rode it through the lonely streets of London again, now thoroughly confused.

I reached Greenwich just as the sky, formerly swept by wispy clouds, had closed in with darkened faces and began a rain that turned to a light and silent snow, and I was never so glad to reach the inside of the palace and the warmth it offered.

And it offered it in the person of Nicholas Pachett, who happened to be by the entry when I returned and shook off the flakes of snow from my travelling cloak and stomped my frozen feet to awaken them, for I had not the forethought to don my boots.

'Will,' he said, surprised to see me. 'What have you been doing? Were you . . . travelling?'

'Eliminating suspects. Do you have a moment to talk?'

He swept his gaze about the entry and through the next arch full of people, and nodded, leading me through the court to his lodgings.

The fire in his hearth burned bright and I stood before it, thawing m'self. Oh, the simple pleasure of a warm fire when one was frozen to the bone!

'Will you tell me where you went?'

And there sat Nicholas. Handsome as ever, as close to domestic bliss as I could get besides Marion. Wicked world! *My strange Saviour and Lord*, thought I for not the first time in me head. *Why do this to good men? Make them sinners. For I would not choose such a life, always afraid, always in the wrong.* It would be a pleasant thing only thinking of my wife and our love, and perhaps looking upon this man as a friend of the bosom. Why could it not be so?

I shook the thoughts loose. It was useless to think about it.

'I have spoken to Doctor Ellis Dawlish, envoy to the queen's charities, and to Eustace Edgar, Viscount FitzAllen, the queen's purse – two "E" names on our list – and found them to be innocent.'

'How so?'

'What mean you?'

'How did you find their innocence?'

'Well . . . I . . . I . . .' Cuds-me. Was I relying too much on my own instinct? 'I felt their sincerity, and they didn't flinch at all when I brought some of the evidence to light.'

He looked at me hard. 'You *felt* it?'

'Christ, Nick. I must rely on my instincts in most things, else I would never be able to do my job as a jester. And doing so has served me well as an inquisitor.'

He sighed. 'It does not seem to be adequate to the occasion. One could be duped by a good playactor.'

'Not me, they can't. Look, Nicholas, I have been a jester for some years now, and if I had not my instinct into men's hearts, I would have been forced into some other occupation by now. I trust my gut.'

'I suppose,' he muttered, running a finger along his mouth. Oh, traitorous mouth!

Looking away from those tasty lips, I said, 'I think my best course now would be to meet with Lady Horsman and talk to her of the queen's jewellery.'

'You must be careful. What will you say to her?'

'Let me see. I shall flatter her first to ease into my inquisition and then enquire as to what had been missing and how and when it was returned.'

'Very well.'

'I am so glad you approve.'

'Now, now. You have a way about you that endears some and troubles others. Especially if you are too direct. This much I have learned in my dealings at court.'

'You have the right of it. I can often be too direct, as you say. But, Nick, I tell you, there is something stuck in my mind like a piece of meat between my teeth. The more I poke at it, the more stubborn it remains. There is something I can get nearly close to before it scuttles away. It gnaws at me.'

'The solution, you mean.'

'Aye. If only I can recall what it was that sparked this feeling. Aye, marry. There is nothing for it but to proceed.' I made to move from the hearth when I said, 'By the way, I want you to know that you did *not* displease Henry when you made your query to Aske.'

He shuffled his feet and looked down on them. 'I do not know, Will. He looked angry. And so the rise of Nicholas Pachett, Lord Hammond, was brief.'

'Not so. I told you. I *know* Henry. He was glad you asked . . . because *he* could not.'

His expression evolved from one of shame and hurt to one of relief and hope. 'Do you truly think so?'

'I know so! You will be invited back to the *sanctum sanctorum*, I assure you.'

He looked happier, so I hated to ask, 'When do you think Robert Aske will be leaving court?'

'I know not. No one speaks of it.'

'Nick . . . do you think he will be allowed to leave?'

He considered, stroking his beard, and he wandered towards the hearth himself and stared into the flickering fire. 'After all the ceremony and exchange of gifts and promises, it would be more than foolish to keep him here under lock and key. The king *must* let him leave now.'

'Because . . . the court made such a fuss at his coming here?'

'Exactly. It would seem . . . erm, disingenuous now. It would appear to all the world that our king is devious when dealing with those who approach him with humility and sincerity. It would raise the north, to be sure.'

I could not help the smile that curled my mouth. 'You are so very attractive when you spew political knowledge.'

That brought him up short at first, until he mellowed to my words. He sauntered towards me and grabbed my lapels. 'Oh? Should I always talk politics to spur your interest, Will?'

'Not always, no.' I let him kiss me, but I was not so far gone that I forgot my mission. I gently pushed him back. 'I must go.'

He sighed again and turned back to the hearth. 'Yes, you must. Will I see you later this evening?'

'Of course,' I said, and made it to the door before I turned in the entry. 'I will be entertaining in the watching chamber.'

Closing the door after and leaning against it gave me a touch of satisfaction. It proved to me that I could tell him nay when necessary. And I felt – with my damned instincts again – that I had best attend to my wife for these Twelve Days. Nick could wait. She could not. Marital bliss with her was more permanent than a frolic with a lord who was ambitious. He would wake up one day and see the folly of risking his life and fortune with someone like me. I expected that sometime in the new year he would find a wife himself. It had to be. I have always known it.

And so. Off to find Lady Margery Horsman. After all, I had the wherewithal to tempt her to tell me the truth: my knowledge that she was carrying on with the trumpeter. Not that I would ever reveal such to anyone else. I liked John Blanke too much. Or, should I say, *Ekene*. And then I realized the meaning of his entire Christian name. No doubt, he was a pagan, living in the wilds of an uncivilized country with difficult names to pronounce, and who knew if saying them aloud would not be some sort of incantation to condemn a good Christian to Hell? And so they blotted out his pedigree, even his surname if his people had such. He was now quite literally 'blank' where a surname could have been. By baptizing him, most of us would think he was given a shiny new Christian identity.

Or one could look at it another way. That they had taken away his old life, his old country and kin, and he was not to speak of it again. It saddened me. Maybe he had not realized the fullness of it, the responsibility to be a Christian and travel unspeakably far. He was a proud man, a man who garnered much respect from his fellows. But he'd had to sacrifice much to take on the mantle of a follower of Christ. He was rewarded for it, of course. He served two kings in the most singular of ways. It was not just any man who could be a trumpeter, nor one who served as long.

Yet still.

Would I have ever been as brave? Would I have done it and not looked back, as he had done? Willingly, I hoped.

For my part, my past held little to be proud of. My father, who had died a few months ago, was a wicked, miserly man who had owned property. A farm. But he had also owed too many debts, and that farm was taken in payment. Oh, I could have made a fuss, paid the debts, even asked Henry to help me, and he would have done so, but when I talked it over with Marion, she convinced me to leave it be, to let it be forgot. Aye, I had loved my mother, but neither my father nor his farm needed my remembrance. And so, having no child of my own and never to have one since Marion could not, I had no one to bequeath a legacy to. I was disinherited by choice.

And I wondered if I would regret it someday.

I wondered if John-Ekene had.

NINETEEN

S ince the queen was with her own ladies, that was where I decided to go to find Lady Margery. Ah, Twelve Days was certainly in the air, even with the spectre of Robert Aske hovering over all our doings. The scents, the greenery, the Kissing Boughs wherever one turned, Christmas songs, plays, foods . . . it was definitely enough to make one merry. I was hardly needed at all, but I knew that I would still be required to perform for Henry and the court. I did not fret. I had my jests and rhymes prepared.

My Marion was also there amongst the ladies. It was almost as if she were a courtier as she should have been. But had she been Lord Heyward's legitimate heir, I certainly would never have been able to catch her eye, let alone her hand in marriage.

Fate is a ridiculous goddess.

All the maids of honour and ladies were there, including one Margery Horsman, Dallier with Trumpeters. I could sometimes be cruel with my jests – mostly only to rivals, for a man must protect his job – but to jest about the dalliance of a *maid* was to ruin the lady's chances of a good marriage, and so never would I . . . unless I disliked her. And I had naught against Lady Horsman. Naught that I knew of.

I could not go directly to her. And so, instead, I bowed before the queen. 'My gracious lady,' I said, putting on my sweetest face.

'Will,' she said kindly. 'Do you have entertainments for us today? For I do not see our Jane Foole.'

No, she was absent. Unusual of itself.

'My queen, I will entertain the toes right off all your court . . . but first,' and I said this last in a whisper for only her ears, 'first I must speak with one of your ladies.'

'Oh? To what purpose?'

'I must remind you that the king had asked me to investigate the murder of your servant . . .' She frowned and I tried to assuage her fears. 'It is only that this person might know something that would help.'

She nodded. 'Which of my ladies?'

'Lady Horsman.'

There was something in the queen's eyes when I said the name. We both knew that she was the Keeper of the Queen's Jewels and a jewel of hers did seem to be in the heart of these doings. Her gaze on me was steady before she raised her head again to her court. 'Lady Horsman.'

The lady raised her head. Not a beautiful woman as such – not like my Marion, whose features were delicate and adorable – but a handsome woman with sharp cheekbones, a pointed nose and dark eyes, alert and aware like a bird of prey.

'Please accompany the jester for a moment.'

Though the ladies sewed, eyes sprung up at such a request, and Lady Margery rose with covert gazes upon her, gently laid down her sewing on her seat and walked with her head held high towards me. I bowed to her and led her to the outer dining chamber.

I closed the door and her formality disappeared. 'What do you want of me, Fool?'

'My lady. I know it is an inconvenience to take you from the queen's court, but it is of the utmost importance for to find a murderer.'

'Geoffrey Payne.'

'Indeed. I knew you would understand.'

'But I do not. What could you possibly want with me?'

'Ah . . . this is a delicate matter. You are the Keeper of the Queen's Jewels and therefore you keep an inventory, I would imagine.'

Her eyes narrowed just that much. My instincts brightened. Aye, I trusted them.

'I do.' She volunteered naught more than that.

'Then, lady, do you recall a certain brooch—'

'That cursed brooch!' she hissed. She paced, her hands firmly within the opposite sleeves, keeping her arms close to her body.

'Why cursed?'

She stopped at the other end of the chamber and whirled to face me. 'Do not play coy with me, Fool. I have watched you with Jane Foole. I have seen her play with the queen's baubles even as I warned Her Majesty against the practice of allowing it.'

I was always more painfully aware of my crooked shoulders when I was in the presence of a lady or male courtier. When with servants, I never seemed to mind much. But with the aristocracy, whether they said aught about it or not, their keen eyes seemed to rake over me with barely disguised revulsion. Had I been as empty-headed as Janie, they would never have minded it. Perhaps expected it. But with a man as aware as they were, they somehow allowed themselves to disparage me. And so she looked at me now, and I longed to fidget.

'And so. You worried something would happen to that particular brooch?' I said, straightening said shoulders as much as I could.

'I feared, at first, that the fool would break it. And then . . .'

'And then?'

She stayed as she was, far from me. 'And then . . . there were other mishaps I feared.'

'Mishaps?'

'You are no raven to keep echoing my words, so why do you?'

'Forgive me, lady. It is my way of thinking things through. But I am curious as to what the other, what you call "mishaps", would be.'

'That particular brooch had gone missing more than once.'

'Might it have been purloined by Geoffrey Payne?'

'I do not believe so.'

'Oh. You surprise me, lady. I was under the impression that he had tried to take it before.'

'Under what impression? Who has been filling you with . . . Oh, I see. You have been listening to Jane Foole. You surely must know that she lies.'

'Madam! Janie might mix up some things on occasion, but I do not know that she has ever uttered a falsehood intentionally.'

'Then you do not know her as you purport.' She stood with her head tilted back so that she could look down her nose at me. I was not certain if that was intentional or not, or if it was her usual posture, only that she did it now. 'She is a child in her mind, never to grow to adulthood, though her outward appearance is that of a young woman. And children lie. Did you not know that?'

Even dim, sweet Janie might lie, for she did know right from wrong. Most of the time. 'Then . . . are you saying that Geoffrey Payne did *not* steal the brooch on various occasions?'

'Had that been the case, he would have been immediately sent to the Fleet and thence to the noose.'

Why had Janie lied? Cod-pate! I slapped my forehead. '*She* was stealing it.'

'Yes. And each time it went missing, I spoke to her and made her surrender it.'

Christ mend me. I was one of those men in morality tales showing the fault of too trusting a person. But I couldn't help it. I would rather think good of a person than ill.

'Oh dear. Lady Margery, you are a loyal subject and serve your queen well. May I confide in you?'

She did not move, did not step closer, did not change her posture. 'You may.'

'It is something that must be kept between you, me and God. Will you swear on the love of Christ that you will not reveal what I will tell you?'

Her face grew sombre, and she did take a step closer then. 'I so swear it.'

Could I trust her? Could I trust what Janie had told me, for now I doubted some of the things she said. I took a deep breath as one would before plunging into the water. 'It appears that . . . well, the queen herself may have given it to Geoffrey Payne, possibly one of the last acts of his life. Did you know that?'

Her eyes ticked from side to side as she pondered my words. 'I did not *know* it . . .' she said slowly.

'But . . . it isn't entirely unexpected?'

'I can say no more.'

'Lady, it is not my intention to implicate the queen. No, indeed. If you know me at all, you can be certain that I am loyal to the Crown and all who wear one.' I took a cautious step towards her and stopped. 'Please, if you know aught, you know I will keep mention of Queen Jane out of it.'

Her hands disappeared even further into her fur-cuffed sleeves. 'I knew . . . that she wanted to help the pilgrimage.' Her voice was steady but quiet. It pained her to say it, and by that I knew it was the truth.

'Aye. I suspected this. And so. In giving it to Geoffrey, he would have done her bidding, got a horse and set out to where the rebels were.'

'He . . . he was loyal. But . . .'

I waited. I would not parrot her again, though I sorely wanted to.

'He was loyal to the queen,' she began once more, 'but he did not agree with the rebels. He was Protestant and did not want the king to capitulate to them.'

'He would not have taken it to the rebels, then?'

She shook her head and her one veil not pinned to her gable hood swayed across her shoulder. 'But he would have left the palace to look as if he did. I am certain of it. Else it would have looked as if he had not complied with her command.'

'Then what would he have done with the brooch?'

She suddenly seemed weary and shrugged. She sank on to a stool by the window, the bland light of a wintry sun bathing her in muted tones. 'I do not know. He would not have kept it. He would not have wanted to profit by it. He might have donated it to some parish far from here, one that would never recognize it.'

'And yet it was not found on him; at least, I must surmise that. For it was returned to her jewellery casket.'

'Yes.'

'Now, lady, think. Who might have known what the queen was going to do?'

She did not hesitate. 'Her brother, the Viscount Beauchamp.'

Edward Seymour. 'He would have approved.'

'Indeed. You do know the court, sir.'

'I do. Would he have known that Geoffrey was no Catholic?'

'Of that I am uncertain.'

If he had known, he would have left the man to his duty, unless he suspected that he would *not* travel to the rebels with it. In that event, he surely would have taken the brooch off him. He could have ordered him to surrender it. He did not need to kill him. Unless it was in a struggle. Had he been in an awkward position and that was why the strange stroke to Geoffrey's neck?

'Lady, can you think of anyone . . . anyone at all who might have had cause to kill him?'

'Master Somers,' she said. I was of a sudden *Master* Somers. We had come far in the little time we talked. 'Master Somers, I have wracked my mind on the matter, and not one name comes to light. Everyone seemed to like and enjoy Geoffrey's company. He was a merry fellow, much like you are, and always with his little tricks and jests. He could entertain the ladies almost as well as you.'

'I did not know this about him. What a pity I was not better acquainted with him.' I paused, thinking about it, for I had seen his cleverness. But jealous as I was of my vocation, I do not know that I would have helped or encouraged him, for if he was truly clever, he might have had thoughts of supplanting *me*. Our lives were in competition, and it is a sad fact that men must scrabble about in the mud, if necessary, to keep their place in the world.

But there were other Fools at court, younger, more inexperienced and inexpert who might have been jealous of their place as well. Could they have dispatched him in a completely unrelated case of murder?

'There was the foul deed a fortnight later of digging up the poor man and desecrating his corpse,' I wondered aloud.

'And the brooch was returned.' She finally withdrew one hand from the fur of her sleeve to tap her lip in thought.

'Do you think that one has to do with the other?'

'Alas, good jester. I do not know for certain.'

But in my mind, it did. It couldn't be any of the other Fools. They were private Fools, in the service of lords, and they might never have known about Geoffrey. I couldn't see how anything else would signify.

Did I think that his disembowelment had to do with the return of the brooch? Aye. How, I did not know either, but by the Rood, it did.

TWENTY

Lady Margery offered more small points, but we had exhausted the extent of her knowledge or consideration. I thanked her for her time, and she reassured me again of her oath and left me. I stayed a while longer, simply thinking on it, until I feared Henry might be looking for me. Off I went to seek him.

He was in his presence chamber, and Robert Aske was still there with his men. Many of Henry's Gentlemen Ushers were also there, amongst them Thomas Giffard and Peter Meutas.

Meutas was standing apart from the others, observing the room, and I sidled over to him before he noticed me. 'Baaaaa,' I bleated to him.

He glared at me as if I were the biggest idiot.

'I only greeted you in your language, sir,' I said, flipping the bottom edge of his long beard.

He was unamused. 'I easily tire of your antics, Somers. Go harry someone else.'

'Harry, you say? Of course, I shall harry our Harry in due order. But today I am harrying you. Tell me, what think you of this captain of rebels?'

'He's a traitor.'

'Well, some say so. Others say he is sincere.'

He snorted. 'Sincere? Who knows what is in the mind of a traitor when they defy the king.'

'And yet *you* seem to. Know what is in the mind of a traitor, that is.'

'And why not? It is my duty to protect the king and his kingdom. I do not suffer those who try to defy it.'

'Does that also serve for those *of* the court?'

'Wherever it may be, Jester.'

'A servant, perhaps?'

He had no ready reply then, but he turned his head most deliberately to stare at me, laying his hand on his dagger hilt with purpose and in such a way as I could not fail to miss it. 'Anywhere,' he said.

'Ah. That is surely my signal to leave you.' I scampered away, trying to look as silly as I could (not difficult) so as to steer his suspicions away from me. For I did not like the serious look in his eye. If he were an 'E' name, I would be certain he had done the deed.

'Harry, Harry!' I called, and this time it seemed that my appearance was timely, for Henry looked worn out talking with all these men in sombre tones. 'Tell me this! What speaks in all languages in his riding, and his mouth spits the poison of life or death? It is silent when it rests and is deaf like a boy or one of the poor. What is it?'

'Will,' he said. 'This riddle is puzzling.'

''Tis true, Uncle. But is simpler than you think.'

'Speaks all languages,' muttered the king. 'Spits poison. Silent when it rests.' He ruminated on it and then suddenly laughed. 'You clever whoreson. It is a quill.'

I bowed. 'You are correct, Harry. I had no doubt you would find the answer.'

'Where have you been, Will? I was in sore need of you.' He took in his companions, and I winced at the thought of being locked in a room with them.

'I see that, my Harry. Brrr,' I said, and added a shiver. 'It's cold in here, what with all the crows around you. Perhaps you could use a song.'

I had stopped off at my lodgings and grabbed my cittern, which I had thrown on its strap around to the front of me now. 'Any requests?'

'*Departure Is My Chief Pain*,' said Henry. Of course he would suggest his own work. It was a round, but I could make it work as a simple song.

I bowed before I began to pluck and to sing:

> '*Departure is my chief pain,*
> *I trust right well to return again.*
> *Parting is a privy pain,*

> *But old friends cannot be called again!*
> *Adieu sweet Harry, departing is a pain,*
> *But mirth renews when friends meet again.'*

The gathering clapped, including Henry, but he wagged a finger at me too. 'You changed my words, Somers.'

'Harry, I am singing it to you. I can hardly call *you* my lover.'

Chuckles all around.

'The talented Will Somers,' said Aske. 'His Majesty is fortunate indeed to have you at court.'

'I thank you, sir. I do love the man and his friendship. You would be wise to hold his friendship close as well.'

'Yes, good jester. This is my most desired outcome.'

'You have a funny way of going about it. In truth, sir, rebellion is not the way.'

'Somers,' Henry growled.

'Forgive me, Uncle. I wish to protect you, my bosom friend. That is the one thing on my mind.'

He patted my hand that rested on the back of his chair. 'I know, Will. But perhaps you should come back later. I have more business with these gentlemen and your amusements, though welcomed, might get in the way of it.'

A firm dismissal. And so I put on my Thomas Cranmer Archbishop of Canterbury face and voice, thrust my nose into the air and signed the cross upon all in the room, backing away. '*Benedicte, benedicte . . .*' I murmured over the assemblage. 'Serve your king well, my lords,' I said, still drawling like Cranmer. 'And serve yourselves as much of the good wine as you can. My blessings upon the man who drinks the most. He shall be in need of it.' I blessed my way out of the chamber whereupon the guards closed the door after me. I saluted them and went off to find my dog, who was surely wandering about the court and making trouble.

Poor Robert Aske. His only hope was my intervention to Henry to plead for him. Make Henry see Aske meant no harm to him. But any sort of naysaying – like a rebellion – hit Henry hard. He did not like to be questioned. He did not like to be made to feel that he must defend his commands. He firmly believed in the Divine Right of Kings, eschewing Magna Carta. Sometimes I admired him for it, and sometimes I wanted to take the birch to him. I never realized before how much he was like Janie. Both just children trapped in adult bodies, with temper tantrums and fits. But maybe that is why I loved them both so much. I often said how Henry was like an uncle to me, but sometimes he was more like my own son, and I had need to discipline him gently. Princes are raised to lead and so they must not be told that they are wrong in their opinions. Indeed, they are surrounded by courtiers and minders that build them up, but ordinary children are told the limits of their powers and punished when they transgress them. And I can only think that before Henry became the heir, he had more freedoms. It must have been a terrible shock to suddenly be the heir, to be treated so differently. I grieve for that little boy that he was, confused, taken from his playmates and given new ones, made to study for to groom him for his great responsibility, learning only from the miserly King Henry Seven and determined to be the opposite in almost every way. I did not know him as that boy . . . and yet I often felt that I could see that little boy in there, past the ermine and the jewels. A little boy, simply aching for love. It broke my heart, and so I have tried to be that love he so desired, a man, a friend who was unconditionally *his* man and his alone.

But it is dangerous and difficult to tame a lion.

As I left through the many chambers and finally out to the corridors, I ran into Charles Wriothesley again, Windsor Herald of Arms in Ordinary, chronicler for the king. He seemed befuddled at quite literally bumping into me, and I reassured him that I had not been hurt. It appeared to take a moment for him to recognize me, but when he did, he seemed to cheer.

'Well, Master Chronicler,' I said, 'how goes it? Is your writing hand numb from work?'

He looked down at his hand – the right one, fingers stained with ink – and chuckled. 'Oh, I see what you mean. Yes, I observe when I can, take down notes on my slate—' He raised said slate from his robes, showing me his note-taking hand on the wax. 'And then I think about what I have seen and what it may mean. But I shall not set it to parchment before I see the final outcome. When Master Aske is free to leave the court.'

'Do you have your doubts that he will be?'

'It is hard to say. The king is . . .' He appeared to wonder how to proceed with that sentence.

'The king puts on a good face,' I answered – helpfully, I hoped.

'Yes. A good face. A sincere face? That has yet to be determined. But I am cautious what I put into ink. Our King Henry is a great king like those of old, and like the Almighty in that he is a jealous ruler, and will not suffer insurgencies, just as the Almighty did not suffer the fallen angels when they rebelled.'

'That puts an interesting face on it. I can picture in my mind, Henry, wearing a toga and standing on the clouds, hurling down thunderbolts.'

'It sounds as though you are confusing him more with Zeus than the One True God.'

'Cuds-me, maybe I am.' I chuckled. 'It is an apt vision in me head.'

'You know him best.'

I wanted to spend more time with Wriothesley because he was an interesting man, but I had to move on. I needed to find Janie. I hoped she wasn't hiding as she sometimes did when her feelings were hurt or she felt threatened.

That last thought worried me. Had she been threatened by someone she might have spoken out of turn to? Or someone . . . who might have seen her spy the murder?

Maybe the murderer himself.

'My lord,' I said with a bow. 'I wish good work for you, but I must go.'

'You are a busy lad, are you not. Go then, Jester. Good luck to you.'

'Thank you, sir!'

I hurried off without running, but then I did run, for Janie did not have her own lodgings as I had. She slept on a cot in the queen's presence chamber, so she could not go far. She had few possessions. She had tried to keep puppets and such, as had I, but she always lost them and made do with stockings on her hands or sticks with scraps of cloth tied to it. So if she had set out on her own, she hadn't anywhere to go to.

I arrived back to the queen's court and stood in the doorway of the presence chamber, scanning the assembly. The queen's ladies were all in attendance, as was Marion . . . and Nosewise, who was taking treats from each woman there . . . but no Janie.

Marion glanced up and noticed me and she, always solicitous to her husband, must have seen the worry on my face. She rose and put her sewing aside to stand before the queen and curtsey. 'Your Majesty, my husband is here and in need of me.'

Queen Jane cast a glance towards me in the doorway. I could tell from her face that she had forgotten that Marion was married to me. 'You must attend to your husband in all obedience.'

I might have burst out with a laugh, but the situation was too dire for my foolery. Obedience? From *my* wife?

Marion curtseyed again to the queen, motioned for Nosewise to come with her, but like the cur he was, he ignored her for the promise of pats and treats from the ladies.

She rushed through the door with me. 'Marion, have you seen Janie of late?'

'Come to think of it, I have not.'

'I think she is missing. I worry that she is in danger.'

TWENTY-ONE

'If she is hiding,' said Marion, 'then where is she likely to do so? You must know her hiding places.'

'It has been a while since she felt the need to hide, but there are places in the queen's bedchamber.'

'You aren't seriously considering looking in the queen's privy bedchamber? Surely even you are not allowed entrance there.'

'Oh, I have managed from time to time.' I stuck me head back into the presence chamber. 'Do you think I just ask the queen's permission . . . or pardon?'

'Just go!'

The wife has spoken! I crept along the wall, for, after all, there were musicians playing and no one was paying attention to a jester-shaped shadow slinking behind them. I had only to sneak through her dining chamber, withdrawing room and an antechamber before reaching her bedchamber . . . and convince the guards to let me pass.

I made it through the first door and even the second, but the Yeoman Guards stopped me at the bedchamber. 'What is your business here?' asked the wheat-bearded Andrew.

'I have business everywhere in the palace, in every one of Henry's palaces, my good sir. I am leaving a jest I just made up for Her Majesty.'

'Why not just tell it to her?' said the other guard, Walter.

'Because then it would not be a pleasant bedtime surprise. I do it for King Harry as well.'

They regarded one another.

'You can come in with me if you doubt my word.'

They knew my sincerity was true, for they knew I would never harm the royal heads. In the end, they had no real argument.

'Then hasten, Jester,' said Walter impatiently. And they turned their faces forward again, pretending neither had seen me slip through the door.

The curtains were open, washing the room in tones of afternoon grey, and the fire was lit, burning softly. It would be enough light since the candles remained unlit. I followed along the wainscoting and called out a whispered 'Janie!'

Nothing stirred.

I then pulled out the truckle bed beneath the queen's. A doll was there that belonged to Janie, but no sign of her.

My heart began to thump, worrying about what could have happened. I looked in the cupboards, in the coffers that were not locked, thumped on those that were, but I found no sign of her.

I left, thanking the guards as I passed them.

Where else could she be? I quit the rooms as I had entered them, with the same stealth as before and joined my wife out in the corridor.

'She was not there. There are other places in the palace.' And I led her on. Janie liked Marion, trusted her almost more than she trusted me and liked her pretty face. If I could just find her, she might tell more to Marion. But I'd have to find her first.

'Will,' Marion whispered as I tugged her along. 'If something has happened to her, if *someone* has stolen her away, where is the likely place they might stash her?'

'Alive, you mean?'

Her mouth dropped open.

'I am sorry, my love, but it might be that they could not afford for her to tell anyone more than she had.'

Tears sprang to her eyes, for she doted on Janie as much as any courtier.

'Oh, Will, where do we look?'

'Well, you will recall that last time I was so employed to find a murderer, I was stuffed into a cupboard off the corridor. I was heading there now.'

She clutched at the cross at her neck, letting my hand go so that I could run ahead, and followed behind.

I found the hidden door in the wainscoting, something servants knew about, but distracted courtiers did *not* know about – at least most of them – and pried with my fingers into the hidden seam.

'Use your dagger, Will.'

My wife had arrived beside me. Christ, I barely remembered I had a dagger at my hip. I unsheathed it and stuck the blade in where the catch was, and it opened for me. I peered inside. 'Janie? Are you here. Marion, fetch that candle.'

'I am not supposed to say,' said the timid voice of the Fool.

By then, Marion had brought the candle, and its little glow illuminated the dark cupboard. Janie's glossy eyes caught the light and shined back to us.

'Janie,' I said, gently taking her in my arms. 'What happened to you?'

'He grabbed me and put me here and told me to stay until he came for me.'

She was not tied up or secured in any way. 'But, Janie, why didn't you cry out?'

'He told me to be silent.'

'Who, dearest?'

'The man. The man that I think killed Geoffrey.'

I ushered her out of the cupboard and closed it up again. 'Come with us.'

We bundled round her and moved on swift feet back to my lodgings. We dismissed Michael when we entered and sat her in the best chair. Marion brought her wine, and we sat on either side of her, dragging our chairs closer together.

'Now, my dearling,' I said, 'you tell me what transpired. And don't leave anything out. Tell me all you can.'

'But he told me not to.'

'Is he a courtier?'

'Yes, he must be. Dressed with satins and jewels.'

'But you do not know his name?' asked Marion in a calm and soothing tone.

'I do not.'

'Tell me what he looks like.' Surely she would know what Edward Seymour looks like, and if this was not he, then I wondered mightily who.

'He's tall. He has a beard.' She gestured the beard by stroking her chin. 'And young.'

Cuds-me, I could think of no one fitting that description . . . until I did.

'And what did he say to you when he first grabbed you?'

'He said, "Quiet, wench!" and put his hand over my mouth. He walked me through the corridor to the cupboard and shoved me in. I fell.' She raised the palm of her bruised hand to show me. I took it in my own hands and kissed the bruised palm.

'Now it is better,' I said with a soothing smile.

She beamed. Strangely, she did not seem frightened or worried. She did not know the man but did not seem to fear him. Was it a cleric, then? She seemed to trust clerics.

'And then when I got up from the floor,' she went on, 'he told me to say nothing and wait for him.'

'And why should you be made to wait?'

'He said he wanted to ask me some things.'

'But you do not know his name.'

She shrugged. Seeming to have exhausted her words, she began to look round the room. 'This is where you live, Will? It's nice. This whole room is yours?'

'And Marion's. And there is a sleeping chamber, too.'

'A chamber for sleeping and this chamber as well.' She laughed. 'Are you certain you should be here? This is a courtier's room.'

'The king gave us, as a married couple, these rooms. We don't take up much space.'

'Neither do I. I think it would be lonely. I like being in the queen's room, or in the presence chamber, because the other servants are there.'

Marion patted her hand. 'You don't seem frightened at being stolen and locked in a dark room.'

'I am sometimes handled so, by the young men of court.'

Fury rose up in my chest and I shot from my chair. 'What young men? What did they do?'

'They touch me and kiss me. Practice kissing, they said.'

'Janie! These young men should be whipped for that. Tell me their names!'

She rolled her eyes at me, unperturbed. 'I care not. They only want to play.'

'They are not allowed. You are special in this court, and they are not allowed liberties with you. Janie, it is very important that you never leave Queen Jane's side. For your own safety. You mustn't let this courtier or any other abduct you again.'

She rubbed at the bruised palm of her hand. 'He has the right,' she said softly.

'He does not,' I reassured her. 'Janie . . . are you certain he is the man who killed Geoffrey?'

Her eyes were wide and the cog wheels in her scrambled head tried to reckon it. 'Maybe. I think so. I could not see much of his face, but I remembered his voice.'

Now we were getting somewhere. If we could keep Janie safe, then surely we could get her to identify him.

'Well, then . . .' I sank to my chair again, tension unwinding from my shoulders. My fear released, I could ease back. 'You have become a troublesome wench.'

'He said that, too.'

'Aye, marry. He has the right of it. I must talk to you of several things.'

'But I'm tired, Will. I was in there for hours.'

'I imagine so. But you did not fear?'

She shook her head, looking at the painted scene on the wall of people being entertained by a jester. It was another wedding gift from Henry.

'Then listen well to me, girl. One, you must not allow these hobbledehoys to treat you that way again. You tell them that the king will hear of it. Repeat that.'

'The king will hear of it.'

'Aye, just like that, with authority.'

She grinned. I reckoned she would jump at the chance to have some kind of authority. I took mine in my stride, for I could not insult others as I did if I did not have the proper comportment.

'And more. I have heard from Lady Horsman that it was you who stole the brooch the many times it went missing. Is this not so?'

Her grin faded and she looked down at her hands in her lap. 'I thought Geoffrey had . . .'

'You mustn't lie, Janie. It makes Jesus unhappy.'

'Oh!' Her large eyes took no time at all to fill with tears, for she loved God as a good Christian girl should. 'I did not mean to make Jesus unhappy.'

'You must tell the truth.'

She pulled and twisted her fingers and finally, squirming in her seat, she seemed to relent. 'I . . . I did take it. But only to look at on my cot at night. It sparkles with candle-light and with moonlight. I liked to look at it. I always put it back.'

'John Blanke said you'd stolen jewels from others of court. Thou shalt not steal, Janie. Is that true?'

'I didn't steal them. I mean . . . I took them, but only to borrow.'

'Janie, when you take something that is not yours to keep without permission of the owner, then it *is* stealing. And that is breaking one of the Ten Commandments. You don't wish Jesus to weep over that, do you?'

Her eyes shone bright again. 'No,' she offered meekly.

'Good. I knew if it was just explained to you, you would understand. John Blanke returned those things, and that put him in danger. You wouldn't want *him* to be in danger because of something *you* did, now would you?'

'No. He's my friend.'

'He is a good friend to you. And you mustn't take advantage of that friendship again.'

'I swear, Will.' She held up her bruised palm again.

'Good girl. Now. Is there anything you haven't told me before about Geoffrey and the murder?'

'No. I have told you all I can remember. But, Will, some-times when I remember things, they get jumbled, not in the right order.'

'I understand, my turtle dove.'

'So it isn't that I wouldn't tell you. It's just it doesn't always make sense until later.'

'Aye.'

She glanced at Marion and smiled again. Ah, glancing at Marion would make anyone smile. 'Madam Will,' she said. 'Can I show you a trick that Geoffrey showed me?'

'Not now, sweeting. We need to hear what you may have to say about when he was slain, if you can.'

She sighed like a petulant child. 'I *told* you,' she said, waving her hands about. 'I followed Geoffrey to see where he was going with my jewel and then he encountered the man. He made the man angry because of the trick. Let me show you! Do you have a coin?'

Clearly, she would not move on with her details until she showed us this trick, and so I took a coin from my own pouch and handed it to her. She turned it over and over in her hands, for it was newly minted and bright and shiny.

'Pretty,' she muttered. Then she positioned herself, and her words and speech patterns were clearly parroted from another. 'You will observe,' she said, holding the coin so we both could see. 'It is here now, but in the next moment—' She popped it in her mouth and smiled, holding out her hand to show it was empty.

God's teeth, she might choke to death! I leapt forward and slapped her back hard so she would expel it.

'Will!' she cried, twisting, trying to rub her smarting back. 'I didn't put it in my mouth. It is here. Look.' She opened her opposite hand and the coin lay there on her palm undisturbed. 'That's what Geoffrey taught me.'

I froze. Because now I knew all.

TWENTY-TWO

'Christ's toes, Marion!' I cried, on my feet again and pacing about the room.

There was scratching at the door and, absently, I opened it, allowing Nosewise in, who immediately ran to Janie.

I knew what had happened. I couldn't believe it, but I knew. 'Marion, remember how Geoffrey's throat was cut up and down, not from side to side?'

'Yes. It is strange.'

'No, it isn't. Janie.' She was sitting on the floor now, playing with the dog, when she looked up. 'Can you at all recall what Geoffrey and his murderer were arguing about?'

'I couldn't hear it all. But the other man was yelling at him. "You stupid fool. You swallowed it!" I think he said.'

'Could it be that Geoffrey was performing his trick . . . with the brooch?'

Janie sat up, abruptly alert. 'Oh! Yes! That's what he did. He was saying that it was gone now and laughing. But the other man wasn't laughing at all. He grabbed him round the throat and then he took his dagger . . .' She turned back to the dog, gathered him in her arms and held him tight, rocking back and forth. 'I turned away.'

'You see, Marion? He played that trick on his killer, pretending to swallow the brooch—'

She caught on swiftly. 'But the murderer thought he did swallow it and cut open his throat to get it.'

'Precisely!'

'But it wasn't there.'

'No, it wasn't. He'd secreted it somewhere else, but the killer didn't know that. That's why he returned to dig up his body. Oh, how cruel is the murderous mind! He cut open his gut to find it in his stomach.'

'But wait.' Marion perched herself on the edge of the table, fingers to her lips in thought. 'But how could he return the brooch to the jewellery box if it wasn't in his belly?'

I stopped my pacing and stood stock still. 'That's curious, isn't it? And why wait a fortnight? Why not as soon as he was buried?'

'He . . . he hadn't thought about it until later, thinking that if he *had* swallowed it, it would have travelled to his belly?'

'No good, Marion. Because he didn't have it in his belly. So how could the brooch have been returned so quickly?'

'Cuds-me, I do not know.'

'Well . . . you think on it, and I'll take Janie back to the queen's household.'

I helped to drag her to her feet and made her look at me. 'Jane, m'dear, listen to me carefully. You are not to be alone. Do you ken? You are not to be on your own at all. Ever. Stay with the ladies at all times and in the queen's chamber at night if she will have you.'

'You don't want that man to come back and get me.'

'No, I most definitely do not. You must stay safe. And do not worry. I am after this miscreant now and I am close to capturing him.'

She looked at me with head tilted far to the side. Suddenly, she leapt at me and hugged me a bit too tight. 'I knew you would help me. I always say, Will Somers is my bosom friend. And he loves me.'

'I do love you, my daisy. But look you. Take Nosewise and go with Madam Will.'

'Yes, Will.'

Her simple mind took all that in, at least. I reckoned she was safe. For now. I needed to find Nicholas and talk it through with him. There was little else to do. Except that as I was leaving, Michael returned. 'His Majesty is looking for you and roaring it about the halls.'

'Oh, hang me in my face! Thank you, Michael. I must away.'

'Master Somers.' He didn't exactly touch my sleeve but had reached forth just that far from doing so. 'I hope you will pardon me for my actions of the other night. Madam Somers . . . well . . . I have known and served her longer, sir . . .'

I rested my hand gently on his shoulder. I could not believe he was worried as to what I would say. 'Michael, you are loyal and honourable. And you serve this family well. I cannot begrudge you for following what your mistress commands. And I would never punish you for that. You should know me well by now.'

He ducked his head in a nod. 'I know, sir, but . . .'

'Do not fret on it, Michael. All is forgiven.'

He was mollified at last, and we were both content.

Now I had *Henry* to content!

I hadn't realized how late it was. It was nearly feasting time, and I reckoned Henry wanted all his retinue to accompany him in a show of majesty before Aske.

I grabbed my stick with the bladder and, at a run, made it to his presence chamber just as Henry and Queen Jane were being escorted by his Gentlemen Ushers.

'Where have you been, Somers?' he growled out of the side of his mouth. 'I should have you whipped.'

'You'd be in the right, Harry. I hurried as much as I could, but my wife, sir. When she demands I frolic in my bed, well . . . what is a poor sort to do?'

He smirked. 'You were delayed because of bedroom matters?'

'It's a good excuse, you have to admit.'

'Very well, you cur. Your wife is a brave woman.'

'There is no doubt of that.'

I marched, capering around Henry with my bladder stick held aloft like a sceptre, and finally got into line behind him, blessing and nodding to all those watching and cheering, pretending that it was all for me: King William of the Jester Dynasty, conferring laughter to all my subjects.

We processed to the banqueting hall this time, to the sound of trumpets. Could I detect John Blanke's amongst the others? No, for they were all too well practised and it was as if one man blew the horn except for the brilliant changes in harmony.

We entered, and all who were there stood as Henry arrived. He and his queen moved to the high table in its centre, under the canopy of state, and sat in their chairs, Lady Mary and Madam Elizabeth at the queen's left and Henry with his men on his right. I noted that there was still a place for Nicholas, but it had been moved to Henry's side. Proud I was of that accomplishment from my lover lord.

I scampered to my stool set before Henry on the other side of the table. Henry sat, but I continued to stand and wave my hand and my stick to all assembled . . . until Henry threw a manchet loaf at me head.

The prayers intoned, the hands all washed, and the musicians began playing from the gallery, whilst I poured m'self some good wine from the silver flagon set before Henry. 'Ah, another feast, eh, Harry? Our favourite time of year.'

'I do enjoy the food in this season. The spices make all sauces fragrant.'

'Harry, you even know of food. Have you ever tried to cook before?'

'Of course not.'

'You should do it sometime. Yeoman Cook Pero Doux would be pleased to teach you, I'll be bound.' But would certainly *not* thank me for the suggestion.

'What nonsense. Does the man need the king invading his kitchen?'

'It is *your* kitchen, Harry. But perhaps not. It takes a long time to learn the art of cookery. And I know you are not a patient man.'

'The devil you say. I am not a patient man?'

'Harry, Harry, Harry. You know the truth of it. One unrisen cake would send you to burn the kitchen down. Forget I ever mentioned it. Instead, why don't you try embroidery. It is a fine hand skill.'

'Will, I have more than enough to contend with on matters of state without taking up needle and thread. What should the people think? That their king is more concerned with sewing than ruling? Shall I be called the Tapestry King?'

I laughed. 'No, sire, I cannot see it. You are right, after all.'

'Of course I'm right,' he muttered into his goblet. Hadn't he known that all his life?

The dinner proceeded. I winked covertly at Nicholas, who blushed and hid it behind his goblet. Henry from time to time turned to him in conversation, and my heart soared at Nicholas's good fortune. Even as it sorrowed me, for I knew that soon, he and me would be finished. At least it would make Marion happy. I must content myself with that.

After most of the dinner was finished and sweets were served and wine flowed, the dancers began. Henry loved dancing, and since his leg did not seem to hurt today, he rose and escorted Queen Jane to the centre between the lower tables. They stood an arm's length apart holding each other's hand and proceeded from the music above.

Her skirts whirled, his jig was merry, and soon others were invited to form a line of whirling and strutting dancers.

It suddenly reminded me that I had some bawdy songs to sing, but I had, in my haste, forgotten to get my cittern. Henry looked well occupied, and so I slipped away to find it.

I came to my lodgings and found Marion there, crouched over a candle with that cursed blood-stained shirt.

'Good Christ, Marion. What are you doing with that? I wonder what should be done with it. Give it to the Captain of the Guard? Burn it?'

'I shouldn't do that just yet.'

'What are you looking at?' I stood behind her and peered over her shoulder.

'I was just examining this again and noticed something amiss.'

'Oh?'

'When I looked at it the first time, I did recognize the hand of the queen. Or thought I had. But, Will, this *wasn't* done by the queen.'

'Woman, what are you saying? Have I not been querying suspects based on that information?'

'Call me "woman" again and you shall see what transpires.'

I knew I shouldn't like to see that, so I kept silent.

'Here . . . and here. This is good stitchery but not expert like the queen or I can achieve. You see how the stitch does not quite follow the weave of the cloth?'

I did not, but I nodded authoritatively.

'It's strange.' She turned the cuff this way and that. 'If I were to hazard a guess . . .'

'Hazard away, my love.'

She glanced over her shoulder at me with a familiar scolding look to her eye. 'If I were to guess, I would say this is the work of Jane Astley, another of the queen's ladies.'

'The devil you say. Where does this put us?'

'And look here.' She pointed to the letter that put us on the hunt for 'E' names. 'This isn't an "E" at all.'

'What?' Without thinking, I snatched it out of her hand and looked close, bending towards the candle's feeble light. But now I saw. Oh aye, threads were pulled and I could just see the faint memory of holes. The bottom line of the 'E' was shorter, which I had never quite noted before. But the top two lines were never meant to be open.

'You're right, Marion. The letter is not an "E" . . .'

'It's a "P",' she said. 'And do you know who Lady Astley's young gentleman is?'

'I do not.'

She wore a satisfied face, did Marion. For she had got it solved before the jester. 'It is Peter Meutas.'

TWENTY-THREE

'Peter sarding Meutas?' I said, perhaps louder than I should have, for I saw Michael peer at us through the opening in the door between dining chamber and bedchamber. I stepped back, shut the door and modulated my speech to softness. 'I *knew* I liked him for a murderer!'

'It's definitely a "P" now that I look at it closely. So it is Peter Meutas who murdered the man? He must have dispatched him and then fled to the north to meet Robert Aske. It had to be directly before, else how could he have found Aske and made the journey back in a fortnight?'

'Aye. He must have . . . Ah, Christ mend me! It's impossible, Marion. He hadn't returned before poor Geoffrey was found disembowelled. It doesn't work.'

She blew out a huff of exasperation. 'But it *has* to be him!'

I caught sight of my cittern and hurried to grab it. 'I have to go.'

'Oh, Will. How will we ever solve this?'

'We have. It's him. Has to be. We just have to figure out how he can be in two places at once.'

I kissed her forehead and scurried out, running through the halls like a . . . well, a Fool. And made it back to the watching chamber before Henry was done with his dance. He was flushed and happy with the exertion and escorted his queen back to her seat. Whereupon, with a lull in the music from above, I set my foot on my stool and had my cittern in hand.

'I have a song to sing for His and Her Majesty, and *all* the court!' And I gave a nod to them. 'In this most festive time of year, it is meet to have . . . a different kind of cheer! With my compliments to my fellow musicians—'

Those in the gallery above cheered me and I waved back.

'They have played quiet songs, dancing tunes and gentle music throughout our meal. But now it is time for something a bit more earthy.'

I began:

> *'I plough my lover's field*
> *Though dense brush detours me*
> *She does not wish to yield*
> *Yet none of that deters me*
> *Two hillocks before the plough*
> *And a valley before me*
> *Makes merry there and now*
> *In ploughing love's glory . . .'*

Some ladies, including the queen, blushed as the song went on, whilst others smirked across the room . . . to their own lovers and *his* 'plough', perhaps. I finished with a flourish, and Henry clapped the loudest. He never wrote songs of a bawdy nature, only sighing love ballads that are fair enough, but sometimes a man . . . or a woman . . . would hear something more unsophisticated than his visions in the clouds.

And then I caught sight of Nick, who was moving slowly through the crowd. The evening was coming to a close, and I did wish to speak with him about the new developments in the murder enquiry. Yet he seemed to be avoiding my eye. But of course he was, for he knew my mind on this. Still, I needed his help, for accusing a courtier of a crime was tricky business.

Henry, having filled his belly with good wine and good food and having shown the court how well he could dance, thanked his courtiers, his musicians and even me as he retired for the evening with his ushers . . . and not his wife.

The people drifted away to their various apartments. Robert Aske took his retinue with him, always accompanied by guards, and I looked round anxiously for Nicholas Pachett . . . and could not see him. Aye, marry. He betook it rightly to his heart and deemed it fruitless to woo me. My heart hurt at that.

And just as I had secured my cittern over my back and straightened my coat, hands grabbed me from behind. I think I might have let out a slightly unmanly yelp. And when I turned, it was Nick.

'God's beard, Nicholas,' I gasped. 'For the sake of this beating heart, do not ever do that again.'

'I'm sorry, Will. But I . . . I had to see you, talk to you.'

He looked as if he was moving to take me in his arms, but despite the emptiness of the place, it still felt too exposed.

'Not here, Nick,' I said, taking a step back.

'You are the most frustrating man I ever met.'

'I don't doubt it.' Some of the chandlers were extinguished, leaving the corners of the hall to fall to darkness. But I knew the guards were not far away. 'It's to save both our necks.'

'I know. But I do love you, as well *you* know.'

'Aye.' His words always befuddled me where Marion's loving words had not. I reckoned there was nothing to lose from Marion's sighs of love, whereas with Nick . . .

'Do you . . . do you have anything to report about the investigation?'

Ah, firmer ground. I looked up at him again and urged him to walk out of the hall with me. 'My lord,' I said for the benefit of the guards as we passed them, 'there is a thing or two that has developed since last we talked.'

Once we were in the corridor again, our loud talk lowered to intimate whispers. 'Nick, Marion and I discovered it is not an "E" name, after all – that the "E" was instead a "P".'

'A "P"? That is strange.'

'Not so strange when I reckoned it was Peter Meutas all along.'

'Meutas? But why?'

'He's a fierce Protestant, and any whiff of a Catholic conspiracy was never to be borne. He knew of Geoffrey's cargo somehow and tried to get the brooch away from him. But Geoffrey had a trick that Jane Foole told me of. He would pretend to swallow a jewel or a coin and then produce it suddenly in his hand, as if it were magic. And that's what he did when Peter Meutas confronted him, not sensing his imminent danger. That's why he was throttled and that's why Meutas sliced him, cut his throat from north to south. He was looking for the brooch. And that is also why, having not found the brooch in the man's throat, Geoffrey was dug up and disembowelled a fortnight later.'

He was speechless for a moment, until he stopped and shook his head. 'God and all His angels,' he muttered. 'How can such a vile thing be? But . . . hold, Will. Meutas was gone on his mission to retrieve Aske. He couldn't have done the disembowelling.'

'Aye, that is a puzzle. He had to have an accomplice. And I believe that accomplice to be Edward Seymour.'

'Christ, Will!'

I hushed him with imploring hands and he mastered the volume of his speech again. 'Must you accuse the highest courtiers in the land?'

'What does it matter? I cannot bring this to Henry. If his brother-in-law is accused, he will either brush it off his shoulders or might end up accusing the queen as well. But Meutas might take his punishment himself . . . and be just as quickly pardoned by the king. Oh, how I wish for a simple merchant to have done the deed. His like would more easily get his just punishment.'

Nick threw up his hands and paced. 'If you are certain of this, then your inquisition is done. You cannot accuse either one of them.'

'I know. It's damnable.'

'I suppose the only satisfaction we can get now is to know ourselves what transpired. And give poor Payne our prayers.'

'My heart is sore on it.'

His hand lighted on my shoulder and squeezed gently. 'You did a fine job of it, Will. Content yourself in that. There is little more to be done.'

'Surely . . . surely *something* could be—'

'You know as well as I do that there is nothing.'

'You are right, of course, Nick. Then . . . I shall say good night.'

'Won't you . . . will you . . .'

'I must go home. To my wife.'

His expression was hurt, but it soon turned to resolve. He straightened his shoulders. 'Very well, then. Good night, Will. Sweet dreams.'

'I think that an unwarranted expectation.' Drearily, I turned away from him and trudged down the corridor to where it turned. I wanted very badly to look back, but either he had gone or I should be saddened had he been standing there.

How could such a merry fellow as me end up with so much melancholy?

I turned the corner again and wondered where the candles had gone to. The gloom that was presented before me certainly fit my mood, but I smelled the burnt and smoky ends of snuffed candles in their sconces, and I wondered which servant would get a beating for that lack. For only one or two were lit and they a distance from each other. It was all shadows and darkness.

I should have been more cautious. I should have thought more clearly about it. But for all my inattention, all I got was something smacking the back of my head which sent me to the floor and blackness closing in . . .

TWENTY-FOUR

I t was very like waking after a night of too much wine, or from that brandywine that Henry gave me once whilst we, morose in our pasts, exchanged tales late into the night.

But this was different. The pain was in the back of my head. Though it did leave me with a sour stomach. And then I remembered. Some varlet had struck me, and when I snapped open my eyes, it was still dark. But I was no longer in the corridor. I was in that sarding cupboard where I had found Janie!

I sat up much too fast and eased m'self against the wall, rubbing the back of me head. I looked at my hand. No blood, thank Christ. But as I sat, all the aches and pains coursing through me, I became aware of a presence, and it wasn't the Almighty.

'You were out a long while, Jester,' said the voice. 'I thought I might have killed you.'

'Nothing new to you, eh, Master Meutas?'

My eyes had adjusted to the darkness, and I saw the figure of Peter Meutas bent towards me, studying my face this way and that. 'You stole away my captive from this cupboard,' he said. 'But I reckon you got out of her what I had wanted to. So the bitch told you.'

'I wouldn't be tossing about insults, my lord. You have assaulted and kidnapped the king's jester. If you murder me, others know you are guilty of the murder of the queen's servant as well.'

He stood up again and measured me, stroking that long beard of his.

'Didn't think it through, did you?' I was so used to poking Henry that poking any old badger would do. He frowned.

'You have proved yourself to be a wearisome fellow. What *shall* I do with you? Beat you into silence?'

'And yet again, there is the troublesome aspect of my having told my compatriots what you already did.'

He released an agitated sigh. 'Yes, there is that.' He leaned against the opposite wall and folded his arms over his chest.

'How did you know that Geoffrey was given the brooch to take to Robert Aske in the first place? Was it perhaps the lovely Lady Margery, Keeper of the Queen's Jewels? No, no. It wouldn't have been her. Perhaps it was the striking Jane Astley, a woman who is said to be of interest to you . . . and you to her. As one of the queen's ladies, she could witness much.'

He stood stiffly, stone-faced.

'You will not answer? Maybe it *was* someone else. Well, no matter, your silence serves as assent. But why kill Geoffrey at all? Over some bauble? He was no Catholic to take it to Robert Aske. Or didn't you bother to learn that?'

By the look on his face, he did not.

'He hadn't swallowed it anyway. It was a trick he did, pretending to, but you didn't allow him to finish the trick.'

He hadn't known that either.

'You seem to be a hasty fellow, my lord. Act first, think later. Not very efficient.'

Ah, one remark too many. He jolted forward and the back of his hand struck me across my face, bloodying my lip. I licked the blood away. 'Your opinion on the matter is now crystal clear, my lord.'

'And my dilemma, Fool. What to do with you?'

Why wasn't I more afraid? Because I was on the righteous course? I had God on my side? That he had hit me too hard on my head? I was more afraid facing Cromwell and his cronies than this instance. How could I use my fearlessness to my advantage?

'So, you didn't realize that Geoffrey Payne, being no Catholic, would never have actually delivered the brooch to Aske and his ilk? And then you didn't realize that poor Geoffrey hadn't actually swallowed the thing? God's breeches! Why did you not simply clout him upon his head like you did mine?'

'He was just a servant. As are you.'

'As are *you* . . . my lord.'

'You are equating your prating and jesting and making a full arse of yourself to *my* service to the king?'

I cocked my sore head at him. 'Aye.'

He burst out laughing at that. 'And so you think.'

'And so I *know*. I *help* His Majesty. I calm his anger and raise questions he had not had before in his mind. I make him *aware*. Do I make him aware of your activities?'

'Would the king wish to know that his wife the queen supports rebels?'

I stalled him by reaching back and using the wall to help me to my feet. I stood unsteadily. 'The woman has a kind heart. She did not see it as defiance of the king. She saw it as helping those in the kingdom who were saddened by the loss of their religion. You know she is an innocent creature, much like Jane Foole.'

'We don't need two Jane Fooles, especially when one sits on the throne.'

'And so now *you* would decide this like your own inquisitor? Would you see such a disaster as Anne Boleyn repeat itself?'

His argument held no weight. I could see that he didn't want to bring any of this to Henry's attention. We were at a stalemate. But I tried one last move. 'Who did you tell about the brooch being swallowed? Did you send your missive to Viscount Beauchamp?'

It seemed for but a heartbeat that he was not going to answer me. The pause was long, until . . . 'He needed to know.'

'So that he could disembowel the poor soul himself?' I shook my head. There was little to say on that matter but my own disgust. Until the idea occurred to me. 'He did not want the missing brooch to become a way of accusing his sister the queen. God's body, I can see it now.' I said it more to myself than to him. 'Were it missing, it would be an accusation that anyone could use against her. But found and returned, she was safe. And so would his position at court be. But, of course, he did not – could not – find it in Geoffrey's lifeless body . . . for it wasn't there at all.'

'And do you have an answer to that?'

Oh, aye, he must have been biting his lip over that as well. For how could it have been returned when Seymour didn't find it?

I pushed away from the wall and moved carefully towards

the door. 'I am going now, my lord, since we seem to have exhausted our conversation.'

He jerked towards me for a moment, then halted himself. What more was there to do? He knew I would say nothing, and I knew that he could *do* nothing. Still, I rested my hand on my dagger hilt. Not that I would have the gall to use it.

'Fare you well, my lord. My advice to you is to think before you act next time.'

'And my advice to you is . . . keep your mouth shut.'

'Terrible advice to a jester,' I muttered and left him. Once I reached the corridor, I hurried my steps from that dreadful place and then ran the rest of the way home.

Michael was there as I dropped into a chair, and I asked him for wine. Marion stood over me and with fists at her hips. 'And where were you?' And then those fists dropped away as she could only guess where I was. Unfortunately, I was not in love's embrace with Nicholas Pachett.

I waited for Michael to quit fussing, and once he left us, I leaned back . . . except that the back of my head smarted when I did so, and I pressed my hand there. 'No, I was not with Nick. I was snatched from the corridor by getting smote on the head and confronted by our murderer, Peter Meutas.'

She let out a squeak and ran to me, kneading my head with her fingers and finding the bump. 'People are always hitting you on the head,' she muttered as she rushed to get a towel wetted at the basin. She placed the cold cloth to the lump there and eased me back. It did feel better.

'My least vulnerable spot, as it happens.'

'Will, Will, Will. You must stop this investigating. It's not what the king hired you for.'

'And yet, this time, he asked me to do so. Oh, Marion. What am I to do? I cannot accuse him.'

'These courtiers, getting away with murder.'

'Alas. It shall always be so. If you are rich enough and high enough, the hangman cannot reach you.'

'There has to be a way.'

'I cannot see it. Oh Christ, my head hurts.' I lowered it to my hand and massaged my forehead.

She took the goblet from my other hand and set it aside. Her hand was under my arm, and she lifted me from the chair. 'You must go to bed. I will keep watch of you.'

'You will? Ah, that is a comfort, my sweet. I would like to go to bed.'

She helped me undress, helped me put on my night shift and tucked me under the covers. I felt a tender kiss drop to my temple and, in a while, the bed dipped as she joined me.

We slumbered. My dreams were nightmarish and confused, and always filled with a pounding headache. Even Nan Boleyn made an appearance, scolding me for getting into trouble. I awoke when Marion's gasp alerted me, and, at first, I thought that she, too, had a nightmare.

But it was the voice in the dark that had startled her to waking, and I jolted up against the headboard and stared at the shadowy figure in our bedchamber.

'You will cease interfering.'

I pulled up the bedclothes to cover my wife. 'You . . . . you have the bollocks to stand in the chamber of the king's jester and threaten me, Viscount Beauchamp?'

'You are certainly an impudent fellow.'

'It's my job.'

'And perhaps it is my job to throttle you.'

'You must commit two murders then, my lord,' said Marion, rising in the bed. 'For I shall not stand by whilst you do so. And that will be the murder of the daughter of Lord Heyward, another of the king's servants *and* a courtier.'

Beauchamp stood silently, appraising his situation. He thought to burst into my chambers to threaten me when I had already been threatened by Meutas, and both were equally foolish. I had friends. A courtier whom I have told these tales to. But Beauchamp could not hope to guess who they were.

'I'm curious, my lord,' I said, bold as a knight, 'after you dug up and disembowelled Geoffrey Payne and found no brooch in his belly, how did you acquire it at last and return it to the queen's jewel casket?'

I got an elbow in the ribs from my wife for the trouble of speaking out.

He dropped his face to his palm and breathed into it for a while, breath fogging around his hand. 'And so you are the clever fellow they say you are. A pity.'

Now *that* last word did put the fear of God Almighty in me. For, still being one of the highest courtiers in the land, Seymour could very well do his will on me and my wife, and no one could naysay him.

I slipped out of the bedclothes and stood with naked feet on the cold floor. 'Your presence is unwelcome, my lord. You must leave now.'

He laughed, as I knew he would. 'You think you can order *me* about, Fool?'

'I . . . I am damned well going to try. Michael!'

Our servant, who had had no choice in preventing this lord from entering, stumbled into the room, hair askew, coat buttoned wrong.

'Michael, show this gentleman out.'

Michael's eyes grew as wide as moons as he stood, immobile in the doorway. After all, what was *he* to do? I reckoned it was time to posture as much as we could.

And then Marion slipped from the bed, held her neckline closed and stood beside me. 'I shall scream loud and long, your grace, and the guards *will* come running.'

I hoped to the Devil they would. They were all good friends to me, and this was the same corridor as the king's.

Beauchamp still hesitated. 'You have something in your possession that I must have back. Something that belonged to . . . to Peter Meutas.'

The sarding shirt. I had forgotten about it.

But it was Marion who moved. She knelt at our coffer and pulled it out, showing the stained shirt to Seymour. Before he could snatch it from her, she tossed it into the fire. It smoked at first, and then it caught a meagre flame from the glowing coals and was soon consumed.

She stayed by the hearth, chin still lifted defiantly. Oh, what a noble lady she would have made! What a chatelaine, defending an entire castle from capture.

In the end, Beauchamp saw the futility in remaining. He witnessed the evidence go up in smoke and naught more needed

to be said. Though Michael would not put hands on him for
fear of losing them, Marion's screams would do the trick, and
she would make good on her promise to do so. He snorted
discontentedly, cast his cloak aside in a swirl of cloth like
some Devil in a morality play, then pushed his way past
Michael and out the front door, slamming it for good measure
as he left.

We all breathed a collective sigh of relief.

'Thank you, Michael.' I reached for my pouch lying on the
chair where Marion had thrown my clothes, and retrieved a
silver penny. 'Here, my man. You are a loyal and honest servant.'

He was dazed as he took it and then shuffled back to the
outer room, where we heard him bolt the door and snuff out
the candle.

Marion was already bringing us goblets of wine. She sidled
back under the covers as I was doing and handed me my
cup. We drank in silence, sitting up against the headboard
in the dark.

'Marion, would you prefer I become a merchant somewhere
in a faraway city?'

She licked the wine from her upper lip. 'Sometimes. But
that is not the man I married.'

'Aye me. Well. The man you married puts you in peril. And
once is too many. This is twice. Or is it thrice?'

'I'm not counting.'

'Thank Christ.'

'Will. You must do a better job of protecting *yourself*. You
must not let them know what you know in future.'

'Future? You think I have a future if this continues?'

She knocked back the goblet, finished her wine with
another pass of her pink tongue over her lips and set the
empty cup on the small table beside her. 'I am going to try
to sleep the rest of the night, for I do not know the hour,
except that it is late.'

I finished my wine, set the cup aside and crawled down
under the quilts with her. The cold of the room, which was
blissful whilst we slept, was now colder from this encounter.
She was right. I had no business bringing doom upon us. I
had to learn to curb my tongue, but I didn't know if I could.

'Marion, I am sorry.'

She wrapped herself about me, and I felt the warmth slowly return to my body. And . . . something more. 'Marion . . .'

'Will Somers. Do not tell me you wish to make love *now* of all times.'

Well . . .

In the end, Marion clung fast to me as much as I clung to her. And her ardour matched my own.

When the bleary light of dawn seeped into the room with a grey flush, we both rose. Sleepy-eyed, dreadfully tired, we joined Michael, equally exhausted, in the outer room. We took wine and urged him to take some with us, and then left for the servants' hall.

I wanted dearly to tell them all that transpired, and if the jester was somehow missing one day, or found stabbed to death in the corridors, it was this man or that one that did it. But I could not. It would be foolish, for those words would become the gossip that the court thrived on and reach all the *wrong* people. No, as aggravating as it was, I had to keep silent to protect Henry and his reign. His closest ministers should not be known as murderers . . . though they surely did their best to people London Bridge with heads.

Sometimes I wish Henry was the country squire he reckoned himself to be, albeit one who had few responsibilities. I wish I could always talk true with him like a bosom friend, laugh with him, drink with him, play games with him. But I was not a courtier. I was not a lord of the land. I could never be his equal.

And maybe that was just as well.

TWENTY-FIVE

nd as if nothing happened, I was back in Henry's company, cavorting, prating, telling jokes and rhymes, and entertaining Henry and that damned Aske fellow again. How I tired of him and all that came with it. I longed for a moment alone with Henry. Oh, I couldn't tell him all that transpired, but . . . I wanted just to be with him, as I used to be. For he was a comfort of the familiar for me, just as I was to him.

But these were the Twelve Days, and he was never alone. And through all my antics, I worried. For Edward Seymour was there as well, and I couldn't help but feel his steely eyes boring into me, watching me with a predatory glint, looking for ways to dispatch me.

'Harry,' I said abruptly, 'A riddle! Are you ready? Now. Truly, no one is outstanding without me, nor fortunate. I embrace all those whose hearts ask for me. He who goes without me goes about in the company of death, and he who bears me will remain lucky forever. But I stand lower than earth and higher than heaven. What am I?'

Henry scratched at his ginger beard and screwed up his eyes in thought. 'I think you are being too clever to make it harder.'

'I might be at that, Harry. But it is for you to try to parse it.'

'Troublesome Fool,' he muttered.

The king looked to his courtiers, amongst which was my Nicholas, but they were stumped as well.

I looked straight at Edward Seymour as I gave the answer. 'It is "humility", my lords.' And I bowed, keeping my eyes on him. 'I knew that the privy council would be unaware of such a thing, but one must be mindful.'

'And what of you, Will?' said Henry. 'How is your humility?'

'Me? A jester cannot be humble all the time, though a humble person am I. To be a proper Fool, one must be bold and bawdy. Is that not right,' I said turning to Seymour, 'my lord Beauchamp?'

He merely lifted his chin and stared down his nose at me whilst the gentlemen around him laughed. All but Nicholas, that is. For he was looking at me and trying to discern the meaning of this directed barb.

The king begged me for a song, and so I played and sang, and amused the gentlemen more with my clever words and lusty meanings.

But soon, as it seemed to happen in these Twelve Days, Henry turned to serious matters of state. Aske was dismissed, and the conversation turned to the pilgrimage. The gentlemen were not inclined to entertain their demands any more than was the king, but they talked round it and to other matters that needed attending to before the new year. I was soon forgot, and Henry, seeing that I was making to leave, nodded to me his permission, and I took my basket and cittern with me out the door.

As I made my way through the corridor, a hand touched my shoulder, and like a skittish cat, I leapt into the air and twisted round. Hand to wildly beating heart, my relief that it was Nick slowed that thumping to a trickle. 'God's bollocks, Nicholas!' And I had forgot myself as I said it, and searched the corridor for any ears a mite late. None, thank *Jesu*. 'Don't do that.'

'You are tetchy today,' he said.

'And rightly so. Where can we talk?'

'My rooms.' Oh, that glint in his eye meant more than solicitousness.

'Just to talk.'

He bowed. 'As you wish.'

I let him move ahead of me and pretended to organize my basket, always keeping an eye out now for Meutas or Seymour. One couldn't be too careful.

Once Nick was far enough ahead, I slowly made my way forth. I stopped briefly in my nearly abandoned old rooms to deposit my foolery and set out again for Nick's rooms. He should have cleared out his servants by now.

When I reached it, I still scanned the empty corridor before I knocked. The passage was still filled with the fragrant scent of pine for all the swagged boughs, and though it usually cheered me, it only reminded of the current deadly situation. It was as if these Twelve Days would never end, for this was only the third day of them. Oh, when would Aske leave!

Nicholas opened the door, dressed this time, and ushered me in. And once the door was closed, he rushed me and kissed me full. I wanted, needed, that comfort and had no mind to push him away. I moved in, in fact, and let him embrace me, and it was marvellous.

He touched my face, stroking my cheek. 'I could tell your merry-making was somewhat forced.'

'Aye, it was. Oh, Nick.' I pushed my fingers over my shorn head. 'Yesterday, I was smote over the head and dragged into a cupboard to be confronted by our murderer, Peter Meutas.'

'No!' He grabbed me again and ran his hands over my skull. 'Are you well now? Did he admit to the murder?'

'I still have a sore head, but it will pass. And yes, he admitted to the murder.'

His mouth had fallen open as he breathed out. 'I'll be damned.'

'Not you, my love.' I couldn't help but kiss him again.

'Will, what will you do?'

'Nothing. Nothing can be done as we have witnessed before.'

'But I know Meutas to be a good man.'

'And so he was being a good servant to the king and trying to prevent the rebels from getting their booty. But he did not have to kill the man. He could have struck him right well as he did me.' I rubbed the back of my head. 'It was just that Geoffrey, in his playful way, pretended to swallow the brooch, and Meutas wanted to get it back. It happened so quickly that he had little time to think. Unless this is his natural course in things.'

He ran his hands down his bearded face. 'What a complete mess. What a disaster.'

'For poor Geoffrey certainly, and for my poor head.'

His gaze settled on me. 'Your poor head indeed. Come.' He opened his arms again and I gratefully fell into them. He held me tight and kissed my temple. 'No ill effects?'

I shook my head against his shoulder. 'Even if I am knocked silly and cannot be the same Will, at least I have a home here as a natural fool.'

'I think your head is far too hard for that.'

'Sirrah!' I cried, raising said head from his neck.

He gently pushed it back in place. 'Hush. I only meant to chide you. And what of Beauchamp?'

'The churl came into my private rooms and into my bedchamber late last night and threatened me to silence. With my wife lying in bed beside me!'

He jerked away from me and grasped the hilt of his sword. 'Why that . . .'

Well! I have never had such a champion. And his actions filled my heart with the warmth of pride. I might have even giggled. 'My lord, I would not be so hasty.'

There was a question on his face before he looked down at his hand. He brought up a sheepish expression. 'Can I help it that I would protect you? And Marion,' he added for propriety's sake.

'No.' I stepped forward and laid a hand to his cheek as his sword hand fell away from the hilt. 'It is lovely of you, though.'

Now he blushed full and turned away. 'He threatened you.'

'Aye, and he did not think it through either, for I made it plain to him that we were at a stalemate. He could not act for fear of hurting the king's beloved jester, and I could not act for no one would believe me. Either way, Henry would be aggrieved. We could not have that. But he demanded the shirt . . . and Marion threw it in the fire before his very eyes. And that was that.'

'Is there nothing to be done?'

'If you could think of something, my lord, I would love to hear it.'

'Then damn them both.' He sighed deeply and glanced at me over his shoulder. 'And damn you too for making me *think*. For I might have been just as cruel and unmindful of servants as Meutas is . . . but for your presence in my life. You are like the personification of a conscience. You whisper here and there what is right and what is wrong.'

'Aye, marry, 'tis true. The wealthy seldom see servants as whole people. We must seem quite dull and common to the likes of you. Not quite with the same feelings and sensibilities. It is quite an extraordinary exercise.'

'It shames me.'

'Shame you it might, but you seem to have learned from it.'

'That it takes a Fool to teach the aristocracy courtesy . . .'

'The Fool has the least to lose.'

He studied me in a most peculiar fashion. It was a steady and searching scrutiny. 'I think you have very much to lose. And so do we all from your absence. I want you to live a very long time.'

His words suddenly embarrassed me with the depth of emotion that swirled in his eyes. 'Oh. Well, then . . . aye. I hope to.'

'You can give the king no conclusion.'

'I know that Henry already forgot it and will never ask.'

He laughed. Such was Henry's attention. It amused him to ask for this or that, but if it was not something physical – like food or baubles – he quickly forgot ever mentioning it. The servants found it . . . consoling.

'But wait, Will.' It awakened me from my musing. 'What had Beauchamp to do with this?'

'He did the disembowelling. For he knew that if the queen could not produce this expensive brooch, then it might be used to bring her down.'

'But . . . you said that Geoffrey only pretended to swallow it. Which was why Meutas cut the man's throat as he did. Yes, I see that now. But if he did not truly swallow it, it could not be in his gut. And yet it was returned. Beauchamp could not have found it.'

'I suspect that Janie was still not telling the entire truth of it all. When next I see her, I shall have to ask her. But I am certain that she found it after all on the night the man was killed. Perhaps the ordeal made her forget she had.'

He stroked his beard as he shook his head. 'What will you do now?'

'Oh, I expect I will carry on as usual. And nothing more will be said.'

'What of the threats from Meutas and Beauchamp?'

'They will most likely perspire into the aether. Or . . . I will be found suddenly dead. And if the latter, do me the courtesy of whispering the truth to the king.'

He sputtered. 'How can one merry man find himself in such constant peril?'

'Just lucky, I reckon.'

TWENTY-SIX

I encountered Wriothesley as I made my way through the passages again. He stopped me and enjoined me to sit with him in an alcove. I was pleased to do so since the window seat caught the warmth of the sun and not the cold through the diamond-paned glass.

'I have been listening more carefully to your cavorting and jests, good Master Somers. And now I see what I, in my folly, have missed before. You, sir, have a keen and clever mind, and you insult with intent, even rhyme, riddle and sing to make your point to any man who cares to listen. You are a wit, sir, and the king should be proud to have you.'

'Those are very kind words indeed, Master Wriothesley. I am gratified that you discern my hard work at last. It's a fine line to tread.'

'Indeed it is. Tell me, how has your latest investigation gone?'

'Oh, that.' I held crossed arms over my chest. 'To tell you the truth, good sir, and I know how you value the truth, it is unbearable. I can say only that the murder was committed and abetted by those of high rank and that I am therefore at loose ends about it. I cannot tell the king, and the victim cannot get his justice. He will have to find it instead on the Day of Judgement.'

'That is a very great pity. Does this happen to you often?'

'More often than not, master.'

He tsked and shook his head. 'I cannot but think that something must be done.'

'The only thing I can do, master, is to continue to jeer them and make jokes at their expense. It is a small recompense, but it is all I have.'

'But your own safety . . .'

'True, I have been threatened. Often. Just last night, in fact. But I belong to King Harry, and anyone who has the gall to kill me will suffer for it.'

'That would be a trifle late for your benefit.'

'A man in my position might have a fatalistic streak. There is too much I have seen and heard not to have. A Fool must look at the world in which he lives philosophically. And with a grain of salt.'

'I suppose that is best.'

'It is all I have.'

'Then . . . has your assessment of this Robert Aske situation changed with time, Master Somers?'

'Alas, sir, it has not. He may very well leave the court in good health, but I do not know how long that will last.'

'I believe him to be a man of good character and sincere in his faith. But I agree that he has no reason to expect a good outcome to this.'

'And yet he does. He puts his faith in the king. And though I would never speak ill of my Henry, the king has been known to be . . . swift in his actions to those that oppose him. One must not oppose the majesty of any king, for he must naturally put down any rebellion. He has been put in a very awkward position.'

'I do not think so, good jester. I think the king has known all along his position and that of his subject Robert Aske.'

'You are probably right, sir.'

He rose. 'Well, I must not keep you. But I have enjoyed our conversations.'

'As have I. Your good health, sir.'

He bowed as I left him. An interesting man was our herald.

But now I felt I needed to pursue Jane Foole and ask her some concluding questions.

I encountered her easily enough in the queen's company, where she was, ironically, sitting upon the floor and playing about in the queen's jewellery casket. Lady Horsman was there as well, keeping a careful eye upon it.

All of us at court might be called upon to kill in the name of the king at any time. It was a certainty that many courtiers saw their own deeds in that light. Peter Meutas was such a man as that, and Henry was proud to have him as a Gentleman Usher, for to be in such close proximity to the king was to swear to protect him in any way necessary, and surely Meutas saw giving funds to rebels as a very great threat to His Majesty. Even I, with my little dagger, would freely use it to protect my sovereign. Aye, I would. It would be second nature. And so, in the end, could I truly blame the man for only doing his duty, for surely he thought it so.

But even twisting the information about as I did, I could not justify it for myself. I could not help but think that there could have been a better way to go about stopping Geoffrey other than murder. Ah, well.

I sat on the floor with Janie, and she squealed in delight that I was there, and leaned awkwardly over the casket to hug me. 'Will, I'm glad you've come.'

'And I am glad to be with you, sweeting.'

'What shall we play with? Shall I adorn you again?'

I reached forth and trapped her hands in mine. 'In a moment,' I said quietly so that just we two could hear. 'I do have a question for you. When you saw poor Geoffrey killed in the corridor . . . did you find the brooch yourself?'

'I told you that.' She frowned and tried to pull her hands away, but I held them fast.

'No, my rose, you did not.'

She rolled her eyes as she was wont to do when she felt that a person was lacking in common sense. 'I told you. I saw it spin across the floor. And when the Longbeard left him, I snatched it up.'

'You seemed to have left that part out the last time I asked.'

She shrugged in answer, because her mind had already left the fear and trouble behind. How I envied her!

'Then did *you* replace it here in the casket yourself and simply forgot?'

'No,' she said, as if talking to a simpleton. 'I am certain I told you this, Will. Beauchamp saw me playing with it in the corner there' – and she waved to the far corner of the chamber, almost where Marion was sitting with her embroidery and sewing basket at her feet – 'and he crouched down close to me and said, "What have you there, Fool?" You know, Will, the way he does in that voice that says he doesn't like me.'

'I know the sound of that.'

'And so. He knew right well what I had, and I held it up to show it to him. And that's when he snatched it out of my hand. "You should know better than to play with this,"' she said in a fair imitation of his voice. 'And I told him that the queen said I could, that even though she gave it to Geoffrey to take it far away, it was my favourite, and the queen would want me to play with it if I wanted to. He's a mean man, Will.'

'Indeed he is. Then what did he do with it?'

'He took it and kept it. Then he must have returned it to the casket, for here it remains.' She lifted it from the now tangled necklaces. I snatched a glance at Lady Margery, and her face was none too pleased. I reckoned that every night, Lady Margery untangled the mess that Jane Foole had made in the casket. 'But I told you all this, Will.'

'No, dearling, you forgot to tell me this part.'

'Oh? Ah, well. It is over.'

Aye, it was over for her, and in another day, it would be forgot forever. How lucky she was. But there was one thing more that troubled me.

'Sweeting, when you were so very upset days ago and were wanting to talk to me, I, er, found you outside of Lord Hammond's apartments. How, erm . . . how did you know I was there?'

Again, her look of disgust with the very stupid. '*Because*, Will, you are always talking quietly with him when you think no one is looking. He is your bosom friend, is he not? When you are upset, where else would you be?'

Robert Aske stayed at court for almost all the Twelve Days festival, but sometime in the night of the fifth of January, he and his retinue slipped out of the palace and no doubt headed north. I hope he found what he needed from Henry. I hope he spread the tidings of mercy and pardons to his men, and I hoped that his men would be mindful of that and go on their way again, retreating to their towns and villages from whence they came. I hoped that mercy *would* follow them and that they would take Aske's sound advice on the matter.

But Hope was often a fleeting thing, and bold men don't always listen to sound advice, much to their detriment.

AFTERWORD

So much to talk about. Where should we begin?

Let's first talk about Margery Horsman. She was not made Keeper of the Queen's Jewels until 1537 when she married Sir Michael Lyster of Hurstbourne. It was a little stretching of events to get her into the story, though she had been well known as a maid of honour to Catherine of Aragon, Anne Boleyn and Jane Seymour, and bringing in and training some ladies to serve in the queen's court. So I hope you will forgive that small breach in factual etiquette.

Jane Beden known as Jane Foole was a real person, probably with a learning disability, and served as Fool to Catherine of Aragon, Princess Mary, Anne Boleyn, Catherine Parr and then Mary when she became Mary I. I know it seems odd to modern sensibilities to have someone with a learning disability around to play the Fool, possibly to even laugh at. But in Tudor times, people with learning disabilities were not kept at court as objects of ridicule. It was believed that such persons were completely without guile or evil, and to have them as close companions was a blessing to both the Fool and the master or mistress. Many Fools had learning disabilities or were people with restricted growth or physically disabled. And just as many were like Will, the witty sort.

Edward Seymour was not a nice chap. He and his father did push Jane before Henry, hoping to entice him to marry her, and it worked. He was used to pushing her around, so it isn't unfeasible that he would continue as he did in this novel. In fact, some instances of this were documented. Edward Seymour, created 1st Viscount Beauchamp and later 1st Earl of Hertford, 1st Duke of Somerset, Warden of the Scottish Marches and Lord High Admiral, stuck around throughout Henry's reign to its end and then became the Lord Protector of Edward VI, too young yet to rule on his own. But it was found that Seymour took control of the protectorate and acted as the monarch, pushing through unpopular laws and wielding autocratic authority. It wasn't until Edward VI was almost to his majority that he ousted Seymour from the protectorate, and he was arrested and brought before the king who sent him to the Tower on the charges of 'ambition, vainglory, entering into rash wars in mine youth . . . enriching himself of my treasure, following his own opinion, and doing all by his own authority, etc'. He was released from the Tower in 1550 only to return, this time on a charge of treason, and was executed. So I don't feel too bad throwing him under the bus.

Peter Meutas or Mewtas or Mewtis or Meautis or Meautys – spelling was not codified till much later – did serve in Henry's court. He was the grandson of Henry VII's French secretary John Meutas and spoke French excellently, which made him a good spy. He was a gentleman of the privy chamber and an expert on handguns, like the arquebus, an early long gun. He may also have been sent by Henry in 1537 to assassinate Cardinal Pole, a royal supremacy denier. If he attempted it, it failed. But he was a staunch Protestant and an unquestionably loyal dogsbody. He did not do well under Mary I's reign, but regained his place at court under Elizabeth I. As far as I know, he did not murder any servants, but since Henry considered that he would make a good assassin, it is not outside the realm of possibility, hence his being the murderer in my 'what if'.

Now let's talk about John Blanke. In the 1520s, in the Tudor court, a black man called John Blanke was trumpeter to Henry VII and later to Henry VIII. This was not just any musician. This was a most prestigious position in the royal retinue, the fellows that trumpeted announcements at spectacles, at royal baptisms, weddings and coronations. And there were other such African musicians at other European courts. In fact, in a tapestry depicting the Field of the Cloth of Gold, one can see a dark-skinned trumpeter in French livery.

It can only be assumed that in Henry VII's time, he wanted to be as cosmopolitan as the other monarchs and brought into his retinue an African trumpeter. We don't actually know where he came from, but it was my fiction to bestow on him the Nigerian name 'Ekene'.

So besides John Blanke as an 'E' name, all the others mentioned were real to the court except my fictional Eustace Edgar, Viscount FitzAllen, the 'queen's purse', and Doctor Ellis Dawlish, 'envoy to the queen's charities'. They didn't exist. Whenever I add people that weren't there or make my villains from those that did exist, it is always with the thought in mind that they *could* have been involved and served as they did in the story. The 'what if' of fiction.

Robert Aske. He was indeed the person who captained the Pilgrimage of Grace. Nine thousand citizens of the north marched and did perpetrate a bit of violence. Indeed, they suggested more violence on Cromwell and those visitors who had taken inventory of the monasteries and found them wanting. The dissolution of the monasteries was a foregone conclusion anyway. All the monasteries were to be shut, the roof taken down; some convents were sold, and some were left to rot. Many people wanted their old religion back and with it all the familiar accoutrements including the clergy and the mass that so moved through their lives. Though it had to be said, the majority in England was already primed for Protestantism for some years and they only wanted forward movement, not backwards.

Aske was indeed invited to court and spent Christmas to 5th January, when he slipped quietly away back to the north to tell them all about the pardons and the king's generosity and mercy. His followers did not believe what the king had promised – and rightly so – and continued their march and their raids. Henry and his men used this as the excuse to not go through with the pardons they promised. Henry VIII wrote to the Duke of Suffolk, saying, 'if it appear to you by due proof that the rebels have since their retires from Lincoln attempted any new rebellion, you shall, with your forces run upon them and with all extremity destroy, burn, and kill man, woman, and child the terrible example of all others, and specially the town of Louth because to this rebellion took his beginning in the same.' And writing to the Earl of Derby, he said, 'we now desire you immediately to repress it, to apprehend the captains and either have them immediately executed as traitors or sent up to us. We leave it, however, to your discretion to go elsewhere in case of greater emergency. You are to take the said abbot and monks forth (who were returned to their monasteries) with violence and have them hanged without delay in their monks' apparel, and see that no town or village begin to assemble.'

Aske and the other leaders were eventually captured, tried and condemned. Aske's last request was to be quickly dispatched instead of the usual brutal and lengthy execution for traitors, but again he was naïve and had been taken in by Henry's former vows of mercy. 'Let me be full dead ere I be dismembered,' pleaded Aske. Henry didn't dismember him alive. Instead, he ordered that Aske be hanged in chains in York till he died, a pretty gruesome way to go as well.

And finally, Jane Seymour. Was she the most beloved of queens to Henry VIII? Most people think so, since he was buried with her. But those who have studied the era see a more subtle situation. Henry, as was stated by Will in this book, picked Jane because she was put before him from his reliable courtiers – mainly Edward Seymour and Gertrude, Marchioness of Exeter – but, as was Henry's way, he immediately regretted marrying her when there were so many other women at court more beautiful than she. Also, she wasn't the lusty, broad-humoured kind of woman that he liked, but a bit on the mousy side. He tolerated her and spent as much time as necessary with her. The fact that she gave him his longed-for son made her the best wife at the time, and he probably would have remained married to her. He didn't rush to get married after her death, which made some historians assume he was mourning for his lost love. I have to imagine that he was rather tired of married life, got his son and felt he didn't need to bother anymore. But he did eventually get a little lonely, I think, and decided that he should use the next marriage for some European alliances, as Cromwell suggested he do. And so in the next instalment of the King's Fool mysteries, we will meet Anne of Cleves of Germany, Henry's quickest and cleanest divorce. And Will Somers will again find himself stuck in the centre of the action in the fourth book, *Beloved Sister*.

As always, if you like a book, please review it. See my other books and sign up for my monthly newsletter at JeriWesterson.com.

Acknowledgements

Much thanks to editor Sara Porter for her help and guidance; to the expertise of the copyeditors for keeping it British; and to the amazing Jem Butcher for his cover design. Smashing!